The Californians

by

Gertrude Atherton

Double 9 BOOKS

The Californians
by Gertrude Atherton

Copyright © 2023

All Rights reserved.

ISBN: 978-93-60461-79-9

Published by

DOUBLE 9 BOOKS

2/13-B, Ansari Road
Daryaganj, New Delhi – 110002
info@double9books.com
www.double9books.com
Tel. 011-40042856

This book is under public domain

ABOUT THE AUTHOR

American author Gertrude Franklin Horn Atherton lived from October 30, 1857, to June 14, 1948. A lot of her books take place in California, which is where she lives. In 1923, her best-selling book Black Oxen was turned into a silent movie with the same name. Besides novels, she also wrote short stories, essays, and news stories for magazines and newspapers about war, women, and politics. Gertrude Franklin Horn was born in San Francisco, California, on October 30, 1857. Her parents were Thomas Ludovich Horn and his wife, who used to be Gertrude Franklin. As a tobacco dealer, her father had become well-known in San Francisco, even though he was from Stonington, Connecticut. New Orleans was where her mom was from. When she was two years old, her parents split up. Her maternal grandpa, Stephen Franklin, who was a devout Presbyterian and a relative of Benjamin Franklin, raised her. Grandfather Franklin told her she had to read a lot, which had a big effect on her. She went to high school at St. Mary's Hall in Benicia, California, and for a short time at the Sayre School in Lexington, Kentucky.

CONTENTS

BOOK II

BOOK I

I

"I won't study another word to-day!" Helena tipped the table, spilling the books to the floor. "I want to go out in the sun. Go home, Miss Phelps, that's a dear. Anyhow, it won't do you a bit of good to stay."

Miss Phelps, young herself, glanced angrily at her briery charge, longingly at the brilliant blue of sky and bay beyond the long window.

"I leave it to Miss Yorba." Her voice, fashioned to cut, vibrated a little with the vigour of its roots. "You seem to forget, Miss Belmont, that this is not your house."

"But you are just as much my teacher as hers. Besides, I always know what Magdaléna wants, and I know that she has had enough United States history for one afternoon. When I go to England I'll get their version of it. We're brought up to love their literature and hate them! Such nonsense—"

"My dear Miss Belmont, I beg you to remember that you have but recently passed your sixteenth birthday—"

"Oh, of course! If I'd been brought up in Boston, I'd be giving points to Socrates and wondering why there were so many old maids in the world. However, that's not the question at present. 'Léna, do tell *dear* Miss Phelps that she needs an afternoon off, and that if she doesn't take it—I'll walk downstairs on my head."

Helena, even at indeterminate sixteen, showed promise of great beauty, and her eyes sparkled with the insolence of the spoiled child who already knew the power of wealth. The girl she addressed had only a pair of dark intelligent eyes to reclaim an uncomely face. Her skin was swarthy, her nose crude, her mouth wide. The outline of her head was fine, and she wore her black hair parted and banded closely below her ears. Her forehead was large, her expression sad and thoughtful. Don Roberto Yorba was many times more a millionaire than "Jack" Belmont, but Magdaléna was not a spoiled child.

"I don't know," she said, with a marked hesitation of speech; "I'd like to go out, but it doesn't seem right to take advantage of the fact that papa and mamma are away—"

"What they don't know won't hurt them. I'd like to have Don Roberto under my thumb for just one week. He'd get some of the tyranny knocked out of him. Jack is a model parent—"

Magdaléna flushed a dark ugly red. "I wish you would not speak in that way of papa," she said. "I—I—well—I'm afraid he wouldn't let you come here to study with me if he knew it."

"Well, I won't." Helena flung her arms round her friend and kissed her warmly. "I wouldn't hurt his Spanish dignity for the world; only I do wish you happened to be my real own cousin, or—that would be much nicer—my sister."

Magdaléna's troubled inner self echoed the wish; but few wishes, few words, indeed, passed her lips.

"Well?" demanded Miss Phelps, coldly. "What is it to be? Do you girls intend to study any more to-day, or not? Because—"

"We don't," said Helena, emphatically. And Magdaléna, who invariably gave way to her friend's imperious will, nodded deprecatingly. Miss Phelps immediately left the room.

"She's glad to get out," said Helena, wisely. "She hates me, and I know she's got a beau. Come! Come!" She pulled Magdaléna from her chair, and the two girls ran to the balcony beyond the windows and leaned over the railing.

"There's nothing in all the world," announced Helena, "so beautiful as California—San Francisco included—in spite of whirlwinds of dust, and wooden houses, and cobblestone streets, and wooden sidewalks. One can always live on a hill, and then you don't see the ugly things below. For instance, from here you see nothing but that dark blue bay with the dark blue sky above it, and opposite the pink mountains with the patches of light blue, and on that side the hills of Sausalito covered with willows, and the breakers down below. And the ferry-boats are like great white swans, with long soft throats bending backwards. I don't express myself very well; but I shall some day. Just you wait; I'm going to be a scholar and a lot of other things too."

"What, Helena?" Magdaléna drew closer. She thought Helena already the most eloquent person alive, and she envied her deeply, although without bitterness, loving her devotedly. The great gifts of expression and of personal magnetism had been denied her. She had no hope, and at that time little wish, that the last paucity could ever be made good by the power of will; but that articulate inner self had registered a vow that hard study and close attention to the methods of Helena and others as—or nearly as— brilliant should one day invest her brain and tongue with suppleness.

"What other things are you going to be, Helena?" she asked. "I know that you can be anything you like."

"Well, in the first place, I am going to New York to school,—now, don't look so sad: I've told you twenty times that I *know* Don Roberto will let you go. Then I'm going to Europe. I'm going to study hard—but not hard enough to spoil my eyes. I'm going to finish off in Paris, and then I'm going to travel. Incidentally, I'm going to learn how to dress, so that when I come back here I'll astonish the natives and be the best-dressed woman in San Francisco; which won't be saying much, to be sure. Then, when I do come back, I'm going to just rule things, and, what is more, make all the old fogies let me. And—*and*—I am going to be the greatest belle this State has ever seen; and that *is* saying something."

"Of course you will do all that, Helena. It will be so interesting to watch you. Ila and Tiny will never compare with you. Some people are made like that,—some one way and some another, I mean. Shall—shall—you ever marry, Helena?"

"Yes. After I have been engaged a dozen times or so I shall marry a great man."

"A great man?"

"Yes; I don't know any, but they are charming in history and memoirs. I'd have a simply gorgeous time in Washington, and ever after I'd have my picture in 'Famous Women' books."

"Shall you marry a president?" asked Magdaléna, deferentially. She was convinced that Helena could marry a reigning sovereign if she wished.

"I haven't made up my mind about that yet. Presidents' wives are usually such dreary-looking frumps I'd hate to be in the same book with them. Besides, most of the presidents don't amount to much. Truthful George must have been a deadly bore. I prefer Benjamin Franklin—although I never could stand that nose—or Clay or Calhoun or Patrick Henry or Webster. They're dead, but there must be lots more. I'll find one for you, too."

Again the dark flush mounted to Magdaléna's hair, as with an alertness of motion unusual to her, she shook her head.

"Aha!" cried the astute Helena, "you've been thinking the matter over, too, have you? Who is he? Tell me."

Magdaléna shook her head again, but slowly this time. Helena embraced and coaxed, but to no effect. Even with her chosen friend, Magdaléna was reticent, not from choice, but necessity. But Helena, whose love was great and whose intuitions were diabolical, leaped to the secret. "I know!" she exclaimed triumphantly. "It's a caballero!"

This time Magdaléna's face turned almost purple; but she had neither her sex's quick instinct of self-protection nor its proneness to dissemble, secretive as she was. She lifted her head haughtily and turned away. For a moment she looked very Spanish, not the unfortunate result of coupled races that she was. Helena, who was in her naughtiest humour, threw back her head and laughed scornfully. "A caballero!" she cried: "who will serenade you at two o'clock in the morning when you are dying with sleep, and lie in a hammock smoking cigaritos all day; who will roll out rhetoric by the yard, and look like an idiot when you talk common-sense to him; who is too lazy to walk across the plaza, and too proud to work, and too silly to keep the Americans from grabbing all he's got. I met a few dilapidated specimens when I was in Los Angeles last year. One beauty with long hair, a sombrero, and a head about as big as my fist, used to serenade me in intervals of gambling until I appealed to Jack, and he threatened to have him put in the calaboose if he didn't let me alone—"

Magdaléna turned upon her. Her face was livid. Her eyes stared as if she had seen the dead walking. "Hush!" she said. "You—you cruel—you have everything—"

Helena, whose intuitions never failed her, when she chose to exercise them, knew what she had done, caught a flashing glimpse of the shattered dreams of the girl who said so little, whose only happiness was in the ideal world she had built in the jealously guarded depths of her soul. "Oh, Magdaléna, I'm so sorry," she stammered. "I was only joking. And my statesmen will probably be horrid old boors. I *know* I'll never find one that comes up to my ideal." She burst into tears and flung her arms about Magdaléna's neck: she was always miserable when those she loved were angry with her, much as she delighted to shock the misprized. "Say you forgive me," she sobbed, "or I sha'n't eat or sleep for a week." And Magdaléna, who always took her mercurial friend literally, forgave her immediately and dried her tears.

II

Don Roberto Yorba had escaped the pecuniary extinction that had overtaken his race. Of all the old grandees who, not forty years before, had called the Californias their own: living a life of Arcadian magnificence, troubled by few cares, a life of riding over vast estates clad in silk and lace, botas and sombrero, mounted upon steeds as gorgeously caparisoned as themselves, eating, drinking, serenading at the gratings of beautiful women, gambling, horse-racing, taking part in splendid religious festivals, with only the languid excitement of an occasional war between rival governors to disturb the placid surface of their lives, — of them all Don Roberto was a man of wealth and consequence to-day. But through no original virtue of his. He had been as princely in his hospitality, as reckless with his gold, as meagrely equipped to cope with the enterprising United Statesian who first conquered the Californian, then, nefariously, or righteously, appropriated his acres. When Commodore Sloat ran up the American flag on the Custom House of Monterey on July seventh, 1846, one of the midshipmen who went on shore to seal the victory with the strength of his lungs was a clever and restless youth named Polk. As his sharpness and fund of dry New England anecdote had made him a distinctive position on board ship, he was permitted to go to the ball given on the following night by Thomas O. Larkin, United States Consul, in honour of the Commodore and officers of the three warships then in the bay. Having little liking for girls, he quickly fraternised with Don Roberto Yorba, a young hidalgo who had recently lost his wife and had no heart for festivities, although curiosity had brought him to this ball which celebrated the downfall of his country. The two men left the ball-room, — where the handsome and resentful señoritas were preparing to avenge California with a battery of glance, a melody of tongue, and a witchery of grace that was to wreak havoc among these gallant officers, — and after exchanging amenities over a bowl of punch, went out into the high-walled garden to smoke the cigarito. The perfume of the sweet Castilian roses was about them, the old walls were a riot of pink and green; but the youths had no mind for either. The don was fascinated by the quick terse common-sense and the harsh nasal voice of the American, and the American's mind was full of a scheme which he was not long confiding to his friend. A shrewd

Yankee, gifted with insight, and of no small experience, young as he was, Polk felt that the idle pleasure-loving young don was a man to be trusted and magnetic with potentialities of usefulness. He therefore confided his consuming desire to be a rich man, his hatred of the navy, and, finally, his determination to resign and make his way in the world.

"I haven't a red cent to bless myself with," he concluded. "But I've got what's more important as a starter,—brains. What's more, I feel the power in me to make money. It's the only thing on earth I care for; and when you put all your brains and energies to one thing you get it, unless you get paralysis or an ounce of cold lead first."

The Californian, who had a true grandee's contempt for gold, was nevertheless charmed with the engaging frankness and the unmistakable sincerity of the American.

"My house is yours," he exclaimed ardently. "You will living with me, no? until you find the moneys? I am—how you say it?—delighted. Always I like the Americanos—we having a few. All I have is yours, señor."

"Look here," exclaimed Polk. "I won't eat any man's bread for nothing, but I'll strike a bargain with you. If you'll stand by me, I'll stand by you. I mean to make money, and I don't much care how I do make it; this is a new place, anyhow. But there's one thing I never do, and that is to go back on a friend. You'll need me, and my Yankee sharpness may be the greatest godsend that ever came your way. I've seen more or less of this country. It's simply magnificent. Americans will be swarming over the place in less than no time. They've begun already. Then you'll be just nowhere. Is it a bargain?"

"It is!" exclaimed Don Roberto, with enthusiasm; and when Polk had explained his ominations more fully, he wrung the American's hand again.

Polk, after much difficulty, but through personal influence which he was fortunate enough to possess, obtained his discharge. He immediately became the guest of Don Roberto, who lived with his younger sister on a ranch covering three hundred thousand acres, and, his first intention being to take up land, was initiated into the mysteries of horse-raising, tanning hides, and making tallow; the two last-named industries being pursued for purposes of barter with the Boston skippers. But farming was not to Polk's taste; he hated waiting on the slow processes of Nature. He married Magdaléna Yorba, and borrowed from Don Roberto enough money to open a store in Monterey stocked with such necessities and luxuries as could be imported from Boston. When the facile Californians had no ready money to pay for their wholesale purchases, he took a mortgage on the next hide yield, or on a small ranch. His rate of interest was twelve per cent; and as the

Californians were never prepared to pay when the day of reckoning came, he foreclosed with a promptitude which both horrified Don Roberto and made imperious demands upon his admiration.

"My dear Don," Polk would say, "if it isn't I, it will be some one else. I'm not the only one—and look at the squatters. I'm becoming a rich man, and if I were not, I'd be a fool. You had your day, but you were never made to last. Your boots are a comfortable fit, and I propose to wear them. I don't mean yours, by the way. I'm going to look after you. Better think it over and come into partnership."

To this Don Roberto would not hearken; but when the rush to the gold mines began he was persuaded by Polk to take a trip into the San Joaquin valley to "see the circus," as the Yankee phrased it. There, in community with his brother-in-law, he staked off a claim, and there the lust for gold entered his veins and never left it. He returned to Monterey a rich man in something besides land. After that there was little conversation between himself and Polk on any subject but money and the manner of its multiplication; and, as the years passed, and Polk's prophecy was fulfilled, he gave the devotion of a fanatic to the retention of his vast inheritance and to the development of his grafted financial faculty.

Between the mines, his store, and his various enterprises in San Francisco, Polk rapidly became a wealthy man. Even in those days he was accounted an unscrupulous one, but he was powerful enough to hold the opinion of men in contempt and too shrewd to elbow such law as there was. And his gratitude and friendship for Don Roberto never flickered. He advised him to invest his gold in city lots, and as himself bought adjoining ones, Don Roberto invested without hesitation. Polk had acquired a taste for Spanish cooking, cigaritos, and life on horseback; his influences on the Californian were far more subtle and revolutionising. Don Roberto was still hospitable, because it became a grandee so to be; but he had a Yankee major-domo who kept an account of every cent that was expended. He had no miserly love of gold in the concrete, but he had an abiding sense of its illimitable power, all of his brother-in-law's determination to become one of the wealthiest and most influential men in the country, and a ferocious hatred of poverty. He saw his old friends fall about him: advice did them no good, and any permanent alliance with their interests would have meant his own ruin; so he shrugged his shoulders and forgot them. The American flag always floated above his rooms. In time he and Polk opened a bank, and he sat in its parlour for five hours of the day; it was the passion of his maturity and decline. When Polk's sister, some eleven years after the Occupation of California by the United States, came out to visit the brother who had left her teaching a small school in Boston, he married her promptly, feeling himself blessed in another New England relative. She was thirty-two at the time, and her complexion was dark and sallow: but she carried her tall angular figure with impressive dignity, and her chill manners gave her a certain distinction. Don Roberto was delighted with her, and as she was by nature as economical as his familiar could desire, he dismissed the major-domo and gave her *carte blanche* at the largest shops in the city; even if he had wished it, she could not have been induced to buy more than four gowns a year. But she was a very ambitious woman. As the wife of a great Californian grandee, she had seen herself the future leader of San Francisco society. Her ambitions were realised in a degree only. Don Roberto built her a huge wooden palace on Nob Hill,—on which was the highest flagstaff and the biggest flag in San Francisco,—placed a suitable number of servants at her command, and gave her a carriage. But he only permitted her to give two large dinners and one ball during the season, and would go to other people's entertainments but seldom. As their ideas of duty were equally rigid, she would not go without him; but they had a circle of intimate and aristocratic friends with whom they lunched and dined informally,—the Polks, the Belmonts, the Montgomerys, the Tarltons, the Brannans, the Gearys, and the Folsoms.

They had been married ten years when Magdaléna, their only child, was born.

III

Mrs. Yorba was so ill when her daughter came that the child struggled miserably into existence, and, failing to cry, was put away as dead, and forgotten for a time. It was discovered to be breathing by Mrs. Polk, who coaxed it through several months of puny existence with all a native Californian woman's resource. During this time it never cried, only whimpered miserably at rare intervals. It was finally discovered to be tongue-tied, and as soon as it was old enough an operation was performed. After that the child's health mended, although she seemed in no hurry to use her tongue. As she progressed in years she still spoke but seldom, only mildly remonstrating when Helena Belmont pulled her hair or vented her exuberant vitality upon Magdaléna's inferior person. Once only did she lose her temper,—when Helena hung up all her dolls in a row and slit them that she might have the pleasure of seeing the sawdust pour out,—and then she leaped upon her tormentor with a hoarse growl of rage, and the two pommelled each other black and blue. But as a rule she was gentle and much-enduring, and Helena was very kind and clamoured constantly for her society. As the girls grew older they studied together, and the friendship, born of propinquity, was strengthened by mutual tastes and sympathy. Helena was probably the only person who ever understood the reticent, proud, apparently cold and impassive temperament of the girl who was an unhappy and incongruous mixture of Spanish and New England traits; and Magdaléna was Helena's most enthusiastic admirer and attentive audience.

Magdaléna had one other friend, her aunt, Mrs. Polk, for whom she was named. That lady was enormously stout and something of an invalid, but carried the tokens of early beauty in a skin of brilliant fairness and a pair of magnificent dark eyes fringed with lashes so long and thick that Magdaléna, when a child, found it her greatest pleasure to count them. Mrs. Polk knew little of her husband and liked him less. She had obeyed her brother's orders and married him, loving a dazzling caballero—who had since gambled away his acres—the while. But Polk ministered to the luxury that she loved; and though his high-pitched voice never ceased to shake her nerves, and his hard cold face to inspire active dislike, as the years went on and she saw how it was with her people, she accepted her lot with philosophy, and finally—as youth fled—with gratitude. Mrs. Yorba she detested, but she loved the child she had saved to a life of doubtful happiness, and—she had no children of her own—would gladly have adopted her. She lived a life of retirement, and had a scanty though kindly brain: therefore she never understood Magdaléna as well as Helena did at the age of six; but she could love warmly, and that meant much to her niece.

The three large and aristocratically ugly mansions of Don Roberto Yorba, Hiram Polk, and Colonel "Jack" Belmont stood side by side on Nob Hill. Belmont was not as wealthy as the others, but a "palatial residence" does not mean illimitable riches even yet in San Francisco. Belmont had married a Boston girl of far greater family pretensions than Mrs. Yorba's, but of no more stately appearance nor correct demeanour. The two women were intimate friends until her husband's notorious infidelities and erraticisms when under the periodical influence of alcohol killed Mrs. Belmont. Neither Don Roberto nor Polk drank to excess, and they kept their mistresses in more decent seclusion than is the habit of the average San Franciscan. It would never occur to Mrs. Yorba to suspect her husband or any other man of infidelity, did she live in California an hundred years, and Mrs. Polk was too indifferent to give the matter a thought.

Although she lived in retirement, rarely venturing out into the winds and fogs of San Francisco, Mrs. Polk surrounded herself with all the luxuries of a pampered woman of wealth and fashion. Her house was magnificent, her private apartments almost stifling in their sumptuousness. Polk squeezed every dollar before he parted with it, but his wife had long since accomplished the judicious exercise of a violent Spanish temper, and her bills were seldom disputed.

Magdaléna and Helena loved these scented gorgeous apartments, and ran through the connecting gardens daily to see her. Their delight was to sit at her feet and listen to the tales of California when the grandee owned the land, when the caballero, in gorgeous attire, sang at the gratings of the beauties of Monterey. Mrs. Polk would sing these old love-songs of Spain to the accompaniment of the guitar which had entranced her caballeros in the *sala* of her girlhood; and Helena, who had a charming voice, learned them all—to the undoing of her own admirers later on. It was she who asked a thousand questions of that Arcadian time, and Mrs. Polk responded with enthusiasm. Doubtless she exaggerated the splendours, the brilliancy, the unleavened pleasure; but it was a time far behind her, and she was happy again in the rememoration. As for Magdaléna, she seldom spoke. She listened with fixed eyes and bated breath to those descriptions of the beautiful women of her race, seeing for the time her soul's face as beautiful, gazing at her reflected image aghast when she turned suddenly upon one of the long mirrors. Her soul sang in accompaniment to her aunt's rich voice, and her hands moved unconsciously as those listless Spanish fingers swept the guitar. When Helena imperiously demanded to be taught, and quickly became as proficient as her teacher, Magdaléna kept her eyes on the floor lest the others should see the dismay in them. Had it occurred to Mrs. Polk to ask her niece if she would like to learn these old songs of her race, Magdaléna would have shaken her head shyly, realising even sooner than she did that there was no medium for the music in her soul, as there was none for the thoughts in her mind. Although her aunt loved her, she did not scruple to tell her that she was not to be either a beautiful or a brilliant woman; but although Magdaléna made no reply, she had a profound belief that the Virgin would in time grant her passionate nightly prayers for a beautiful face and an agile tongue. Beauty was her right; no woman of her father's house had ever been plain, and she had convinced herself that if she were a good girl the Virgin would acknowledge her rights by her eighteenth birthday. As her intellect developed, she was haunted by an uneasy scepticism of miracles, particularly after she learned to draw, but she still prayed; it was a dream she could not relinquish. Nor was this all she prayed for. She had all the Californian's indolence, which was ever at war with the intellect she had inherited from her New England ancestors. Her most delectable instinct was to lie in the sun or on the rug by the fire all day and dream; and she was thoroughly convinced that the Virgin aided her in the fight for mental energy, and was the prime factor in the long periods of victory of mind over temperament.

And only her deathless ambition enabled her to keep pace with Helena. She sat up late into the night poring over lessons that her brilliant friend danced through while dressing in the morning. Her memory was bad, and she never mastered spelling; even after her schooldays were over, she always carried a little dictionary in her pocket. She laboured for years at the piano, not only under her father's orders, but because she passionately loved music, but she had neither ear nor facility, and to her importunities for both the Virgin gave no heed.

And the bitterness of it all lay in the fact that she was not stupid; she was fully aware that her intellect was something more than commonplace; but the machinery was heavy, and, so far as she could see, there was not a drop of cleverness with which to oil the wheels. She had read extensively even before she was sixteen,—letters, essays, biographies, histories, and a number of novels by classic authors; and although she was obliged to read each book three times in order to write it on her memory, she slowly assimilated it and developed her brain cells. Up to this age she was seldom actively unhappy, for she had the hopes of youth and religion, her aunt, Helena, and, above all, her sweet inner life, which was an almost constant dwelling upon the poetical past, linked to a future of exalted ideals: not only should she be more beautiful than Helena or Tiny Montgomery or Ila Brannan, but she should hold rooms spell-bound with her eloquence, or the music in her finger-tips; and when in solitude her soul would rise to such heights as her fettered mind hinted at vaguely but insistently. Wild imaginings for a plain tongue-tied little hybrid, but what man's inner life is like unto the husk to whose making he gave no hand?

IV

Helena remained an hour longer, then ran home to don a white frock and Roman sash. Her father, with all his vagaries, seldom failed to dine at home; and he expected to find his little daughter, smartly dressed, presiding at his table. His sister, Mrs. Cartright, who had managed his house since his wife's death, made no attempt to manage Helena, and never thought of taking the head of the table.

Magdaléna stood for some time looking out over the darkening bay, at the white mist riding in to hang before the mountains beyond. She had seen California wet under blinding rain-storms, but never ugly. Even the fogs were beautiful, the great waves of sand whirling through the streets of San Francisco picturesque. California was associated in her mind, however, with perpetual blue skies and floods of yellow light. She had wondered occasionally if all people were not happy in such a country,—where the sun shone for eight months in the year, where flowers grew more thickly than weeds, and fruit was abundant and luscious. She had read of the portion to which man was born, and had decided that if Thackeray and Dickens had lived in California they would have been more cheerful; but to-day, assailed by a presentiment general rather than specific, she accepted, for the first time, life in something like its true proportions.

"There are no more caballeros," she thought, putting into form such sense of the change as she could grasp. "And Helena is going away, for years; and papa will not let me go, I know, although I mean to ask him; and aunt is way down in Santa Barbara, and writes that she may not return for months. And I don't know my music lesson for to-morrow, and papa will be so angry, because he pays five dollars a lesson; and Mrs. Price is so cross." She paused and shivered as the white fog crept up to the verandah. It was very quiet. She could hear the ocean roaring through the Golden Gate. Again the presentiment assailed her. "None of those things was it," she thought in terror. "Uncle Jack Belmont says, according to Balzac, our presentiments always mean something." She noticed anew how beautiful the night was: the white wreaths floating on the water, the dark blue sky that was bursting into stars, the mysterious outline of the hills, the ravishing perfumes rising from the garden below. "It is like a poem," she thought. "Why does no one write about it? Oh!" with a hard gasp, "if I could—if I could only write!" A meteor shot down the heavens. For the moment it seemed that the fallen star flashed through her brow and lodged, effulgent, in her brain. "I—I—think I could," she thought. "I—I—am sure that I could." And so, the cruel desires of art, and the tree of her crucifix were born.

She went inside hastily, afraid of her thoughts. She changed her frock for a white one, smoothed her sleek hair, and walked downstairs. She never ran, like Helena—unless, to be sure, Helena dragged her; she had all the dignity of her father's race, all its iron sense of convention.

She went into the big parlours to await her parents' return; they had been spending a day or two at their country house in Menlo Park, and would return in time for dinner. The gas had been lighted and turned low; Magdaléna had never seen any rooms but her own in this house sufficiently lighted by day or by night, except when guests were present. Mrs. Yorba would waste neither gas nor carpets; in consequence, the house had a somewhat sepulchral air; even its silence was never broken, save when Helena gave a sudden furious war-whoop and slid down the banisters.

The walls of the parlour were tinted a pale buff, the ceilings frescoed with cherubs and flowers. On the great plate-glass windows were curtains of dark red velvet trimmed with gold fringe. The large square pieces of furniture were upholstered with red velvet. The floor was covered with a red Brussels carpet with a design of squirming devil-fish. Three or four small chairs were covered with Indian embroidery, and there were two Chinese tables of teak-wood and mottled marble. Gas having been an afterthought, the pipes were visible, although painted to match the walls. Magdaléna had seen few rooms and had not awakened to the hideousness of these; her aunt had mingled little taste with her splendour, and the Belmont mansion was furnished throughout its lower part in satin damask with no attempt at art's variousness. Magdaléna opened the piano and felt vaguely for the music in the keys. She forgot the star, remembered only her passionate love of exultant sound, her longing to find the soul of this most mysterious of all instruments. But her stiff fingers only sprawled helplessly over the keys, and after a few moments she desisted and sat staring with dilating eyes, the presentiment again assailing her. Her shattered caballeros rose before her, but she shook her head; they, under what influence she knew not, had faded out into ghost-land.

A carriage drove up to the door. She went forward and stood in the hall, awaiting her parents. They entered almost immediately. Both kissed her lightly, her mother inquiring absently if she had been a good girl, and remarking that she had neuralgia and should go to bed at once. Her father grunted and asked her if she and Helena Belmont had behaved themselves, and, more particularly, if she had been outside the house without an attendant; he never failed to ask this when he had been away from the house for twenty-four hours. Magdaléna replied in the negative, and did not feel called upon to confess her minor sins. She had a conscience, but she had also a strong distaste for her father's temper.

Don Roberto had been a handsome caballero in his youth, but his face, like that of most Californians, had coarsened as it receded from its prime. The nose was thick, the outlines of the jaw lost in rolls of flesh. But the full curves of his mouth had been compressed into a straight line, and the consequent elevation of the lower lip had almost obliterated an originally weak chin. He was bald and wore a skull-cap, but his black eyes were fiery and restless, his skin fair with the fairness of Castile. He went to his room, and Magdaléna did not see him again until dinner was announced. She saw little of her parents. There is not much fireside life in California. There was none in the Yorba household. Mrs. Yorba was a martyr to neuralgia, and such time as was not passed in the seclusion of her chamber was devoted to the manifold cares of her household and to her small circle of friends. Don Roberto would not permit her to belong to charitable associations, nor to organisations of any kind, and although she regretted the prestige she might have enjoyed as president of such concerns, she had long since found herself indemnified: Don Roberto's social restrictions had unwittingly given her the position of the most exclusive woman in San Francisco. As time went on, it gave people a certain distinction to be on her visiting list. When Mrs. Yorba realised this, she looked it over carefully and cut it down to ninety names. After that, hostesses whose position was as secure as her own begged her personally to go to their balls. Her own yearly contribution to the season's socialities was looked forward to with deep anxiety. It was the stiffest and dullest affair of the year, but not to be there was to be written down as second of the first. So was greatness thrust upon Mrs. Yorba, who never returned to her native Boston, lest she might once more feel the pangs of nothingness. She loved her daughter from a sense of duty rather than from any animal instinct, but never petted nor made a companion of her. Nevertheless she watched over her studies, literary excursions, and associates with a vigilant eye.

Magdaléna's companions were the objects of her severe maternal care. Once a year in town and once during the summer in Menlo Park, Magdaléna had a luncheon party, the guests chosen from the very inner circle of Mrs. Yorba's acquaintance. The youngsters loathed this function, but were forced to attend by their distinguished parents. Magdaléna sat at one end of the table and never uttered a word. The only relief was

Helena, who talked bravely, but far less than was her wont; the big dark dining-room, panelled to the ceiling with redwood, and hung with the progenitors of the haughty house of Yorba, the gliding Chinese servants, the eight stiff miserable little girls, with their starched white frocks, crimped hair, and vacant glances, oppressed even that indomitable spirit. On one awful occasion when even Helena's courage had failed her, and she was eating rapidly and nervously, the children with one accord burst into wild hysterical laughter. They stopped as abruptly as they had begun, staring at one another with expanded, horrified eyes, then simultaneously burst into tears. Helena went off into shrieks of laughter, and Magdaléna hurriedly left the room, and in the privacy of her own wept bitterly. When she went downstairs again, she found Helena making a brave attempt to entertain the others in the large garden behind the house. They were swinging and playing games, and looked much ashamed of themselves. When they went home each kissed Magdaléna warmly, and she forgave them and wished that she could see them oftener. She was never allowed to go to lunch-parties herself. Occasionally she met them at Helena's, where they romped delightedly, appropriating the entire house and yelling like demons, but taking little notice of the quiet child who sat by Mrs. Cartright, listening to that voluble dame's tales of the South before the war, too shy and too Spanish to romp. Even at that early age, they respected and rather feared her. As she grew older, it became known that she was "booky,"—a social crime in San Francisco. As for Helena, she was one of those favoured mortals who are permitted to be anything they please. She, too, devoured books, but she did so many other things besides that people forgot the idiosyncrasy, or were willing to overlook it.

Don Roberto spent his leisure hours with his friends Hiram Polk and Jack Belmont. There was no resource of the town unknown to these elderly rakes; and the older they grew the more they enjoyed themselves. On fine evenings they always rode out to the Presidio or to the Cliff House; and it was one of the sights of the town,—these three leading citizens and founders of the city's prosperity: Don Roberto, fat, but riding his big chestnut with all the unalterable grace of the Californian; Polk, stiff and spare, his narrow grey face unchanged from year to year, ambling along on a piebald; dashing Jack Belmont, a cavalry officer to his death, his long black moustachios flying in the wind, a flapping hat pulled low over his abundant curls, bestriding a mighty black. All three men were somewhat old-fashioned in their attire; they went little into society, preferring the more various life beyond its pale.

V

Half of the dinner passed in unbroken silence. Magdaléna sat at one end of the table, her father at the other, their wants attended to by three Chinese servants. Magdaléna was not eating: she was summoning up courage to speak on a subject that was fast conquering her reticence. Her thoughts were not interrupted. Don Roberto was a man of few words. He had been an eloquent caballero in his youth, but had grown to be as careful of words as of investments. He liked to be amused by women; but, as he rightly judged, no amount of development could make his wife and daughter amusing, so he encouraged them to hold their tongues. He deeply resented Magdaléna's lack of beauty; all the women of his house had been famous throughout the Californias for their beauty. It was the duty of a Yorba to be beautiful—while young; after thirty it mattered nothing.

Magdaléna had completed the structure of her courage. She did nothing by halves, and she knew that she should not break down.

"Papa," she said.

"Well?"

"Helena is going to New York and to Paris to school. She is going to live with relatives, but she will attend school."

"She need."

"I thought you liked Helena."

"I like; but she need the discipline more than all the girls in California."

"I shall be very lonely without her."

"Suppose so; but now is the time to learn plenty, and no think so much by the play."

"I should like to go with her."

"Suppose so."

"May I?"

"No."

"But you would not miss me, nor mamma either."

"I choose you shall be educate at home. I no approve of the schools. Si Helena Belmont was my daughter, I take the green hide reata to her every morning; but Belmont so soffit, the school is better for her. You stay here. No say any more about it."

"Could I not travel with her after? I want to travel."

"Si I find time one day go abroad, I take you; but you no go with Helena Belmont. I no am surprise si she make herself the talk of Europe."

"Could not mamma go with me?"

"Your mother no leave the husband! Never she propose such a thing!"

"Do you think you will be able to go soon?"

"Very doubt. The Californian who leave the business for a year working like the dog for five after. Si he find one red cent when he come back, he is lucky. The man no knowing just where he is even when he stand over the spot."

"Then when Helena goes, can I go to Santa Barbara for awhile and visit aunt?"

"You no can! I no wish you ask the reason. You never go to the South! Never before you talk so much, by Scott!"

VI

Magdaléna had failed at every point. She had expected to fail, but she felt miserable and discouraged, nevertheless. After dinner she went up to her room and prayed to the Virgin. In time she felt comforted, her tears ceased, and she sat thinking for some time at the foot of her little altar. With the sad philosophy of her nature she put the impossible from her, and considered the future. It had been arranged long ago that she and Helena, Ila and Tiny, were to come out at the same time; the great function which should introduce to San Francisco three of its most beautiful girls, and its most favoured by lineage and fortune, was to be given by Mrs. Yorba. The other girls would come out a year earlier or later. Ila and Tiny were already in Europe. She had three uninterrupted years before her. In those years she could do much. When she was not studying, she would read the best authors and learn their secret. Her father had no library, but Colonel Belmont had, and she was a life member of the Mercantile Library; the membership had been presented to her two birthdays ago by her luncheon guests, who respected what they would not emulate. She pressed her face into her hands, striving to arrange the nebulous thoughts and ambitions which burned in her brain.

There was a wild ringing of bells. She raised her head and saw a red glare, then rose and walked over to the window. She thought a fire very beautiful; and as there were many in that city of wood and wind, she had had full opportunity to observe their manifold phases. Her bedroom adjoined the schoolroom, but was on the corner of the house at the back, and overlooked -- not only the business part of the city between the foot of the hill and the bay, but the region known as "South of Market Street." This large valley had its aristocratic quarter, but it was now largely given over to warehouses, dépôts, and streets of the poor. A month seldom passed without a big blaze in this closely built combustible section. To-night there was a long narrow ribbon of flame twisting in the wind, which in a few moments would leap from block to block, licking up the flimsy dwellings as a cat licks up milk. Above the ribbon flew a million sparks, turning the stars from gold to white. Every moment the wind twisted the ribbon into wonderful fantastic shapes, which beset Magdaléna's brain for words as beautiful.

She listened intently. Some one was climbing a pillar of the balcony. It was Helena, of course: she often chose that laborious method of entering a house whose doors were always open to her. Magdaléna opened the back window and stepped out onto the balcony.

"Is that you, Helena?" she whispered.

"Is it? Just you wait till you see me!"

A moment later she had clambered over the railing and stood before the astonished Magdaléna.

"What—what—"

"Boys' clothes. Can't you see for yourself? I'm going to the fire, and you're going with me."

"Of course I shall not. What possessed you—"

But the astute Helena detected a lack of decision in her friend's voice. "You're just dying to go," she said coaxingly. "You adore fires, and you'd love to see one close to. Put a waterproof on and a black shawl over your head. Then if anybody notices you, they'll think you're a *muchacha* from Spanish town. As I am a boy, I can protect you beautifully. We'll go to the livery stable and I'll make old Duff give me a hack. I've a pocket full of boodle; papa gave me my allowance to-day. Here, come in." She dragged the unresisting Magdaléna into the room, arrayed her in a waterproof, and pinned a black shawl tightly about the small brown face. "There!" she said triumphantly, "you look like a poor little greaser, for all the world. Don Roberto would have a fit. Do you think you can slide down the pillar?"

"I don't know—yes, I am sure I can if you can." Her Spanish dignity was aghast, but her newborn creative instinct stung her spirit into a sudden overpowering desire for dramatic incident. "Yes, I'll go," she whispered, closer to excitement than Helena had ever, save once, seen her. "I'll go."

"Of course! I knew you would. I always knew you were a brick; come! Quick! I'll go first." She slid down the pillar, which she could easily clasp with her long arms and legs; and Magdaléna, after a gasp, followed, shivering with terror, but too proud to utter a sound. Before she had reached the bottom she had lost all interest in the fire; she no longer wanted to write poetry; she wished frantically to be back in the security of her room. But she reached the ground safely; and although she fell in a heap, she quickly pulled herself together and stood up, holding her head higher than ever. And when she was on the sidewalk, in disguise, unattended for the first time in her life, her very nerves sang with exultation, and she was filled with a wild longing for a night replete with adventure.

"'Léna!" whispered Helena, ecstatically. "Isn't this gorgeous?"

Magdaléna nodded. Her brain and heart were throbbing too loud for speech.

"I'm going to fires for the rest of my life," announced Helena, as they turned the corner and walked swiftly down the hill. She was not of the order which is content with one experience, even while that initial experience is yet a matter of delightful anticipation.

When they reached the livery stable, Helena marched in, holding Magdaléna firmly by the hand. "I want a hack," she said peremptorily to the man in charge. "And double quick, too." The man stared, but Helena rattled the gold in her pocket, and he called to two men to hitch up.

"Upon my soul," he whispered to his associates, "it's those kids of Jack Belmont's and old Yorba's, or I'm a dead man. But it ain't none of my business, and I ain't one to peach. I like spirit."

"We're going to the fire, and I wish the hack to wait for us," said Helena, as he signified that all was ready. "I'll pay you now. How much is it?"

"Ten dollars," he replied unblushingly.

Helena paid the money like a blood, Magdaléna horrified at the extravagance. Her own allowance was five dollars a month. "Can you really afford this, Helena?" she asked remonstrantly, as the hack slid down the steep hill.

"I got fifty dollars out of Jack to-night. He's feeling awfully soft over my going away. Poor old Jack, he'll feel so lonesome without me. But we'll have a gay old time travelling together in Europe when I'm through."

Magdaléna did not speak of her conversation with her own parent. She did not want to think of it. This night was to be one of uniform joy. They were a quarter of an hour reaching the fire. As they turned into the great central artery of the city, Market Street, they leaned forward and gazed eagerly at the dense highly coloured mass of men and women, mostly young, who promenaded the north sidewalk under a blaze of gas.

"What queer-looking girls!" said Magdaléna. "Why do they wear so many frizzes, and sailor hats on one side?"

"They're chippies," said Helena, wisely.

"What's chippies?"

"Girls that live south of Market Street. They work all day and promenade with their beaux all evening. As I live, 'Léna, we're going down Fourth Street. We'll go right through Chippytown."

They had been south of Market Street before, for Ila and Tiny lived on the aristocratic Rincon Hill; but their way had always lain down Second Street, which was old, but stately and respectable. Fourth Street, like Market Street by night, would be a new country; but after a few moments' eager attention Helena sniffed with disappointment. The narrow street and those branching from it were ill-lighted and deserted; there was nothing to be seen but low-browed shops. But there was always the red glare beyond; and in a few moments the holocaust burst upon them in all its terrible magnificence.

They sprang out of the hack and walked rapidly to the edge of the crowd, which filled the street in spite of the warning cries of the firemen and the angry shouts of the policemen. The fire was devouring four large squares and sending leaping branches to isolated dwellings beyond. A great furniture factory and innumerable tenements were vanishing like icicles under a hot sun.

The girls, careless of the severe jostling they received, stared in fascinated amazement at the red tongues darting among the blackened shells, the crashing roofs, the black masses of smoke above, cut with narrow swords of flame, the solid pillar of fire above the factory, the futile streams of water, the gallant efforts of the firemen. Magdaléna, hardly knowing why, reflected with deep satisfaction that a fire was even more wonderful at close quarters than when viewed from a distance. Every detail delighted her; but when a clumsy boy stepped on her toes, she drew Helena into a sand lot opposite, where it was less crowded. It was then that she noticed for the first time the weeping women gathered about their household goods. She stared at them for a moment, then shook the rapt Helena by the arm.

"Look!" she whispered. "What is the matter with those people?"

"What?" asked Helena, absently. "Oh, don't I wish I were on that house with a hose in my hand! What a lovely exciting life a fireman's must be!" Then, yielding to Magdaléna's insistence, she turned and directed her gaze to the people in the lot behind her. "Oh, the poor things!" she said, forgetting the fire. "They've been burnt out. Let's talk to them."

The two girls approached the unfortunate creatures, who were wailing loudly, as if at a wake.

"Poor devils!" exclaimed Helena. "I am so glad I have some silver with me."

"And I have nothing to give them," thought Magdaléna, bitterly; but she was too proud to speak. She stared at them, her brain a medley of new sensations, as Helena went about, questioning, fascinating, sympathising, giving. It was the first time she had seen poverty; she had barely heard of its existence; it had never occurred to her that great romanticists condescended to borrow from life. It was not abject poverty that she witnessed, by any means. There were no hollow cheeks here, no pallid faces, no shrunken limbs. It was, save for the passing distress, to which they were not unaccustomed, a very jolly, hearty, contented poverty. Their belongings were certainly mean, but solid and sufficient. Nevertheless, to Magdaléna, who had been surrounded by luxury from her birth, and had rarely been in a street of less importance than her own, these commonly clad creatures, weeping over their cheap household goods, seemed the very dregs of the earth. Her keen enjoyment fled. She was sure she could never be happy again with so much misery in the world. If her father would only—she recalled his contempt for charities, the prohibition he had laid on her mother. She determined to pray all night to the Virgin to soften his heart. When the Virgin had been allowed a reasonable time, she would beg him to give her a monthly allowance to devote to the poor. The Virgin had failed her many times, but must surely hearken to so worthy a petition as this. She stood apart. No one noticed her. She had nothing to give. They were showering blessings upon Helena, who was walking about with a cocky little stride, well pleased with herself.

Suddenly Helena wheeled and ran over to Magdaléna.

"I've given away my last red," she said. "It's lucky I paid for that hack in advance. Let's get out. Those I haven't given any to will be down on me in a minute. Besides, it's getting late. A-ou-u!"

A policeman had tapped her roughly on the shoulder. She gazed at him in speechless terror for a half-moment, then gasped, "W-h-a-t do you want?"

"I want you two young uns for the lock-up," he said curtly. The struggling crowd had lashed his pugnacity and ensanguined his temper. As an additional indignity, the saloon had been burned, and he had not had a drink for an hour. "I'll run you in for wearing boys' clothes; have you ever heard the penalty for that, miss? And I'll run in this little greaser as a vagrant."

Helena burst into shrieks of terror, clinging to Magdaléna, who comforted her mechanically, too terrified, herself, to speak. Even in that awful moment it was her father she feared, not the law.

"Shut up!" exclaimed the officer. "None of that." He paused abruptly and regarded Helena closely. She was searching wildly in her pockets. "Oh, if you've got a fiver," he said easily, "I'll call it square."

"I haven't so much as a five-cent piece," sobbed Helena, with a fresh burst of tears. "Oh, 'Léna, what shall we do?"

"You'll come with me! that's what you'll do." He took them firmly by the hand and dragged them through the crowd, a section of which had transferred its attentions to the victims of the officer's wrath. But the three were soon hurrying up a dark cross-street toward a car; and as they went Helena recovered herself, and began to cast about among her plentiful resource. She dared not risk telling this man their names, and bid him take them home in hope of reward, for he would certainly demand that reward of their scandalised parents. No, she decided, she would confide in the dignitary in charge at the station; and as soon as he knew who she was, he would be sure to let them go at once.

They went up town on a street-car. Helena had never been in one before, and the experience interested her; but Magdaléna sat dumb and wretched. She had been a docile child, and her father's anger had never been visited upon her; but she had seen his frightful outbursts at the servants, and once he had horsewhipped a Mexican in his employ until the lad's shrieks had made Magdaléna put her fingers in her ears. He would not whip her, of course; but what would he do? And this horrid man, who was of the class of her father's coachman, had called her a "greaser." She had all the pride of her race. The insult stifled her. She felt smirched and degraded.

Nor was this all: she had had her first signal experience of the pall that lines the golden cloud.

The officer motioned to the conductor to stop in front of a squat building in front of the Old Plaza. The man, whose gall had been slowly rising for want of drink, hurried them roughly off the car and across the sidewalk into a dark passage. Their feet lagged, and he shoved them before him, flourishing his bludgeon.

"Git on! Git on!" he said. "There's no gittin' out of this until you've served your time."

The words and the dark passage made Helena shiver. What if they would not give her a chance to speak, but should lock her up at once? She knew nothing of these dark doings of night. Perhaps the policeman would take them directly to a cell. In that case, she must confide in him.

They entered a room, and her confidence returned. A man sat at a desk, an open ledger before him. He was talking to several tramps who stood in various uneasy attitudes in front of the desk. His face was tired, but his eyes had a humourous twinkle. He did not glance at the new-comers.

"Sit down," commanded the policeman, "and wait your turn."

The girls sat down uncomfortably on the edge of a bench. In a moment they noticed a young man sitting near the desk and writing on a small pad of paper. He looked up, looked again, regarding them intently, then rose and approached the policeman.

"Hello, Tim," he said. "What have you got here? A girl in boys' clothes?"

"That's about the size of it."

Helena pulled her cap over her eyes and reddened to her hair. For the first time she fully realised her position. She was Colonel Jack Belmont's daughter, and she was waiting in the city prison as a common vagrant. Magdaléna bent her head, pulling the shawl more closely about her face.

The young man looked them over sharply. "They are the kids of somebodies," he said audibly. "Look at their hands. There's a 'story' here."

Helena turned cold and set her teeth. She had no idea who the young man might be, but instinct told her that he threatened exposure.

A few moments later the tramps had gone, and the man at the desk asked the policeman what charge he preferred against his arrests.

"This one's a girl in boys' clothes, sir, and both, I take it, are vagrants. The House of Correction is the place for 'em, I'm thinkin'."

Magdaléna's head sank still lower, and she dug her nails into her palms to keep from gasping. But Helena, in this crucial moment, was game. She walked boldly forward and said authoritatively,—

"I wish to speak alone with you."

The sergeant recognised the great I AM of the American maiden; he also recognised her social altitude. But he said, with what severity he could muster,—

"If you have anything private to say, you can whisper it."

Helena stepped behind the desk and put her lips close to his ear. "I am Colonel Jack Belmont's daughter," she whispered. "Send me home, quick, and he'll make it all right with you to-morrow."

"A chip of the old block," muttered the sergeant, with a smile. "I see. And who is your companion?"

Helena hesitated. "Do—do I need to tell you?" she asked.

"You must," firmly.

"She's—you'll never breathe it?"

"You must leave that to my discretion. I shall do what is best."

"She is the daughter of Don Roberto Yorba."

"O Lord! *O* Lord!" He threw back his head and gave a prolonged chuckle.

The young man edged up to the desk.

"Who is that man?" demanded Helena, haughtily. She felt quite mistress of the situation.

"He's a reporter."

"What's that?"

"Why, a reporter for the newspapers."

"I know nothing of the newspapers," said Helena, with an annihilating glance at the reporter. "My father does not permit me to read them."

The sergeant sprang to his feet. "This *is* no place for you," he muttered. "That's the best thing I've heard of Jack Belmont for some time. Here, come along, both of you."

He motioned to the girls to enter the passage, and turned to the officer. "Don't let anybody leave the room till I come back," he said; and the reporter, who had started eagerly forward, fell back with a scowl. "There's no 'story' in this, young man," said the sergeant, severely; "and you'll oblige *me*," with significant emphasis, "by making no reference to it."

"I think you're just splendid!" exclaimed Helena, as they went down the passage.

"Oh, well, we all like your father. Although it would be a great joke on him,—Scott, but it would! However, it wouldn't be any joke on you a few years from now, so I'm going to send you home with a little good advice,— don't do it again."

"But it's such fun to run to fires!" replied Helena, who now feared nothing under heaven. "We *did* have a time!"

"Well, if you're set on running to fires, go in your own good clothes, with money enough in your pocket to grease the palm of people like our friend Tim. Here we are."

He called a hack and handed the girls in.

"Please tell him to stop a few doors from the house," said Helena; "and," with her most engaging smile, "I'm afraid I'll have to ask you to pay him. If you'll give me your address, I'll send you the amount first thing to-morrow."

"Oh, don't mention it. Just ask your father to vote for Tom Shannon when he runs for sheriff. It's no use asking anything of old Yorba," he added, with some viciousness. "And I'd advise you, young lady, to keep this night's lark pretty dark."

The remark was addressed to Magdaléna, but she only lifted her head haughtily and turned it away. Helena replied hastily,—

"My father shall vote for you and make all his friends vote, too. I won't tell him about this until next Wednesday, the day before I leave for New York; then he'll be feeling so badly he won't say a word, and he'll be so grateful to you that he'll do anything. Good-night."

"Good-night, miss, and I guess you'll get along in this world."

As the carriage drove off, Helena threw her arms about Magdaléna, who was sitting stiffly in the corner. "Oh, darling, dearest!" she exclaimed. "*What* have I made you go through? And you're so generous, you'll never tell me what a villain I am. But you will forgive me, won't you?"

"I am just as much to blame as you are. I was not obliged to go."

"But it was dreadful, wasn't it? That horrid low policeman! The idea of his daring to put his hand on my shoulder. But we'll just forget it, and next week, to-morrow, it will be as if it never had happened."

Magdaléna made no reply.

"'Léna!" exclaimed Helena, sharply. "You're never going to own up?"

"I must," said Magdaléna, firmly. "I've done a wicked thing. I've disobeyed my father, who thinks it's horrible for girls to be on the street even in the daytime alone, and I've nearly disgraced him. I've no right not to tell him. I must!"

"That's your crazy old New England conscience! If you were all Spanish, you'd look as innocent as a madonna for a week, and if you were my kind of Californian you'd cheek it and make your elders feel that they were impertinent for taking you to task."

"You are half New England."

"So I am, but I'm half Southerner, too, and all Californian. I'm just beautifully mixed. You're not mixed at all; you're just hooked together. Come now, say you won't tell him. He's a terror when he gets angry."

"I must tell him. I'd never respect myself again if I didn't. I've done lots of other things and didn't tell, but they didn't matter,—that is, not so much. He's got a *right* to know."

"It's a pity you're not more like him, then you wouldn't tell."

"What do you mean, Helena? I am sure my father never told a lie."

Helena was too generous to tell what she knew. She asked instead, "I wonder would your conscience hurt you so hard if everything had turned out all right, and we were coming home in our own hack?"

Magdaléna thought a moment. "It might not to-night, but it would to-morrow. I am sure of that," she said.

Helena groaned. "You are hopeless. Thank Heaven, I was born without a conscience,—that kind, anyhow. I intend to be a law all to myself. I'm Californian clear through into my backbone."

The hack stopped. The girls alighted and walked slowly forward. Mr. Belmont's house was the first of the three.

"Well," said Helena, "here we are. I'm going to climb up the pillar and walk along the ledge. How are you going in?"

"Through the front door."

"Well, if you will, you will, I suppose. Kiss me good-night."

Magdaléna kissed her and walked on. A half-moment later Helena called after her in a loud whisper,—

"Take off that shawl!"

Magdaléna lifted her hand to her chin, then dropped it. When she reached her own home, she rang the bell firmly. The Chinaman who opened the door stared at her, the dawn of an expression on his face.

"Where is Don Roberto?" she asked.

"In loffice, missee."

Magdaléna crossed the hall and tapped at the door of the small room her father called his office. Don Roberto grunted, and she opened the door and went in. He was writing, and wheeled about sharply.

"What?" he exclaimed. "What the devil! Take that shawl off the head."

Magdaléna removed the shawl and sat down.

"I went to a fire," she said. "I got taken up by a policeman and went to the station. A man named Tom Shannon said he wouldn't lock me up, and sent me home. He paid for the carriage." She paused, looking at her father with white lips.

His face had turned livid, then purple. "*Dios!*" he gasped. "*Dios!*" And then she knew how furious her father was. When his life was in even tenor he never used his native tongue. "*Dios!*" he repeated. "Tell that again. You go with that little devil, Helena Belmont, I suppose. *Madre de Dios!* Again! Again!"

"I went to a fire—south of Market Street. A policeman arrested me for a vagrant. He called me a greaser—"

Her father sprang to his feet with a yell of rage. He caught his riding-whip from the mantel.

She stumbled to her feet. "Papa!" she said. "Papa! You will not do that!"

A few moments later she was in her own room. The stars shone full on her pretty altar. She turned her back on it and sat down on the floor. She had not uttered a word as her father beat her. Even now she barely felt the welts on her back. But her self-respect had been cut through at every blow, and it quivered and writhed within her. She hated her father and she hated life with an intensity which added to her misery, and she decided that she had made her last confession to any one but the priest, who always forgave her. If she did wrong in the future and her father found it out, well and good; but she would not be the one to tell him.

VII

It was a part of her punishment that she was to be locked in her room until Helena left for New York; but Helena visited her every night in her time-honoured fashion. Magdaléna never told of the blows, but confinement was a sufficient excuse to her restless friend for any amount of depression; and Helena coaxed twenty dollars out of her father and bought books and bonbons for the prisoner, which she carefully disposed about her person before making the ascent. Magdaléna hid her presents in a bureau drawer; and it is idle to deny that they comforted her. One of the books was "Jane Eyre," and another Mrs. Gaskell's Life of Charlotte Brontë. They fired her with enthusiasm, and although she cried all night after the equally tearful Helena had said good-bye to her, she returned to them next day with undiminished enthusiasm.

The Sunday after Helena's departure she was permitted to go to church. She was attended by her mother's maid, a French girl and a fervid Catholic. St. Mary's Cathedral, in which Don Roberto owned a pew that he never occupied, was at that time on the corner of California and Dupont streets.

Magdaléna prayed devoutly, but only for the reestablishment of her self-respect, and the grace of oblivion for the degradation to which her father had subjected her. Later, she intended to pray that he might be forgiven, both by herself and God, and that his heart should be softened to the poor; but not yet. She must be herself again first.

Her head had been aching for two days, the result of long confinement and too many bonbons. It throbbed so during service that she slipped out, whispering to the maid that she only wanted a breath of fresh air and would be back shortly.

She stood for a few moments on the steps. Her head felt better, and she noticed how peaceful the city looked; yet, as ever, with its suggestion of latent feverishness. She had heard Colonel Belmont say that there was no other city in the world like it, and as she stood there and regarded the precipitous heights with their odd assortment of flimsy "palaces" and dilapidated structures dating back to the Fifties, she felt the vague restlessness that brooded over everything, and understood what he had meant; and she also knew that she understood as he had not. Above was the dazzling sky, not a fleck in its blue fire. There was not a breath of wind in the city. She had never known a more peaceful day. And yet, if at any moment the earth had rocked beneath her feet, she would have felt no surprise.

She felt the necessity for exercise. It was now over a week since she had been out of her room, and during that time she had not only studied as usual, but read and read and read. She did not remember to have ever felt so nervous before. She could not go back into the Cathedral; it was musty in itself and crowded with the Great Unwashed. But it would not be right to disturb Julie. There could be no harm in the least bit of a walk alone, particularly as her father was in Menlo Park. She glanced about her dubiously. Chinatown, which began a block to her right, was out of the question, although she would have liked to see the women and the funny little Chinese babies that she had heard of: the fortunate Helena had been escorted through Chinatown by her adoring parent and a policeman. She did not care to climb twice the almost perpendicular hill which led to her home, and at the foot of the hill was the business portion of the city. There was only one other way, and it looked quiet and deserted and generally inviting.

She crossed California Street and walked along Dupont Street. She saw to her surprise that the houses were small and mean; those the fire had eaten had hardly been worse. They had green outside blinds and appeared to date from the discovery of gold at least.

"There are poor people so near us," she thought. "Even Helena never guessed it. I am glad the plate had not been handed round; I will give some one my quarter."

The houses were very quiet. The shutters were closed, but the slats were open. She glanced in, but saw no one.

"Probably they are all in the Cathedral," she thought. "I am glad it is so close to them."

She walked on, forgetting the houses for the minute, absorbed in her new appreciation of the strange suggestiveness of San Francisco. Again, something was shaping itself in her mind, demanding expression. She felt that it would have the power to make her forget all that she did not wish to remember, and thought that perhaps this was the sponge for the slate the Virgin was sending in answer to her prayers.

Suddenly, almost in her ear, she heard a low chuckle. She started violently; in all her life she had never heard anything so evil, so appalling, as that chuckle. It had come from the window at her left. She turned mechanically, her spirits sinking with nameless terror.

Her expanded eyes fastened upon the open shutters. A woman sat behind them; at least, she was cast in woman's mould. Her sticky black hair was piled high in puffs,—an exaggeration of the mode of the day. Her thick lips were painted a violent red. Rouge and whitewash covered the rest of her face. There was black paint beneath her eyes. She wore a dirty pink silk dress cut shamefully low.

The blood burned into Magdaléna's cheeks. Of sin she had never heard. She had no name for the creature before her, but her woman's instinct whispered that she was vile.

The woman, who was regarding her malevolently, spoke. Magdaléna did not understand the purport of her words, but she turned and fled whence she had come. As she did so, the chuckle, multiplied a dozen-fold, surrounded her. She stopped for a second and cast a swift glance about her, fascinated, with all her protesting horror.

Behind every shutter which met her gaze was the duplicate of the creature who had startled her first. As they saw her dismay, their chuckle broke into a roar, then split into vocabulary. Magdaléna ran faster than she had ever run in her life before. Suddenly she saw Colonel Belmont sauntering down California Street, debonair as ever. His long moustaches swept his shoulders. His soft hat was on the back of his head, framing his bold handsome dissipated face. His frock-coat, but for the lower button, was open, and stood out about the dazzling shirt, well revealed by a low vest.

"Uncle Jack!" screamed Magdaléna. "Uncle Jack!"

Colonel Belmont jumped as if a battery had ripped up the ground in front of him. Then he dashed across the street. "Good God!" he shouted. "Good God!" He caught Magdaléna in his arms and carried her back to the shadow of the cross.

"You two have been possessed by the devil of late," he began wrathfully, but Magdaléna interrupted him.

"No! no!" she exclaimed. "I didn't know there was anything different there from any other street. I didn't mean to."

"Well, I don't suppose you did. You never know where you are in this infernal town, anyhow. Where's your maid?"

But Magdaléna had fainted.

VIII

After that, Magdaléna had brain fever. It was a sharp but brief attack, and when she was convalescent the doctor ordered her to go to the country at once and let her school-books alone. As Mrs. Yorba never left her husband for any consideration, Magdaléna was sent to Menlo Park with Miss Phelps. The time came when Magdaléna hated the monotony of Menlo, with its ceaseless calling and driving, its sameness of days and conversation; but at that age she loved the country in any form.

Menlo Park, originally a large Spanish grant, had long since been cut up into country places for what may be termed the "Old Families of San Francisco." The eight or ten families who owned this haughty precinct were as exclusive, as conservative, as any group of ancient county families in Europe. Many of them had been established here for twenty years, none for less than fifteen. That fact set the seal of gentle blood upon them for all time in the annals of California,—a fact in which there is nothing humourous if you look at it logically; there is really no reason why a new country should not take itself seriously.

Don Roberto owned a square mile known as Fair Oaks, in honour of the ancient and magnificent woods upon it. These woods were in three sections, separated by meadows, and there was a broad road through each, but not a twig of the riotous underbrush had been sacrificed to a foot-path. A hundred acres about the house—which was a mile from the entrance to the estate—had been cleared for extensive lawns, ornamental trees, and a deer park.

Directly in front of the house, across the driveway and starting from a narrow walk between two great lawns, was a solitary eucalyptus-tree, one of the few in the State at the time of its planting. It was some two hundred feet high and creaked alarmingly in heavy winds; but Don Roberto, despite Mrs. Yorba's protestations, would not have it uprooted: he had a particular fondness for it because it was so little like the palms and magnolias of his youth.

To the left of the house at the end of an avenue of cherry-trees was an immense orchard surrounded by an avenue of fig-trees, and English walnut-trees.

The house was as unlike the adobe mansions of the old grandees as was the eucalyptus the palms. It was large, square, two-storied, and although of wood, of massive appearance. It was, indeed, the most solid-looking structure in California at that time. A deep verandah traversed three sides of the house, its roof making another beneath the bedroom windows. Its pillars were hidden under rose vines and wistaria. The thirty rooms were somewhat superfluous, as Don Roberto would have none of house-parties, but he could not have breathed in a small house. The rooms were very large and lofty, the floors covered with matting, the furniture light and plain. Above, as from the town house, floated the American flag.

Colonel Belmont's estate adjoined Fair Oaks on one side, the Montgomerys' on the other; and the Brannans, Kearneys, Gearys, Washingtons, and Folsoms all spent their summers in that sleepy valley between the waters of the San Francisco and the redwood-covered mountains; these and others who have nothing to do with this tale. Hiram Polk had no home in Menlo, excepting in his brother-in-law's house. Some of his wife's happiest memories were of the Rancho de los Pulgas, and she refused to witness its possession by the hated American. So Polk had bought her one of the old adobe houses in Santa Barbara, and each year she extended the limit of her sojourn in a town where memories were still sacred.

IX

Magdaléna was languid and content. She put the terrible experiences which had preceded her illness behind her without effort. Her mind dwelt upon the joy of living in the sunshine, and upon the hopes of the future. She admitted frankly that she was glad to be rid of her parents, and only longed for Helena. That faithful youngster wrote, twice a week, letters which were a succession of fireworks embellished by caricatures of such of her teachers and acquaintance as had incurred her disapproval. Her aunt, Mrs. Edward Forbes, who was one of the leaders of New York society and a beauty, was giving her much petting and would take her abroad later.

Magdaléna read these letters with delight stabbed with doubt. More than once she had wondered if Helena had been born to realise all her own ambitions. Even her letters were clever and original.

In a week Magdaléna was strong enough to walk in the woods, and Miss Phelps placed no restraint upon her. She re-read what books she had, then made out a list and sent it to her father to purchase, believing that he would refuse her nothing after her illness. Don Roberto read the note, grunted, and threw it into the waste-paper basket. He abominated erudite women, and had the scorn of the financial mind for the superfluous attributes of the intellectual. Magdaléna waited a reasonable time, then after a day's hard fight with the reticence of her nature, wrote and asked Colonel Belmont for the books. He sent them at once, with a penitent note and an order on the principal bookseller of the city for all that she might want in the future. "I will say a prayer to the Virgin for him," thought Magdaléna, with a glow at her heart, oblivious that the Virgin had refused to intercede with her father.

The packet contained the lives of a number of men and women who had distinguished themselves in letters; but although Magdaléna read them twice they told her little, save that she must read the works of the masters and puzzle out their methods if she could.

Meanwhile, in spite of her studies, she was growing strong, for she spent the day out of doors; and when her parents came down on the first of June, they found her as shy and cold as ever, but with sparkling eyes and a faint glow in her cheeks.

"But never she is beauty," said Don Roberto, that evening to Polk, as the two men sat on the verandah, smoking. "Before, I resent very much, and say damnation, damnation, damnation. But now I think I no mind. Si she is beauty I think more often by that time—no can help. I wonder si there are the beautiful women in the South now, like before; but, by Jimminy! I like forget the place exeest. I am an American. Yes, Great Scott!"

He stretched out his little fat legs and rested his third chin on his inflexible shirt-front. He felt an American, every inch of him, and hated anything that reminded him of what he might become did he yield to the natural indolence and extravagance of his nature. He would gladly have drained his veins and packed them with galloping American blood. It grieved him that he could not eliminate his native accent, and he was persuaded that he spoke the American tongue in all its purity, being especially proud of a large assortment of expletives peculiar to the land of his adoption.

Polk gave a short dry laugh and stretched out his long hard Yankee legs. Even in the dusk his lantern jaws stood out. There was no doubt about his nationality. Those legs and jaws were the objects of Don Roberto's abiding envy.

"Pretty women in the family are a nuisance," said Polk. "They want the earth, and don't see why they shouldn't get it. I wouldn't have that Helena for another million. By the way, Jack told me a good story on you yesterday."

Don Roberto grunted. His Spanish pride had not abated an inch. He resented being discussed.

Polk continued: "There were seven or eight men talking over old times in the Union Club the other night; that is to say, they were reminiscing over the various enterprises they had been engaged in, and the piles they had made and lost. Our names naturally came up, and Brannan said, slowly, as if he were thinking it over hard, 'I—don't—think—I—had—any—dealings—with—Yorba—ever.' Whereupon Washington replied, quick as a shot, 'You'd remember it if you had.'"

Don Roberto scowled heavily. It was one of his fictions that he hoodwinked the world. He never snapped his fingers in its face as Polk did: exteriorly a Yorba must always be a Yorba.

"Some day when the bank have lend Meester Washington one hundred thousand dollars, I turn on the screw when he no is prepare to pay," he said. And he did.

X

During the following week all Menlo, which had moved down before Mrs. Yorba, called on that august leader. She received every afternoon on the verandah, clad in black or grey lawn, stiff, silent, but sufficiently gracious. On the day after her arrival, as the first visitor's carriage appeared at the bend of the avenue, its advent heralded by the furious barking of two mastiffs, a bloodhound, and an English carriage dog, Magdaléna gathered up her books and prepared to retreat, but her mother turned to her peremptorily.

"I wish you to stay," she said. "You must begin now to see something of society. Otherwise you will have no ease when you come out. And try to talk. Young people must talk."

"But I can't talk," faltered Magdaléna.

"You must learn. Say anything, and in time it will be easy."

Magdaléna realised that her mother was right. If she was to overcome her natural lack of facile speech, she could not begin too soon. Although she was terrified at the prospect of talking to these people who had alighted and were exchanging platitudes with her mother, she resolved anew that the time should come when she should be as ready of tongue and as graceful of speech as her position and her pride demanded.

She sat down by one of the guests and stammered out something about the violets. The young woman she addressed was of delicate and excessive beauty: her brunette face, under a hat covered with corn-coloured plumes, was almost faultless in its outline. She wore an elaborate and dainty French gown the shade of her feathers, and her small hands and feet were dressed to perfection. Magdaléna had heard of the beautiful Mrs. Washington, and felt it a privilege to sun herself in such loveliness. The three elderly ladies she had brought with her—Mrs. Cartright, Mrs. Geary, and Mrs. Brannan—were dressed with extreme simplicity.

"Yes," replied Mrs. Washington, "they are lovely,—they are, for a fact. Mine have chilblains or something this year, and won't bloom for a cent. Hang the luck! I'm as cross as a bear with a sore head about it."

"Would you like me to pick some of ours for you?" asked Magdaléna, wondering if she had better model her verbal accomplishments on Mrs. Washington's. She thought them even more picturesque than Helena's.

"Do; that's a jolly good fellow."

When Magdaléna returned with the violets, they were received with a bewitching but absent smile; another carriage-load had arrived, and all were discussing the advent of a "Bonanza" family, whose huge fortune, made out of the Nevada mines, had recently lifted it from obscurity to social fame.

"It's just too hateful that I've got to call," said Mrs. Washington, in her refined melodious voice. "Teddy says that I must, because sooner or later we've all got to know them,—old Dillon's a red Indian chief in the financial world; and there's no use kicking against money, anyhow. But I can't cotton to that sort of people, and I just cried last night when Teddy—the old darling! I'd do anything to please him—told me I must call."

"It's a great pity we old families can't keep together," said Mrs. Brannan, a stout high-nosed dame. "There are plenty of others for them to know. Why can't they let us alone?"

"That's just what they won't do," cried Mrs. Washington. "We're what they're after. What's the reason they've come to Menlo Park? They'll be 'landed aristocracy' in less than no time. Hang the luck!"

"Shall you call, Hannah?" asked Mrs. Cartright. "Dear Jack never imposes any restrictions on me,—he's so handsome about everything; so I shall be guided by you."

"In time," replied Mrs. Yorba, who also had had a meaning conference with her husband. "But I shall not rush. Toward the end of the summer, perhaps. It would be unwise to take them up too quickly."

"I've got to give them a dinner," said Mrs. Washington, with gloom. "But I'll put it off till the last gun fires. And you've all got to come. Otherwise you'll see me on the war-path."

"Of course we shall all go, Nelly," said Mrs. Yorba. "We will always stand in together."

The conversation flowed on. Other personalities were discussed, the difficulty of getting servants to stay in the country, where there was such a dearth of "me gentleman frien'," the appearance of the various gardens, and the atrocious amount of water they consumed.

"I wish to goodness the water-works on top wouldn't shut off for eight months in the year," exclaimed Mrs. Washington. "Whenever I want something in summer that costs a pile, Teddy groans and tells me that his water bill is four hundred dollars a month." And Mrs. Washington, whose elderly and doting husband had never refused to grant her most exorbitant whim, sighed profoundly.

Magdaléna did not find the conversation very interesting, nor was she called upon to contribute to it. Nevertheless, she received every day with her mother and went with her to return the calls. At the end of the summer she loathed the small talk and its art, but felt that she was improving. Her manner was certainly easier. She had decided not to emulate Mrs. Washington's vernacular, but she attempted to copy her ease and graciousness of manner. In time she learned to unbend a little, to acquire a certain gentle dignity in place of her natural haughty stiffness, and to utter the phrases that are necessary to keep conversation going; but her reticence never left her for a moment, her eyes looked beyond the people in whom she strove to be interested, and few noticed or cared whether or not she was present. But at the end of the summer she was full of hope; society might not interest her, but the pride which was her chief characteristic commanded that she should hold a triumphant place among her peers.

She had told neither of her parents of the books Colonel Belmont had given her, knowing that the result would be a violent scene and an interdiction. At this stage of her development she had no defined ideas of right and wrong. Upon such occasions as she had followed the dictates of her conscience, the consequences had been extremely unpleasant, and in one instance hideous. She was indolent and secretive by nature, and she slipped along comfortably and did not bother her head with problems.

XI

The Yorbas returned to town on the first of November. It was decided that Magdaléna should continue her studies, but the rainy days and winter evenings gave her long hours for her books. She found, to her delight, that her brain was losing something of its inflexibility; that, by reading slowly, one perusal of an ordinary book was sufficient. Her memory was still incomplete, but it was improving. Her mother had ceased to overlook her choice of books, being satisfied that Magdaléna would never care for trash.

Magdaléna always found the big dark house oppressive after the months in Menlo Park, and went out as often as she could. On fine days, attended by Julie, she usually walked down to the Mercantile Library, and prowled among the dusty shelves. The old Mercantile Library in Bush Street, almost in the heart of the business portion of the city, had the most venerable air of any building in California. There was, indeed, danger of coming out covered with blue mould. And it was very dark and very gloomy. It has always been suspected that it was a favourite resort for suicides, but this, happily, has never been proved.

But Magdaléna loved it, for it held many thousand volumes, and they were all at her disposal. Her membership was worth more to her than all her father's riches. Julie, who hated the library, always carried a chair at once to the register and closed her eyes, that she might not be depressed to tears by the gloom and the walls of books, which were bound as became all that was left of the dead.

It was during one of these visits that Magdaléna approached another crisis of her inner life. She was wandering about aimlessly, hardly knowing what she wanted, when her eye was caught by the title of a book on an upper shelf: "Conflict between Religion and Science." She knew nothing about science, but she wondered in what manner religion could conflict with anything. She took the book down and read the first few lines, then the page, then the chapter, still standing. When she had finished she made as if to replace the book, then put it resolutely under her arm, called Julie, and went home.

She read during the remainder of the afternoon, and as far into the night as she dared. Before she went to bed she said her prayers more fervently than ever, and the next morning considered deeply whether or not she should return the book half read. She finally concluded to finish it. Her intellect was voracious, and she had no other companion but her religion. Moreover, if she was to aspire to a position in the world of letters, she must equip her mind with the best that had gone before. She had every faith in the power of the Catholic religion to hold its own; her hesitation had been induced, not by fear of disturbing her faith, but because she doubted, pricked by the bigotry in her veins, if it was loyal to recognise the existence of the enemy.

However, she finished the book. On the following Saturday morning she went down to the library and asked the librarian, who took some interest in her, what he would advise her to read in the way of science; she had lost all taste for anything else.

"Well, Darwin is about the best to begin on, I should say," he replied. "He's easy reading on account of his style. And then I should advise you to read Fiske's 'Outlines of Cosmic Philosophy' before you tackle Herbert Spencer or Huxley or Tyndall."

Magdaléna took home Darwin's "Origin of Species" and "Descent of Man." They so fascinated her that not until their contents had become a permanent part of her mental furnishing did she realise their warfare on revealed religion. But by this time science had her in its mighty grip.

She read all that the librarian had recommended, and much more. It was some six months later that she fully realised that her faith was gone. There came a time when her simple appeals to the Virgin stuck in her throat; when she realised that her beloved masters, if they could have seen her telling a rosary at the foot of her altar, would have thought her a fool.

There was no struggle, for the work was done, and finally. But her grief was deep and bitter. Religion had been a strong inherited instinct, and it had been three fourths of her existence for nearly eighteen years. She felt as if the very roots of her spirit had been torn up and lay wilting and shrivelling in the cold light of her reason. She was terrified at her new position. How was she, a mere girl, to think for herself, to make her way through life, which every great writer told her was a complex and crucifying ordeal, with no guide but her own poor reason?

For the first time she felt her isolation. She had no one to go to for sympathy, no one to advise her. Of all she knew, her parents were the last she could have approached on any subject involving the surrender of her reticence.

She lost interest in her books, and brooded, her mind struggling toward will-o'-the-wisps in a fog-bank, until she could endure her solitary position no longer; she felt that she must speak to some one or her brain would fall to ashes. Her aunt was still in Santa Barbara, and showed no disposition to return. A priest was out of the question. There was no one but Colonel Belmont. Magdaléna knew nothing of his private life: not a whisper had reached her secluded ears; but she doubted if religion were his strong point. But he had always been kind, and she knew him to be clever. It took her a week to make up her mind to speak to him and to decide what to say; but when her decision was finally reached, she walked through the connecting gardens one evening with firm tread and set lips.

She entered the house by a side door and went to the library, where she knew Colonel Belmont smoked his after-dinner cigar when at home. A cordial voice answered her knock. When she entered he rose and came forward with the graceful hospitality which never failed him in the moments of his liveliest possession, and with the acute interest which anything feminine and young never failed to inspire.

"Well, honey!" he exclaimed, kissing her warmly and handing her to a chair; "you might have done this before. I'm such a lonely childless old widower."

"Oh!" said Magdaléna, with contrition; "I never thought you'd care to see me." She could not know that he seldom permitted himself to be alone.

"Well, now you know it, you'll come oftener, won't you? Have you heard from my baby lately? I had a letter a yard long this morning. She can write!"

"I had one too." She hesitated a moment, then determined to speak at once. She could not hold this nor any man's attention in ordinary conversation, and she wanted to finish before she wearied him.

"Uncle Jack," she said, "I've come to see you about something in particular. I know so few people, or I wouldn't bore you—"

"Don't you talk about boring me, honey,—you! Why, your old Uncle Jack would do anything for you."

A light sprang into Magdaléna's eyes. Colonel Belmont forgot for the moment that she was not beautiful, and warmed to interest at once. Few people had ever withstood Jack Belmont's magnetism, and Magdaléna found it easy to speak.

"It is this," she said. "I have been reading books lately that have taken my religion from me; it has gone utterly. I want to ask you what I shall do,—if there is anything to take its place. I—I—feel as if I could not get along without something."

Colonel Belmont made a faint exclamation and wheeled about, staring at the fire. His first impulse was to laugh, so ludicrous was the idea that anyone should come to him for spiritual advice; his second to get out of the room. He did neither, however, and ordered his intelligence to work.

He did not speak for some time; and Magdaléna, for the first moment, watched him intently, scarcely breathing. Then her attention wandered from herself, and she studied his profile. She noted for the first time how worn it was, the bags under the injected eyes, the heavy lines about the mouth. She had no name for what she saw written in that face, but she suddenly felt herself in the presence of one of life's mysteries. Of man's life she knew nothing—nothing. What did this man do when he was not at home? Who were his friends besides her morose father, her cold dry uncle? She felt Belmont's difference from both, and could not know that they had much in common. What circumstances had imprinted that face so differently from the few faces familiar to her? For the first time man in the concrete interested her. She suddenly realised how profound was her ignorance, despite the lore she had gathered from books,—realised dimly but surely that there was a vast region called life for her yet to explore, and that what bloomed for a little on its surface was called human nature. She gave an involuntary shiver and sank back in her chair. At the same moment Colonel Belmont looked round.

"Someone walking over your grave?" he asked, smiling. "What you asked came on me right suddenly, 'Léna. I couldn't answer it all in a minute. You didn't say much—you never do; so I understand how you've been taking this thing to heart. I'm sorry you've lost your religion, for it stands a woman in mighty well. They have the worst of it in this life." Perhaps he was thinking of his wife. His face was very sober. "But if you have lost it, that is the end of the chapter as far as you are concerned. All I can think of is this—" the words nearly choked him, but he went on heroically: "Do what you think is right in little matters as well as in great. You've been properly brought up; you know the difference between right and wrong; and all your instincts are naturally good, if I know anything about women. As you grow older, you will see your way more clearly. You won't have the temptations that many women have, so that it will be easier for you than for some of the poor little devils. And you'll never be poor. You'll find it easier than most— and I'm glad of it!" he added with a burst of warm sympathy. Emotional by nature, the unaccustomed experience had brought him to the verge of tears; and Magdaléna, forlorn and lonely, but thanking him mutely with her eloquent eyes, appealed to the great measure of chivalry in him.

"I am glad I spoke to you, Uncle Jack," she said after a moment. "You have given me much to think about, and I am sure I shall get along much better. Thanks, ever so much."

She did not rise to go, but was silent for several moments. Then she asked abruptly, —

"What do you mean by women having temptations? I know by the way you said it that you don't mean just ordinary every-day temptations."

Colonel Belmont glanced about helplessly. His eloquence had carried him away; he had not paused to take feminine curiosity into account. He encountered Magdaléna's eyes. They were fixed on him with solemn inquiry, and they were very intelligent eyes. Did he take refuge in verbiage, she would not be deceived. Did he refuse to continue the conversation, she would be hurt. In either case her imagination would have been set at work, and she might go far, and in the wrong direction, to satisfy her curiosity. Once more he stared at the fire.

To his daughter he could have said nothing on such a subject: he was too old-fashioned, too imbued with the chivalrous idea of the South of his generation that women were of two kinds only, and that those who had been segregated for men to love and worship and marry must never brush the skirts of their thought against the sin of the world. They were ideal creatures who would produce others like themselves, and men—like himself.

But as he considered he realised that he had a duty toward Magdaléna, which grew as he thought: she needed help and advice and had come to him, having literally no one else to go to. After all, might she not have temptations which would pass his beautiful, quick-witted, triumphant daughter by? Helena, with the world at her feet, would have little time for brooding, little time for anything but the lighter pleasures of life under his watchful eye, until she loved and passed to the keeping of a man who, he hoped, would be far stronger and finer than himself. But Magdaléna? Repressed, unloved, intellectual, disappointed at every turn, passionate undoubtedly,—there was no knowing to what sudden extremes desperation might drive her. And the woman, no matter how plain, had yet to be born who could not be utterly bad if she put her mind to it. It was not only his duty to warn Magdaléna, but to give her such advice as no mortal had ever heard from his lips before, nor ever would hear again.

He drew a long breath and wheeled about. Magdaléna was leaning forward, staring at him intently. There was no self-consciousness in her face, and he realised in a flash that he would merely talk into a brain. Her woman's nature would not be awakened by the homily of an elderly man. The task became suddenly light.

"Well, it's just this: There's no moral law governing the animal kingdom; but men and women were allowed to develop into speaking, reasoning, generally intelligent beings for one purpose only: to make the world better, not worse. Their reasoning faculty may or may not be a spark of the divine force behind the universe; but there's no doubt about the fact, not the least, that every intelligent being knows that he ought to be at least two thirds good, and in his better moments—which come to the worst—he has a desire to be wholly good, or at least better than he has ever been. In other words, the best of men strive more or less constantly toward an ideal (and the second-best strive sometimes) which, if realised, would make this world a very different place. I believe myself that it is this instinct alone which is responsible for religions,—a desire for a concrete form of goodness to which man can cling when his own little atom is overwhelmed by the great measure of weakness in him. Do you follow me?"

Magdaléna nodded, but she did not look satisfied.

"Well, this is the point: The world might be prosaic without sin, but it is right positive that women would suffer less. And if it could be pounded into every woman's head that she was a fool to think twice about any man she could not marry, and that she threatened the whole social structure every time she brought a fatherless child into the world; that she made possible such creatures as you saw in Dupont Street, and a long and still more hideous sequelæ, every time she deliberately violated her own instinct for good,—we'd all begin to develop into what the Almighty intended us to be when He started us off on our long march. Don't misunderstand me! Even if I were not such a sinner myself, I'd be deuced charitable where love was concerned, marriage or no marriage—O Lord! I didn't mean to say that. Forget it until you're thirty; then remember it if you like, for your brain is a good one. Look, promise me something, 'Léna;" he leaned forward eagerly and took her hand. "Promise me, swear it, that until you are thirty you'll never do anything your instincts and your intelligence don't assure you is right,—really right without any sophistry. Of course I mean in regard to men. I don't want you to make yourself into a prig—but I am sure you understand."

"I think I do," said Magdaléna. "I promise."

"Thank goodness, for you'll never break your word. You may be tempted more than once to kick the whole stupid game of life to the deuce and go out on a bat like a man, but console yourself with this: you'd be a long sight worse off when you got through than when you started, and you'd either go to smash altogether or spend the rest of your life trying to get back where you were before; and sackcloth hurts. There isn't one bit of joy to be got out of it. If you can't get the very best in this world, take nothing. That's the only religion for a woman to cling to, and if she does cling to it she can do without any other."

Magdaléna rose. "Good-night," she said. "I'll never forget a word of it, and I'm very much obliged."

She kissed him and had half crossed the room before he sprang to his feet and went hastily forward to open the door. He went to her father's house with her, then returned to his library fire. To the surprise of his servants, he spent the evening quietly at home.

XII

A year from the following June, and two days after her arrival in Menlo, Magdaléna went into the middle woods. The great oaks were dusty already, their brilliant greens were dimming: but the depths of the woods were full of the warm shimmer of summer, of the mysterious noises produced by creatures never seen, by the very heat itself, perchance by the riotous sap in the young trees which had sprung to life from the roots of their mighty parents.

Magdaléna left the driveway and pushed in among the brush. Poison oak did not affect her; and she separated the beautiful creeper fearlessly until she reached a spot where she was as sure of being alone and unseen as if she had entered the bowels of the earth. She sat down on the warm dry ground and looked about her for a moment, glad in the sense of absolute freedom. Above the fragrant brush of many greens rose the old twisted oaks, a light breeze rustling their brittle leaves, their arms lifted eagerly to the warm yellow bath from above. Near her was a high pile of branches and leaves, the home of a wood-rat. No sound came from it, and mortal had nothing to fear from him. A few birds moved among the leaves, but the heat made them lazy, and they did not sing.

After a few moments, Magdaléna's glance swept the wall of leaves that surrounded her; then she took a pencil and a roll of foolscap from her pocket. She had made up her mind that the time had come for her first essay in fiction. For two years and a half she had studied and thought to this end; too reverent to criticise, but taking the creators' structures to pieces as best she could and giving all attention to parts and details.

She had had a nebulous idea in her mind for some time. It had troubled her that it did not assume definite form, but she trusted to that inspiration of the pen of which she had read much.

Her hand trembled so that she could not write for a few moments. She put the pencil down, not covering her face with her hands as a more demonstrative girl would have done, but biting her lips. Her heart beat suffocatingly. For the first time she fully realised what the power to write would mean to her. Her religion had gone, that dear companion of many years; she had practised faithfully until six months ago, when she had asked her teacher to tell her father that she could never become even a third-rate musician; and Don Roberto had, after a caustic hour, concluded that he would "throw no more good money after bad;" she had had long and meaning conferences with her mirror, conjuring up phantasms of the beautiful dead women of her race, and decided sadly that the worship of man was not for her. She had never talked for ten consecutive minutes with a young man; but she had a woman's instincts, she had read, she had listened to the tales of her aunt, and she knew that what man most valued in woman she did not possess. Her great position and the graces she hoped to cultivate might gratify her ambitions in a measure, but they would not companion her soul. Books were left; but books are too heterogeneous an interest to furnish a vital one in life, a reason for being alive. She had read of the jealous absorption of art, of the intense exclusive love with which it inspired its votaries. She had read of the joys of creation, and her whole being had responded; she felt that did her brain obey her will and shape itself to achievement, she too would know ecstasy and ask nothing more of life.

Her nerves settled, and she began to write. Her reading had been confined to the classics of the old world: not only had she not read a modern novel, but of the regnant lights of her own country, Mr. Howells and Mr. James, she had never heard. She may have seen their names in the "Literary Bulletin" her bookseller sent her, but had probably gathered that they were biologists. There was no one to tell her that the actors and happenings within her horizon were the proper substance for her creative faculty. California had whispered to her, but she had not understood. Her intention was to write a story of England in the reigns of Oliver Cromwell and Charles the Second. The romance of England appealed to her irresistibly. The mass of virgin ore which lay at her hand did not provoke a flash of magnetism from her brain.

She wrote very slowly. An hour passed, and she had only covered a page. Her head ached a little from the intense concentration of mind. Her fingers were stiff. Finally, she laid her pencil aside and read what she had written. It was a laboured introduction to the story, an attempt to give a picture of the times. She was only nineteen and a novice, but she knew that what she had written was rubbish. It was a trite synopsis of what she had read, of what everybody knew; and the English, although correct, was commonplace, the vocabulary cheap. She set her lips, tore it up, and began again. At the end of another hour she destroyed the second result.

Then she determined to skip the prologue for the present and begin the story. For many long moments she sat staring into the brush, her brain plodding toward an opening scene, an opening sentence. At last she began to write. She described the hero. He was walking down the great staircase of a baronial hall,—in which he had lain concealed,—and the company below were struck dumb with terror and amazement at the apparition. She got him to the middle of the stair; she described his costume with fidelity; she wrote of the temper of the people in the great hall. Then she dropped the pencil. What was to happen thereafter was a blank.

She read what she had written. It was lifeless. It was not fiction. The least of Helena's letters was more virile and objective than this.

Again that mysterious indefinable presentiment assailed her. It was the first time that it had come since that night she had stood on the balcony and opened her brain to literary desire. Had that presentiment meant anything since compassed? Her father's cruel treatment? Her terrible experience in the street of painted women? Her illness? The loss of her religion? It was none of these things. So far, it had not been fulfilled; and it had struck its warning note again. She shivered, then discovered that the yellow light was no longer about her, and that her head ached. She rose stiffly and put the torn scraps of paper in her pocket. As she left, she cast a curious glance about her retreat, not knowing what prompted it. The scent of newly upturned earth came to her nostrils; a bird flew down on the rat's nest, starting along the sides a shower of loose earth; the frogs were chanting hoarsely.

XIII

The next morning the natural buoyancy of youth asserted itself; she reasoned that a long hard apprenticeship had been the lot of many authors, and determined that she would write a page a day for years, if need be, until her tardy faculty had been coaxed from its hard soil and trained to use.

She could not go to the woods that day: her mother expected callers.

"Your birthday is a week from Wednesday," Mrs. Yorba said as they sat on the verandah. "Your father and I have decided to give a dinner. You will not come out formally, of course, until winter; but a little society during the summer will take off the stiffness."

Magdaléna turned cold. "But, mamma! I cannot talk to young men."

"You expect to begin sometime, do you not? I shall also take you to any little entertainment that is given in Menlo this summer; and as the Brannans and Montgomerys are back from Europe,—they arrived last Thursday,— there may be several. The older girls gave little parties before they married; but there have not been any grown girls in Menlo for some years now. Rose Geary and Caro Folsom, who spent last summer in the East, will spend this in Menlo, so that there will be five of you, besides Nelly Washington."

Magdaléna knew that the matter was settled. She had given a good deal of imagination to the time when she should be a young lady, but the immediate prospect filled her with dismay. Then, out of the knowledge that her lines had been chosen for her, she adapted herself, as mortals do, and experienced some of the pleasures of anticipation.

"I believe I did not tell you," her mother resumed, "that I wrote to Helena some time ago asking her to bring back four dresses for you,—a ball dress for your début, an English walking suit, a calling dress, and a dinner dress."

Magdaléna had never given a thought to dress; but this sudden announcement that she was to have four gowns from Paris and London pricked her with an intimation that the interests of life were more varied than she had suspected. She wondered vividly what they would be like, and recalled several of Nelly Washington's notable gowns.

"You are to have forty dollars a month after your birthday, and your father will permit me to get you three dresses a year; everything else must come out of your allowance. You will keep an account-book and show it to your father every month, as I do. Oh—and there is another thing: a Mr. Trennahan of New York has brought letters to your father. He is a man of some importance,—is wealthy and has been Secretary of Legation twice, and comes of a distinguished family; we must do something for him, and have decided to ask him down to your dinner. That will kill two birds with one stone. He can also stay a day or two, and we will show him the different places."

"A strange man in the house for two days," gasped Magdaléna, forgetting that she was to have forty dollars a month.

"He can take care of himself most of the time. Here come Nelly."

Mrs. Washington's ponies were rounding the deer park. Magdaléna craned her neck.

"She has some one with her," she said. And in another half-moment: "Tiny Montgomery and Ila Brannan."

Magdaléna clasped her hands tightly to keep them from trembling. What would they think of her? She saw that they were smartly dressed. Doubtless they were very grand and clever indeed, and would think her more trying than ever. But although all her shyness threatened for a moment, it was summarily routed by her Spanish pride.

She rose as the phaeton drew up, and went to the head of the steps, smiling. They might find her uninteresting, but not *gauche*.

The girls came gracefully forward and kissed her warmly.

"*Dear* 'Léna," said Miss Montgomery. "We wouldn't wait: we wanted so much to see you again. And besides, you know," with a mischievous smile, "we owe you a great many luncheon calls."

Miss Brannan exclaimed almost simultaneously, "How you have improved, 'Léna! I should never have known you." And if her tone was conventional, it fell upon ears untuned to conventions.

It was Magdaléna's first compliment, and she thrilled with pleasure. "My face looks very much the same in the glass," she said. "But I am glad to see you back. Let us sit on this side."

She led the girls a little distance down the verandah; she was trembling inwardly, but felt that she should get along better if relieved of her mother's ear. Tiny began at once to talk of her delight in being home again, and Magdaléna had time to recover herself.

Tiny Montgomery was an exquisitely pretty little creature, very small but admirably proportioned, although thin. Her brown eyes were very sweet under well-pencilled brows, her nose aquiline and fine. The mouth was barely rubbed in, but the teeth were beautiful, the smile as sweet as the eyes. She had the smallest feet and hands in California, and to-day they were clad in white *suède* with no detriment to their fame. She wore a frock of white embroidered nainsook and a leghorn covered with white feathers. She talked rather slowly, in language carefully chosen, although plentifully laden with superlatives. Her voice was very sweet, and highly cultivated.

Ila Brannan was taller, with a slender full figure, and very smart. She wore a closely fitting frock of tan-coloured cloth, a small toque, and a veil covered with large velvet dots. She was very olive, and her cheeks were deeply coloured. Her black eyes had a slanting expression. Young as she was, there was a vague suggestion of maturity about her. She smiled pleasantly and echoed Tiny's little enthusiasms, which had an air of elaborate rehearsal, but she seemed to have brought something of Paris with her, and to adapt herself but ill to her old surroundings. Magdaléna did not feel at ease with either of them, but concluded that she liked Tiny best.

"Tell me something of Helena," she said finally. "Of course you saw her in Paris."

"Oh, constantly," replied Tiny. "She's perfectly beautiful, 'Léna, *perfectly*. Mamma took her with us one night to the opera, and so many people asked her who the beautiful American was. She has grown *quite* tall, and is wonderfully stylish. Colonel Belmont has simply showered money on her since he went over, and she will have beautiful clothes, and cut us *all* out when she comes back." But Tiny did not look in the least disturbed, and peeped surreptitiously into the polished glass of the window.

"She'll have all the men wild about her," announced Ila; she spoke with a slight French accent, which was not affected, as she had spent the greater part of the last five years in Paris. "And she is going to be a very dashing belle. She informed me that she shall run to fires and do whatever she chooses, and make people like it whether they want to or not. But I doubt if she will ever be fast."

"Fast!" echoed Magdaléna, a street of painted women flashing into memory; she knew of no degrees. "Helena! How can you think of such a thing in connection with her!"

Ila laughed softly. "You baby!" she said.

Tiny frowned. "You know, Ila," she said coldly, "that I do not like to talk of such things."

"Well, you need not," said Ila, coolly.

Tiny lifted her brows. "I think you know you cannot talk to me of what I do not wish to hear," she said with great dignity.

Magdaléna turned to her, the warm light of approval in her eyes; and Ila, unabashed, rose and said, "I think I'll go over and talk scandal for awhile," and joined the older women, whose numbers had been reinforced.

Magdaléna longed to ask Tiny if she really had improved, but was too shy. Tiny said almost directly,—

"You look *so* intellectual, 'Léna. Are you? I feel quite afraid "

"Oh, no, no!" replied Magdaléna, hastily, "I really know very little; I wish I knew more." She hesitated a moment; it was difficult for her to expand even to the playmate of her childhood, but an alluring prospect had suddenly opened. "Of course you will have a great deal of leisure this summer," she added. "Shall we read together?"

Tiny rose with a sweet but rather forced smile. "I am not going to let you see how ignorant I am," she said. "But I feel very rude: I should go over and talk to Mrs. Yorba."

When they had gone, Magdaléna sat for a time staring straight before her, unheeding her mother's comments. The snub had been prettily administered, but it had cut deep into her sensitiveness. She realised that she was quite unlike these other girls of her own age, had never been like them; it was not Europe that had made the difference. "I would not care," she thought, "if they would keep away from me altogether. I have what I care much more for. But I must see them nearly every day and try to interest them. And I know they will find me as dull as when I gave those dreadful luncheons."

She was recalled by a direct observation of her mother's.

"Your washed cross-barred muslin looked very plain beside their French things, but I do not think it worth while to get you any new clothes at present. But do not let it worry you. Remember that what *we* do seems right to every one. We can afford to dress exactly as we choose."

"It does not worry me," replied Magdaléna.

XIV

Whether or not to tell her parents of her determination to write had been a matter of momentous consideration to Magdaléna. After the resignation of her faith and her conversation with Colonel Belmont, she had determined to adhere rigidly to the truth and to the right way of living, to conquer the indolence of her moral nature and jealously train her conscience. The result, she felt, would be a religion of her own, from which she could derive strength as well as consolation for what she had lost. She knew, by reading and instinct, that life was full of pitfalls, but her intelligence would dictate what was right, and to its mandates she would conform, if it cost her her life. And she knew that the religion she had formulated for herself in rough outline was far more exacting than the one she had surrendered.

She had finally decided that it was not her duty to tell her parents that she was trying to write. When she was ready to publish she would ask their consent. That would be their right; but so long as they could in no way be affected, the secret might remain her own. And this secret was her most precious possession; it would have been firing her soul at the stake to reveal it to anyone less sympathetic than Helena; she was not sure that she could even speak of it to her.

Her time was her own in the country. Her father and uncle came down three times a week, but rarely before evening; her mother's mornings were taken up with household matters, her afternoons with siesta, calling, and driving; frequently she lunched informally with her friends. How Magdaléna spent her time did not concern her parents, so long as she did not leave the grounds and was within call when visitors came.

Don Roberto would not keep a horse in town for Magdaléna, but in the country she rode through the woods unattended every morning. The exhilaration of these early rides filled Magdaléna's soul with content. The freshness of the golden morning, the drowsy summer sounds, the deep vistas of the woods,—not an outline changed since unhistoried races had possessed them,—the glimpses of mountain and redwood forests beyond, the embracing solitude, laid somnolent fingers on the scars of her inner life, letting free the sweet troubled thoughts of a girl, carried her back to the days when she had dreamed of caballeros serenading beneath her casement. For two years she had dreamed that dream, and then it had curled up and fallen to dust under Helena's ridicule. Magdaléna was fatally clear of vision, and her reason had accepted the facts at once.

Sometimes during those rides she dreamed of a lover in the vague fashion of a girl whose acquaintance of man is confined to a few elderly men and to the creations of masters; but only then. She rarely deluded herself. She was plain; she could not even interest women. She felt that she was wholly without that magnetism which, she had read, made many plain women irresistible to man.

XV

Don Roberto was to bring his guest with him on the train which arrived a few minutes after five. Magdaléna was told to dress early and be in the parlour when Mr. Trennahan came downstairs. She was cold at the thought of talking alone with a man and a stranger; but Mrs. Yorba had neuralgia, and announced her intention to lie down until the last minute.

Magdaléna had received a number of pretty presents from her aunt and friends, a cablegram from Colonel Belmont and Helena, and from her father a small gold watch and fob. Her father's gift was very magnificent to her, and her pleasure was as great in the thought of his generosity as in the beauty of the gift itself. His usual gift was ten dollars; and as it had been decided that she was not to be a young lady until she was nineteen, her eighteenth birthday had been passed over.

Her mother's present was the dress she was to wear to-night, a white organdie of the pearly tint high in favour with blondes of matchless complexion, a white sash, and a white ribbon to be knotted about the throat. The neck of the gown was cut in a small V.

Magdaléna had no natural taste in dress, nor did she know the first principle of the law of colour; but when she had finished her toilette she stood for many moments before the mirror, regarding herself with disapproval. The radiant whiteness of the frock and of the ribbon about her neck made her look as dark as an Indian. She saw no beauty in the noble head with its parted, closely banded hair, in the fine dark eyes. She saw only the wide mouth and indefinite nose, the complexionless skin, the long thin figure and ugly neck. The only thing about her that possessed any claim to beauty, according to her own standards, was her foot. She thrust it out and strove to find encouragement in its pulchritude. It was thin and small and arched, and altogether perfect. She wore her first pair of slippers and silk stockings,—a present from her aunt. Her mother thought silk stockings a sinful waste of money.

Magdaléna sighed and turned to the door. "Feet don't talk," she thought. "What am I to say to Mr. Trennahan?"

She walked slowly down the stair. He was before her, standing on the verandah directly in front of the doors. His back was to her. She saw that he was very tall and thin, not unlike her uncle in build, but with a distinction that gentleman did not possess. Her father was strutting up and down the drive, taking his ante-dinner constitutional.

She went along the hall as slowly as she could, her hands clenched, her mind in travail for a few words of appropriate greeting. When she had nearly reached the door, Trennahan turned suddenly and saw her. He came forward at once, his hand extended.

"This is Miss Yorba, of course," he said. "How good of you to come down so soon!"

He had a large warm hand. It closed firmly over Magdaléna's, and gave her confidence. She could hardly see his face in the gloom of the hall, but she felt his cordial grace, his magnetism.

"I am glad you have come down to my birthday dinner," she said, thankful to be able to say anything.

"I am highly honoured, I am sure. Shall we go outside? I hope you prefer it out there. I never stay in the house if I can help it."

"Oh, I much prefer to be out."

They sat facing each other in two of the wicker chairs. He was a man skilled in woman, and he divined her shyness and apprehension. He talked lightly for some time, making her feel that politeness compelled her to be silent and listen. She raised her eyes after a time and looked at him. He was, perhaps, thirty-five, possibly more. He looked older and at the same time younger. His shaven chin and lips were sternly cut. His face was thin, his nose arched and fine, his skin and hair neutral in tint. The only colouring about him was in his eyes. They were very blue and deeply set under rather scraggy brows. Magdaléna noted that they had a peculiarly penetrating regard, and that they did not smile with the lips. The latter, when not smiling, looked grim and forbidding, and there was a deep line on either side of the mouth. Her memory turned to Colonel Belmont, and the night she had studied his profile. There was an indefinable resemblance between the two men. Then she realised how old-fashioned and worn Belmont was beside this trim elegant man, who, with no exaggeration of manner, treated her with a deference and attention which had no doubt been his habitual manner with the greatest ladies in Europe.

"Shall you be in California long?" she asked suddenly.

"That is what I am trying to decide. I had heard so much of your California that I came out with a half-formed idea of buying a little place and settling down for the rest of my days."

"The Mark Smith place is for sale," she answered quickly. "It has only two acres, but they are cultivated, and the house is very pretty."

"Your father told me about it; but although Menlo is very beautiful, it seems to have one drawback. I am very fond of rowing, sailing, and fishing, and there is no water."

"There is if you go far enough. The bay is not so very far away, and I have heard that there is salmon-fishing back in the mountains. And Mr. Washington and Uncle Jack Belmont often go duck and snipe shooting down on the marsh." She stopped with a shortening of the breath. She had not made such a long speech since Helena left.

He sat forward eagerly. "You interest me deeply," he said. "I am very much inclined to buy the place. I shall certainly think of it."

"But you—surely—you would rather be—live—in Europe. We are very old-fashioned out here."

The expression about his mouth deepened. "I should like to think that I might spend the rest of my days with a fishing-rod or a gun."

"But you have been at courts!"

He laughed. "I have, and I hope I may never see another."

"And—and you are young."

Her interest and curiosity overcame her reserve. She wanted to know all of this man that he would tell her. She had once seen a picture of a death-mask. His face reminded her of it. *What* lay behind?

"I am forty and some months."

She rose suddenly, her hand seeking her heart. "They are coming," she faltered. "I hear wheels. And mamma is not here to introduce you."

"Well," he said, smiling down on her. "Cannot you introduce me?"

"I—I cannot. I have never introduced anyone. I must seem very ignorant and *gauche* to you."

"You are delightful. And I am sure you are quite equal to anything. Am I to be introduced out here, or in the drawing-room after they have come downstairs?"

"Oh, I am not sure."

"Then perhaps you will let me advise you. When they are all here, I will appear in the drawing-room; and if your mother is not down by that time, we will help each other out. They will all be talking and will hardly notice me. But I must run."

The Geary phaeton drove up. It held Rose and her brother. After they had gone upstairs Magdaléna went into the parlour to wait for them. The large room was very dim—the gasoline was misbehaving—and silent; she shivered with apprehension. There was no sign of her mother. But Trennahan's words and sympathy had given her courage, and she burned with ambition to acquit herself creditably in his eyes.

The guests arrived rapidly. In ten minutes they were all in the parlour, sixteen in number, the men in full dress, the women in organdies or foulards showing little of arm and neck. Mrs. Washington was in pink; Tiny in white and a seraphic expression; Rose wore black net and red slippers, a bunch of red geraniums at her belt, her eyes slanting at the men about her. With the exception of Ned Geary and Charley Rollins, a friend of Helena's, with both of whom she had perhaps exchanged three sentences in the course of her life, Magdaléna knew none of the young men: they had been brought, at Mrs. Yorba's suggestion, by the other guests.

She could find nothing to say to them; she was watching the door. Would her mother never come? Her father was on the front verandah talking to Mr. Washington and her uncle.

Trennahan entered the room.

Magdaléna drew herself up and went forward. She looked very dignified and very Spanish. No one guessed, with the exception of Trennahan, that it was the ordeal of her life.

"Mr. Trennahan," she said in a harsh even voice: "Mrs. Washington, Miss Brannan, Miss Montgomery."

He flashed her a glance of admiration which sent the chill from her veins, and began talking at once to the three women that she might feel excused from further duty. A few moments later Mrs. Yorba entered. She received Trennahan without a smile or a superfluous word. Mrs. Yorba was never deliberately rude; but were she the wife of an ambassador for forty years, her chill nipped New England nature would never even artificially expand; the cast-iron traditions of her youth, when neither she nor any of her acquaintance knew aught of socialities beyond church festivals, could never be torn from the sterile but tenacious soil which had received them.

Dinner was announced almost immediately. Mrs. Yorba signified to Trennahan that he was to have the honour of taking her in; and as she had not intimated how the rest were to be coupled, the women arranged the matter to suit themselves. Mrs. Cartright went in with Don Roberto, Mrs. Washington with Polk; there were no other married women present. As

Charley Rollins was standing by Magdaléna, she took the arm he offered her.

The function was not as melancholy as the Yorba dinners were wont to be. Young people in or approaching their first season are not easily affected by atmosphere; and those present to-night, with the exception of Magdaléna and Tiny Montgomery, chattered incessantly. Tiny had a faculty for making her temporary partner do the talking while she enjoyed her dinner; but she listened sweetly and her superlatives were happily chosen.

Mrs. Cartright always talked incessantly whether anyone listened or not. Mrs. Washington, who sat on Don Roberto's left, amused him with the audacity of her slang. Where she learned the greater number of her discords was an abiding mystery; the rest of Menlo Park relegated slang to the unknown millions who said "mommer" and "popper," got divorces, and used cosmetics. When remonstrated with, she airily responded that her tongue was "made that way," and rattled off her latest acquisition. As she was an especial pet of Mrs. Yorba's—if that august dame could be said to pet anyone—and of distinguished Southern connections, the remonstrances were not serious.

Magdaléna, although she ordered her brain to action, could think of nothing to say to Rollins; but he was a budding lawyer and asked no more of providence than a listener. He talked volubly about Helena's childish pranks, the last Bohemian Club Midsummer Jinks, the epigrams of his rivals at the bar. He appeared very raw and uninteresting to Magdaléna, and she found herself trying to overhear the remarks of Trennahan, who was doing his laborious duty by his hostess. After a time Trennahan allowed his attention to be diverted by Ila, who sat on his right. That he was grateful for the change there could be no doubt. His expression up to this point had been one of grim amusement, which at any moment might become careworn. The lines of his face relaxed under Ila's curved smiles and slanting glances. They laughed gaily, but pitched their voices very low.

Magdaléna wondered if all dinners were as wearisome as this. Rollins finally followed Trennahan's example and devoted himself to Caro Folsom, a yellow-haired girl with babyish green eyes, a lisp, and an astute brain. On Magdaléna's left was a blond and babbling youth named Ellis, who made no secret of the fact that he was afraid of his intellectual neighbour; he stammered and blushed every time she spoke to him. He had gone in with Rose Geary, a blonde fairy-like little creature, as light of foot as of wit, and an accomplished flirt; who regarded men with the eye of the philosopher. They occupied each other admirably.

Opposite, another young lawyer, Eugene Fort, was saying preternaturally bright things to Tiny, who lifted her sweet orbs at intervals and remarked: "How *dreadfully* clever you are, Mr. Fort; I am *so* afraid of you!" or "How *sweet* of you to think I am worth all those *real* epigrams! You ought to keep them for a great law-book." Once she stifled a yawn, but Mr. Fort did not see it.

Little notice was taken of Magdaléna, and she felt superfluous and miserable. Even Trennahan, who had seemed so sympathetic, had barely glanced at her. She wondered, with a little inner laugh, if she were growing conceited. Why should he, with one of the prettiest girls in California beside him? Ila was very young, but she belonged by instinct to his own world.

The dinner came to an end. The older men went to the billiard-room, the younger men followed the girls to the parlour. Trennahan talked to Tiny for a time, then again to Ila, who lay back in a chair with her little red slippers on a footstool. She had carefully disposed herself in an alcove beyond the range of Mrs. Yorba's vision.

Tiny, whose train added to the remarkable dignity of her diminutive person, crossed the room to Magdaléna, who was sitting alone on the window-seat.

"You have done so *well*, 'Léna dear," she said, as she sat down beside her discouraged hostess. "I feel I must tell you that *immediately*. You are not a *bit* shy and nervous, as I should be if I were giving my first dinner."

Magdaléna smiled gratefully. Tiny had always been the kindest of the girls. "I am glad you think I am not so bad," she said. "But I fear that I have bored everybody."

"*Indeed*, you have not. You are so calm and full of natural repose. The rest of us seem *dreadfully* American by contrast."

"You are never fussy."

"I know, but it is *quite* different. I've been very carefully brought up. You would be exactly as you are if you had brought yourself up. The Spanish are the most dignified—What are they going to do, I wonder?"

Mr. Fort approached. "We are going to walk about the grounds and step on the frogs," he said. "I don't know a line of poetry, but I can count stars, and I'll tell you of my aspirations in life. Will you come?"

"I *so* want to hear your aspirations, Mr. Fort," said Tiny. "I did not know that California men had aspirations."

The girls went with him to the verandah, and all started down the driveway together, then paired. To her surprise, Magdaléna found Trennahan beside her.

"I am so glad to be with you again," he said petulantly. "I am tired of types."

"Types?"

"Yes; women that a man has been used to for many long weary years,— to put it in another way."

"But surely you find Ila very fascinating?"

"Oh, yes; but one understands the fascination so well; and it gives so much pleasure to—twenty-two, that it is almost immoral for an old fogy like myself to monopolise it. I don't understand you in the least, so I am here."

Magdaléna trembled a little. The nineteen years of her life suddenly assumed a glad complexion, lifting her spirit to the level of her mates. She tried to recall the sad and bitter experiences of her brief past, but they scampered down into the roots of memory.

He did not speak again for a time, beyond asking if he might smoke. He was quite sincere for the moment; but he understood the much of her that was salient to his trained eye. Her parents, her timid reserve, so unlike that of other American girls favoured by fortune, her ignorance of certain conventionalities, the very fashion of her hair, the very incompatibility of her costume and colouring, told him two thirds of her short history. Of the history of her inner life he guessed little, but believed that she had both depth of mind and intensity of feeling. To get her confidence would be next to impossible; it was therefore well worth the effort. If she proved as interesting as he suspected, he believed that he should feel disposed to marry her did she only have a complexion. He was weary straight down into the depths of his weary soul of the women and the girls of the world; but he also abhorred a sallow skin. He had worshipped beauty in his day, and was by no means impervious to it yet; but he felt that he could overlook Magdaléna's nose and mouth and elementary figure for the sake of her eyes and originality, did she only possess the primary essential of beauty. A man regards a woman's lack of complexion as a personal grievance.

If the American habit of monologue had been a part of Trennahan's inheritance, his foreign training had long since lifted it up by the roots; but he saw that if he was to make progress with this silent girl, he must do the talking. He could be both brilliant and amusing when he chose, and he exerted himself as he had not done for some time. He was rewarded by a rapt attention, a humble and profound admiration that would have flattered a demi-god. And in truth he was a demi-god to this girl, with her experience of elderly old-fashioned men and an occasional callow youth encountered on a verandah in summer.

They followed the driveway that curved between one of the two larger lawns and the deer park. The lawn was set thickly along its edge and sparsely on its sweep with fragrant trees and shrubs. Beyond the deer park was the black mass of the woods. The air was sweet with the mingled breath of June roses, orange blossoms, and the pepper-tree. After a time their way lay through a dark avenue of immense oaks, and the perfumes came from the Mariposa lilies in the fields beyond.

If Trennahan had been with Ila, he would have conducted himself as his surroundings and his companion demanded: he would have made love. But he was a man who rarely made a mistake; he talked to Magdaléna of the difference between California and the many other countries he had visited, and answered her eager questions about life in the great capitals. As they were returning, he said to her,—

"You say you ride before breakfast. Do you think I might join you to-morrow? Your father has been kind enough to place his stable at my disposal."

"Oh—I—I don't know. My father is very—Spanish, although he doesn't like you to call it that."

"May I ask him?"

"Oh, yes, you could ask him."

When they reached the house he sought his host in the billiard-room. The game was over, and Don Roberto, Mr. Polk, and Mr. Washington were seated in front of the mantel-piece with their feet on the shelf. It was Don Roberto's favourite attitude; he felt that it completed the structure of his Americanism. He could only reach the tip of the shelf with the points of his little elegant feet, but he was just as comfortable as Mr. Polk, whose feet, large and booted, were planted against the wall. Mr. Washington, who was a most correct gentleman, with the illustrious forbears his name suggested, had never lifted his feet to one of his own mantels in his life; but Don Roberto's guests always humoured this little hobby, among many others.

"Ay, the Mr. Trennahan," said Don Roberto, graciously. "We make room for you."

The others moved along, and Trennahan, seeing what was expected of him, brought a chair and elevated his feet among the Chinese bric-à-brac. He accepted a choice cigar—there were certain luxuries in which Don

Roberto never economised—and added his quota to the anecdotes of the hearthstone. As his were fresh and the others as worn as an old wedding-ring, it was not long before he had an audience which would brook no interruption but applause.

A Chinaman brought a peremptory message from Mrs. Washington, and the feet on the mantel were reduced to six. When these came down, two hours later, Trennahan said to Don Roberto,—

"May I ride with Miss Yorba to-morrow before breakfast?"

"Yes; I no mind," said the don, beaming with approval of his new friend. "But the boy, he go too. My daughter, no must ride alone with the gentleman. And you no leave the grounds, remember."

XVI

When Magdaléna went up to her room, she spread all her pretty gifts on the table and asked herself if they were the secret of this novel feeling of content with herself and her world. She studied the mirror and fancied that she was not so plain as usual. Her eyes returned to her presents, and she shook her head. Her mind worked slowly, but it worked logically; nor was that imagination hers which keeps woman in a fool's paradise long after all but the husk of her Adam has gone.

"It is Mr. Trennahan," she admitted reluctantly but ruthlessly. "He is so clever and so agreeable—no, fascinating—that for the first time I forgot myself, and when I remembered was not unhappy because I am not beautiful nor clever. The world must be much nicer than I thought if there are many people like that in it."

To love she did not give a thought, but she smiled to herself after the light was out, and, still smiling, fell asleep.

The next morning she was downstairs by six o'clock, but found Trennahan before her. As he approached her,—he had been sauntering up and down the drive,—she wondered what he thought of her costume. As she was not allowed to leave the grounds, a habit had never been thought necessary for the heiress of the house of Yorba. She had worn for the past two years one of her mother's discarded black skirts and a cotton blouse. But it is doubtful if an inspired mind-reader could have made anything of such thoughts as Trennahan wished to conceal.

"You look as fresh as the morning," he said, with a gallantry which was mechanical, but true and delightful to a girl in her first experience of compliments.

"Did you sleep well?" she asked. "I hope the mosquitoes did not keep you awake. They are very bad."

"I believe they are, but I received a friendly warning from Mr. Polk and rubbed the leather which protects my skull with vinegar. I think it was superfluous, but at all events I slept undisturbed."

Magdaléna regarded his skin attentively, much to his amusement. "It is thick," she said, feeling that she could not honestly reassure him, but quite positive that he expected her to answer.

He laughed heartily. "Oh!" he said. "What a pity you must 'come out'! I am a convert to the Old-Californian system. But here are the horses."

The improvised groom, a sulky and intensely self-conscious stable-boy, led up the horses, and Magdaléna put her foot in Trennahan's hand.

"Oh!" he exclaimed, with a note of real admiration in his voice; and Magdaléna nearly fell over the other side of her horse.

They cantered off sharply, the boy following a good thirty yards behind, feeling uncommonly sheepish when he was not thinking angrily of his neglected chores. It was not thought good form in Menlo Park to put on the trappings of Circumstance. Mrs. Washington drove a phaeton and took a boy in the rumble to open the gates; but the coachmen when driving the usual char-à-banc or wagonette performed this office while their mistresses steered the horses through the gates. No one ever thought of wearing a jewel or a décolleté gown to a dinner or a dance. Mrs. Dillon, the Bonanza queen, having heard much of the simplicity of the worshipful Menlo Park folk, had paid her first calls in a blue silk wrapper, but, conceiving that she had done the wrong thing, sheltered her perplexities in black silk thereafter. Her daughter upon the same occasion had worn a voluminous frock of pale blue camel's hair trimmed with flounces of Valenciennes lace, that being the simplest frock in her wardrobe; but she privately thought even Mrs. Washington's apotheosised lawns and organdies very "scrubby," and could never bring herself to anything less expensive than summer silks, made at the greatest house in Paris.

"I am going to see the Mark Smith place this afternoon," said Trennahan. "Your mother has very kindly offered to drive me over. I suppose it has no woods on it. These are beautiful."

"They are the only ones in the San Mateo Valley," replied Magdaléna, experiencing the full pride of possession. "Are there such beautiful ones in Europe?"

"Those at Fontainbleau are not unlike. But in England you stand in the middle of a wood and admire the landscape on either side."

"Helena wrote me something like that. She said that she always put on a veil when she went into an English wood for fear she would get freckled."

"Who is Helena?"

"She is my great friend. She is Colonel Jack Belmont's daughter, and the most beautiful girl in California. At least I think she is, for of course I have not seen them all."

"Are you always as conscientious as that? Why have I not seen this peerless creature?"

"She is in Europe. You will see her in December. Of course I do not know if she is a 'type,' but I don't see how anybody else could be like Helena. Mr. Rollins said last night that she was the concentrated essence of California."

"Describe her to me." He was delighted at the prospect of drawing her out on any subject.

Magdaléna hesitated, wondering if she should have the courage to continue, did she begin a monologue. She recalled the sustained animation of the girls at her dinner, and moved as if to shake her head, then recollected her ambition to shine in conversation. To no one had she ever found it so easy to express herself as to this man. Why not take advantage of that fact? And that represented but the half of her present ambition. If she could only interest him!

He watched her closely, divining some cause of her hesitation, but not all. Her complexion was even less desirable by day than by gas, but her hair was tumbled, her eyes were sparkling softly; and the deep green arbours of the wood were an enchanting aid to youth.

"She has curly shining hair about the colour of mahogany, and big—long—dark blue eyes that look as if they were not afraid of anything, and make you afraid sometimes, and regular features, and a whiter skin than Tiny's, with a beautiful pink colour—" She stopped short, feeling that her attempt at description was as ineffective as the hours wasted upon her much modelled hero.

"That sounds very charming, but still—never mind her appearance. Tell me what you so much admire in her."

"She talks so much, and she isn't afraid of anybody. She says she wouldn't lie because she wouldn't pay anyone that compliment. She loves to 'cheek' and shock people. She walks all round the outside of the house—upstairs—on a narrow ledge, and she runs to fires—at least she ran to one—and she won't study when she doesn't feel like it. And—and—she even snatched off papa's skull-cap once."

Trennahan threw back his head and laughed loud and long. "And you would have me believe that all that is what moves you to admiration. Don't you know, my dear child, that you love your friend in spite of her tomboy eccentricities, not because of them? You wouldn't be or do one of those things if you could."

Again Magdaléna hesitated. The implied approval was delightful; but she would not hold it on false pretences. She answered firmly,—

"I went to the fire with her."

"You? Delightful! Tell me about it. Every detail."

She told him everything except the terrible sequel. It was lamely presented, but he cared nothing for the episode. His sympathies were immediate if temporary, and experience had eaten off the very cover of the book of seals. He followed her through every mental phase she unconsciously rehearsed; and when she brought the story to an abrupt close, lacking the art to run it off into generalities, he inferred something of the last development and did not press her to continue. He pitied her grimly. But he was an intensely practical man.

"You must never think of doing that sort of thing again," he said. "Unless a person is naturally eccentric, the attempt to be so demoralises him, because there is nothing so demoralising as failure—except on one's own particular lines. Did you, for instance, jump on a horse and career barebacked through Menlo Park like a wild Indian,—a performance which your friend would probably carry off with any amount of dash and *chic*— you would feel a hopeless fool; whereas," he gave her a keen side glance, "if you felt that you possessed a talent—for music, say—and failed forty times before achieving success, you would feel that your failures partook of the dignity of their cause, and of your own character."

She turned to him with quickening pulse. "Do you think," she faltered, hunting for phrases that would not commit her, "that if a person loved an art very much, even if he could not be sure that he had genius, that he would be right to go on and on, no matter how often he became discouraged?"

Her eyes were staring at her horse's neck; she did not see him smile. He had felt quite sure that she sought relief for the silences of her life in literary composition. When an unattractive woman has not talent she finds a double revenge in the torture of words, he thought. What shall I say to her? That she is whittling thorns for her own soul? Bah! Did I not find enjoyment once in the very imaginings of all that has scourged me since? Would I have thanked anyone for opening my eyes? And the positive is the one thing that grips the memory. It is as well to have what high lights one can.

She had raised her head and was looking at him expectantly.

"Certainly," he said. "He should go on, by all means. Love of an art presupposes a certain degree of talent."—May Heaven forgive me for that lie, he thought.

She detected his lack of spontaneity, but attributed it to the fact that he had not guessed her personal interest in the question. "Have you met many literary people?" she asked. "But of course you must. Did you like them very much?"

"I have inquired carefully, and ascertained that there are none in Menlo. If there were, I should not think twice about the Mark Smith place."

Magdaléna felt herself burning to her hair. She glanced at him quickly, but he averted his eyes and called her attention to a magnificent oak whose limbs trailed on the ground. Should I tell him? she thought, every nerve quaking. *Should* I? Then she set her lips in scorn. He spoke of "literary" people, she continued. It will be many a day before I am that. Meanwhile, as Helena would say, what he doesn't know won't hurt him.

He had no intention of letting her make any such confidences. "Tell me," he said. "I have heard something of the old Spanish families of California. You, of course, belong to them. That is what gives you your delightful individuality. I should like to hear something of that old life. Of course it interests you?"

"Oh, I love it,—at least, I loved it once. My aunt, my father's sister, used to talk constantly of that time, but I have no one to talk to of it now; she has lived in Santa Barbara for the last three years. She told me many stories of that time. It must have been wonderful."

He drew one leg across the horse's neck and brought him to a stand. They had entered the backwoods and were walking their horses. The groom was nowhere to be seen. He was, in fact, awaiting them at the edge of the woods, his beast tethered, himself prone, the ring-master of a tarantula fight.

"Tell me those stories," commanded Trennahan. He knew they would bore him, but the girl was very interesting.

Magdaléna began the story of Ysabel Herrara. At first she stumbled, and was obliged to begin no less than three times, but when fairly started she told it very well. Many of her aunt's vivid picturesque phrases sprang from their dusty shelves; her own early enthusiasm revived. When she had finished she passed on to the pathetic little histories of Éléna Duncan and Benicia Ortega. She had told over those stories many times to herself; to-day they were little more than the recital of a well-studied lesson. The intense earnestness of Trennahan's gaze magnetised her out of self-consciousness. When she was concluding the third, his horse shied suddenly at a snake, and while he quieted it she tumbled back to the present. She sat with parted lips and thumping heart. Had she talked as well as that? She, Magdaléna Yorba, the dull, the silent, the terrified? She felt a glad pride in herself, and a profound gratitude to the wizard who had worked the spell.

"I have never been more interested," he said in a moment. "How delightfully you talk! What a pity you don't write!"

Magdaléna's heart shook her very throat, but she managed to answer, "And then you wouldn't buy the Mark Smith place?"

"Well, no, perhaps I wouldn't," he answered hurriedly, lest she might be moved to confidence. He had a lively vision of Magdaléna reading her manuscripts to him, or sending them to him for criticism. "But you must tell me a story every time we—I am so fortunate as to have you all to myself like this. I suppose we should be going back now."

Magdaléna took out her watch. The little air of pride in her new possession amused Trennahan, although he saw the pathos of it.

"Yes," she said; "it is nearly eight. We must go. Papa does not like us to be late for breakfast."

As they reached the edge of the woods, Magdaléna gave an exclamation of disgust; but Trennahan leaned forward with much interest. The two tarantulas, after tearing each other's fur and legs off, were locked in the death embrace, leaping and rolling.

"Get on your horse at once," said Magdaléna, sternly. "You are a cruel boy."

"But that is very interesting," said Trennahan; "I never saw it before."

"They are always doing it here. They pour water—" She turned to the boy, who was mounted, and close behind them, now that they were likely to come within the range of the old don's vision at any moment. "Dick," she said sternly, "how did you get those tarantulas up? Have you a whiskey flask about you?"

She spoke with all her father's harsh pride when addressing an inferior: Don Roberto regarded servants, in spite of the heavy wage they commanded, as he had the Indians of his early manhood. Trennahan watched her closely, remarking upon the variety a man might find in a woman if he chose to look for it.

The boy assured Magdaléna that the tarantulas had been above ground. She shrugged her shoulders and turned her back expressively upon him.

"You see those little round holes covered with white film?" she said to Trennahan. "They lead down to the tarantulas' houses,—real little houses, with doors on hinges. People pour water down, and the old tarantula comes up—back first, dragging his legs after him—to see what is the matter. Then they set two of them at each other with sticks, and they—the tarantulas—never stop fighting until they have torn each other to death: they have two curved sharp teeth."

Good sport for variety's sake, thought Trennahan. I see myself engaged on warm afternoons.

XVII

After breakfast Trennahan lay in a long chair on the verandah and smoked undisturbed. Mrs. Yorba was busy, and Magdaléna sat up in her room, longing to go down, but fearing to weary him. She recalled the early hours with vivid pleasure. For the first time in her life she was almost pleased with herself. She took out her writing materials; but her beloved art would not hold her. She went to the window and unfastened the shutter softly. Trennahan was not talking to himself nor even walking up and down the hard boards below, but the aroma of his cigar gave evidence that he was there. It mingled with the perfume of the pink and white roses swarming over the roof of the verandah almost to her window.

She experienced her first impulse to decorate herself, to gather a handful of those roses and place them in her hair. Her aunt had never been without that national adornment, worn with the grace of her slender girlhood.

She stepped over the sill, catching her breath as the tin roof cracked beneath her feet, but gathered the roses and returned to her mirror. With the nimble fingers of her race she arranged the roses at one side of her head, above and behind the ear. Certainly they were becoming. She also discovered that she had her aunt's turn of the head, her graceful way of raising her hand to her ear.

But it is so little, she thought with a sigh; if I could only have the rest!

Her mind wandered back to the heroines of her aunt's tales. If she but had the beauty of those wondrous girls, Trennahan would have taken fire in the hour that he met her, as their caballeros had done. The thought made her sigh again, not with a woman's bitterness,—she had lived too little for that,—but with a girl's romantic sadness. Why had she been defrauded of her birthright? She recalled something Colonel Belmont had once said about "cross-breeding being death on beauty in nine cases out of ten." Why could not her father have married another woman of his race? She dismissed these reflections as unfilial and wicked, and returned to her work; but it was only to bite the end of her pen-holder and dream.

Meanwhile Trennahan fell asleep and dreamed that his Menlo house caught fire one night and that all the maidens of his new acquaintance came in a body to extinguish the flames. Miss Montgomery played a hose considerably larger round than her neck, with indomitable energy and persistence. Miss Brannan, in a dashing red cap and jacket, danced like a bacchante on the roof, albeit manipulating large buckets of water. Mrs. Washington was also there, and, swinging in a hammock, encouraged the workers with her characteristic optimism expressed in picturesque American. Magdaléna, in a suit of her father's old clothes, was handing his books through the library window to Miss Folsom. Miss Geary was scrambling up the ladder, a hose coiled about her like a python. The leader of the company stood on the roof directly above the front door, giving orders with imperious voice and gesture. But although the flames leaped high about her, starting the leaves of a neighbouring tree into sharp relief, he could not see her face.

XVIII

Trennahan did not see Magdaléna until luncheon. She came in late, and her manner was a shade colder and more reserved than usual. After much excogitation, she had decided to leave the roses in her hair, but it had taken her ten minutes to summon up courage to go downstairs.

He understood perfectly, and his soul grinned. Then he sighed. Youth had been very sweet to him, all manifestations of femininity in a woman very dear. There were four long windows in the dining-room, but the roof of the verandah, the thick vines springing from pillar to pillar, the lilac-trees and willows just beyond, chastened the light in the room. Magdaléna looked almost pretty, with her air of proud reserve, the roses nestling in her dark hair. Ten years ago he might have loved her, perhaps, in spite of her complexion.

Mrs. Yorba did not notice the roses. Her mind was blind with wrath: the cream sauce of the chicken was curdled. During at least half the meal she did not utter a word; and Trennahan, wondering if fate were forcing him into the permanent role of the garrulous American, a breed for which he had all the finely bred American's contempt, talked of the weather, the woods, the climate, the beauty of the Californian women, with little or no assistance from Magdaléna. The moment he paused, and he was hungry, the catlike tread of the Chinese butlers was the only sound in the large house; the silence was so oppressive that he reflected with gratitude that his visit would be done with the morrow's morn.

Finally, Mrs. Yorba left the table and stepping through one of the open casements walked up and down the verandah. She was very fond of this little promenade between the last solid course of luncheon and the griddle-cakes and fruit.

"I am glad you wear flowers in your hair," said Trennahan. "Your head was made for them. I am certain your Ysabel What's-her-name must have worn them just so the night her ardent lover conceived the idea of robbing the Mission of its pearls for her fair sake."

Magdaléna's face glowed with its rare smile. "But Ysabel was so beautiful," she said wistfully,—"the most beautiful woman in California."

"All women are beautiful, my dear Miss Yorba—when they are young. If girls could only be made to understand that youth is always beautiful, they would be even prettier than they are."

Magdaléna's eyes were large and radiant for a moment. She was disposed to believe in him implicitly. She determined that she would think no more on the beautiful women of her race, but learn to make herself attractive in other ways. Helena would return soon and would teach her.

"I have read in books that plain women are sometimes more fascinating than beautiful ones," she said. "How can that be? Of course you must know."

"A fascinating ugly woman is one who in the same moment sets the teeth on edge and makes a beauty look like a daub or a statue. Her pitfall is that she is apt to be lacking in pride: she makes too great an effort to please. Your pride is magnificent. I say that in strict truth and without any desire to pay you a compliment. Had fate been so unkind as to make you an ugly woman, you would not have had a jot less; it is the finest part of you, to my way of thinking. You are worrying now because you have less to say than these girls who have travelled and been educated abroad, and who, moreover, are of lighter make. Don't try to imitate them. The knack of making conversation will come with time; and you will always be appreciated by the men who are weary past your power to understand of the women that chatter. If I buy this place, I shall read over some of my favourite old books with you,—that is, if you will let me; and I believe that you will."

Magdaléna's hands were clasped on the edge of the table; she was leaning forward, her soul in her eyes. For the moment she was beautiful, and Trennahan looked his admiration and forgot her lack of complexion. To Magdaléna there had been a sudden blaze of golden light, then a rift, through which she caught a brief flash of heaven. Her vague longings suddenly cohered. She was to be solitary no longer. She was to have a companion, a friend,—perhaps a confidante, a person to whom she might speak out her inmost soul. She had never thought that she should wish to open her reserve to anyone, but in this prospect there was enchantment.

Mrs. Yorba returned to her seat and helped herself to hot cakes.

"When Miss Montgomery and Miss Brannan were leaving last night," she said, "they asked me to stop for them this afternoon, as they wished to persuade you that the Mark Smith place was exactly what you wanted, or something to that effect. So we shall stop for them. The char-à-banc will be at the door at a quarter to four."

That was her last remark, as it had been her first, and some twenty minutes later the repast came to an end.

XIX

Trennahan was again left to his own devices. He amused himself inspecting the stable, a most unpretentious structure, containing all that was absolutely indispensable and no more. Attached to the farmhouse in an adjoining field was a barn for the work-horses. The stable-boy did duty as guide, and conducted Trennahan through the dairy, granary, carpenter shop, and various other outbuildings. It was all very plain, but very substantial, the symbol of a fortune that would last; altogether unlike the accepted idea of California, that State of rockets and sticks.

But, for the matter of that, thought Trennahan, all things should be stable in this land of dreaming nature. He had been told since his arrival that everything had been in a rut since the great Bonanza plague; but assuredly this archaic repose must be its natural atmosphere; its fevers must always be sporadic and artificial.

Yes, he thought, it is a good place to die in. It would have been intolerable ten years ago, but it seems little short of paradise when a man has dry rot in him. And that girl looked remarkably well with those roses in her hair. Poor thing!

Magdaléna came down to the verandah a few moments before the char-à-banc drove up. She wore a buff lawn, simply made by the family seamstress, and a large straw hat trimmed with daisies. She had taken the flowers out of her hair, but had pinned a large cluster of red roses at her waist. Altogether she looked her best, and felt that she might be able to hold her own against the other girls.

One secret of Trennahan's charm for women was that he never overlooked their little efforts to please him. He said immediately, —

"Yellow and red were made for you. You should leave white for those who cannot stand the fury of colour."

She was keenly alive to the pleasures of appreciation, but merely asked if he had managed to amuse himself.

"Fairly well, considering that you deserted me."

"But they almost always leave the men alone down here in the daytime, Tiny says. She says that all they come for is to get away from San Francisco, and that they prefer to go to sleep on the verandah or the lawns."

"I should not have guessed that Miss Montgomery was cynical. I fancy she finds entertaining in the open air rather sleepy work herself. Or perhaps she thinks they are sufficiently honoured in being asked within the sacred precincts of Menlo Park," he added mischievously. "I have been given to understand that it *is* an honour."

"We keep very much to ourselves," said Magdaléna, gravely. "We never care to know new people unless we are sure that we shall like them."

To flirt with her a little, or rather to flirt at her, was irresistible. He bent over her, smiling and compelling her gaze. "And how can I be sure that you will not find me wanting?" he asked; "not like me at all a month hence? I think I should wait at least that time before buying this place."

She shook her head seriously. "I am sure we are all going to like you. While you were with papa last night, Tiny and Ila and Mrs. Washington and Rose and Caro all said they hoped you would buy the Mark Smith place. Ila said she had not come back to California to talk to children; and Tiny — who is not really enthusiastic — said you were one of the few men she ever wanted to see a second time. Mrs. Washington said, 'A man-of-the-world at this last end of creation, stepping off landing—'"

"I am more flattered than I can possibly express, but I want to know what *you* think about it. Shall you tire of me?"

"Oh, I think not. I am sure I shall not."

"Do you want me to buy this place?"

She looked at him helplessly. Instinct whispered that he was unfair, but she had no anger for him. "I—I—think I do," she said. "I—I think you know I do." And then she did feel a little angry with him.

He drew back at once. "You are my first friend, you know," he said in his ordinary manner. "I should not think of settling near you unless I were sure of not boring you. But I believe we have tastes in common, and I hope you will let me come over often."

"You will be always welcome," she said formally. Her anger had gone, leaving a chill in its wake.

The char-à-banc drove up. Mrs. Yorba descended simultaneously. Her virtues were many, and one of them was punctuality.

XX

The Montgomerys' house was next in age to the Yorbas', but neither so large nor so solid. Even its verandah, however, had a more homelike air; its carpets and rugs were old but handsome; and it was full of pretty trifles, and much carved furniture, gathered in Europe. The lawns were small, the grounds carelessly kept, but there were many fine old trees and a wilderness of flowers.

Coralie Brannan and Lee Tarlton, Mrs. Montgomery's little ward, were romping on the lawn as the Yorbas drove up. Tiny and Ila were sitting on the verandah. The former was in her favourite white, and a hat and sash of azure. Ila wore a superlatively smart frock of yellow silk muslin, and a yellow sun-hat covered with red poppies.

Trennahan saw the flash of dismay from Magdaléna's eyes before her face settled into its most stolid expression. He felt genuinely sorry for her, but his only part was to get out and hand these radiant visions into the char-à-banc.

"It is *so* nice to think that you may be a neighbour of ours," said Tiny, sweetly, as Ila was kissing Mrs. Yorba, and asking if she were not a good girl to meet her halfway. "We shall really be glad to have you."

"We shall make him forget that he has not lived here always," said Ila, with her most brilliant smile. She was much elated at the unexpected foil. "He will become quite one of us."

"I am sure he would not think of settling elsewhere in California," said Mrs. Yorba. And then she added with what for her was extreme graciousness, "My husband and I shall be very glad to have him for neighbour."

Trennahan murmured his thanks. He was deeply amused. That he was the representative of one of the proudest families in a State some three hundred years old mattered nothing to these Californians of Menlo Park. Is it catching, I wonder? he thought. If some of my English friends should come out here five years hence, should I patronise them? Doubtless, for it is like living on another planet. Exclusiveness is the very scheme of its nature. It is encouraging to think that I have yet another phase to live through.

Ila claimed his attention and kept it as they rolled down the dusty road toward the Mark Smith place. Tiny, after a futile attempt to engage Magdaléna in conversation, devoted herself prettily to Mrs. Yorba and talked of the plans for the summer.

Magdaléna was acutely miserable. Her exaltation of spirits was a bare memory. She hated her dowdy frock, her glaring contrast to the vivid Ila, accentuated by that grotesque similarity of attire. She listened to Ila's brilliant chatter and recalled her own halting phrases, her narrow vocabulary, and wondered angrily at the conceit which had prompted her to hope that she was overcoming her natural deficiencies.

Then she remembered that she was a Yorba, and drew herself up in lonely pride. It was a privilege for these girls to be intimate with her, to call her 'Léna, great as might be their social superiority over the many in San Francisco whose names she had never heard. In her inordinate pride of birth, in her intimate knowledge of the fact that she was the daughter of a Californian grandee who still possessed the three hundred thousand acres granted his fathers by the Spanish crown, she in all honesty believed no one of these friends of her youth to be her equal, although she never betrayed herself by so much as a lifting of the eyebrow. She had questioned, after her loss of religion, if it were not her duty to train down her pride, but had concluded that it was not; it injured no one, and it was a tribute she owed her race. She liked Trennahan the better that he had discovered and approved this pride.

XXI

Magdaléna did not see Trennahan alone again; he did not ask her to ride with him on the following morning, and left for town immediately after breakfast. But before taking his seat in the char-à-banc he held her hand a moment and assured her with such emphasis that he owed the great pleasure of his visit entirely to her, that her spirits, which had been in weeds, flaunted into colour and song; and she went at once to her nook in the woods, feeling that the fire in her mind was nothing less than creative.

But she did not write for some time. The sun was already intensely hot; even in those depths the air was heavy, the heat waves shimmered among the young green of the undergrowth.

Magdaléna stretched herself out lazily and looked up into the green recesses of the trees. The leaves were rustling in a light hot wind. She fancied that they sang, and strained her ears to catch the tune. It looked so cool and green and dark up there; surely the birds, the squirrels, the very tree-toads, — those polished bits of malachite, — must be happy and fond in their storeyed palace. What a poem might be written about them! but they would not raise their voices above that indefinite murmur, and the straining ears of her soul heard not either.

She sat up and began to write, endeavouring to shake some life into her heroine, but only succeeding in making her express herself in very affected old English, with the air of a marionette.

Then mechanically, almost unconsciously, she began the story again. At the end of an hour she discovered that she had dressed up Trennahan in velvet and gold, doublet and hose. She laughed with grim merriment. Ignorant as she was, she was quick to see the incongruity between modern man in his quintessence and the romantic garments of a buried century. Also, her hero had addressed his startled friends in this wise:

"I can't stand that rat-hole any longer. I'm going to stay down here with the rest of you, whether I'm hanged for it or not."

This was undoubtedly what Trennahan would have said; but not the Cavalier, Lord Hastings of Fairfax. She had a vague prompting that on the whole it was preferable to, —

"Gadsooks, my bold knights, and prithee should a man rot in a rat-ridden cupboard while his friends make merry? Rather let him be drawn and quartered, then fed to ravens, but live while he may."

But she dismissed the thought as treason to letters, and proceeded on her mistaken way with the Lady Eleanora Templemere. Shakspere and Scott were her favourite writers; she felt that she must fumble into the sacred lines of literature by such feeble rays as they cast her. She liked and admired the great realists whose bones were hardly dust; but they did not inspire her, taught her nothing.

XXII

The next morning, as she was starting for the woods, rather later than usual, Dick, the stable-boy, who had just returned from the post-office, detached a letter from a packet he was handing the butler and ran after her. As Helena was her only correspondent, she marvelled at the strange handwriting, but opened the letter more promptly than most women do in the circumstances. It was from Trennahan and read:

> Dear Miss Yorba,—I have virtually bought the place. That is to say, I shall buy it as soon as the deeds are made out. Meanwhile, I am looking for servants and hope to move down on Monday next at latest. Mr. Smith has also consented to sell me his stud, which, your father tells me, is exceptionally fine. So, you see, I am really to be your neighbour, and am hoping you are friendly enough not to be displeased. At all events, I shall give myself the pleasure of riding over on Monday evening, and hope that you will join me in another ride on the following morning. Meanwhile, can I do anything for you in town? Is there anything that you would care to read? Pray command me.
>
> Faithfully,
>
> J. S. Trennahan.

Never was there a more commonplace or business-like note, but it seemed a miracle of easy grace to Magdaléna: it was the first note of any sort that she had received from a man not old enough to be her father. She invested it with all the man's magnetism, and heard it enunciated in his cultivated voice. She imagined it delivered in the nasal tones of her uncle, or in the thick voice of the youth that had sat on her left at the birthday dinner,—she had forgotten his name,—and shuddered.

She recalled that her mother had received an envelope directed by the same hand the night before; but that, doubtless, had been a mere note of politeness. He had written this because he wished to do so!

She spent the entire morning answering the note, and discovered that it was as easy to write a book. After tearing up some twenty epistles, she concluded that the following, when copied on her best note-paper, and compared with the dictionary, would do,—

> Dear Mr. Trennahan,—I am glad that you have bought the Mark Smith place. There is nothing that I want. Many thanks.
>
> Yours truly,
>
> Magdaléna Yorba.

XXIII

On the following Monday Don Roberto had a cold and did not go to town, but sunned himself on the verandah, alternately sipping whiskey and eating quinine pills. Magdaléna dutifully kept him company, and the whiskey having made him unusually amiable, he talked more than was his wont with the women of his family. In his way he was fond of his daughter, deeply as she had disappointed him; and, had she known how to manage him, doubtless her girlish wants would have met with few rebuffs. But that would have meant another Magdaléna.

"I like this Trennahan," he announced. "He prefer talk with me than with the young mens, and he know plenty good stories, by Jimminy! He have call on me at the bank three times, and I have lunch with him one day. Damn good lunch. He is what Jack call thoroughbred, and have the manners very fine. I like have him much for the neighbour. He ask myself and Eeram and Washeengton to have the dinner with him on Thursday and warm the house. He understand the good wine and the tabac, by Scott! I feel please si he ask me plenty time, and I have him here often."

Magdaléna was delighted with these unexpected sentiments. She pressed her lips together twice, then said, —

"He asked me if I could ride again with him to-morrow morning."

"I have not the objection to you ride all you want it with Mr. Trennahan, si you not go outside the place. Need not take that boy, for he have the work; and I have trust in Mr. Trennahan."

He would, indeed, have welcomed Trennahan as a son-in-law. Magdaléna must inherit his wealth as well as the immense fortune of her uncle; neither of these worthy gentlemen had the least ambition to be caricatured in bronze and accumulate green mould as public benefactors. Nor did Don Roberto regret that he had no son, having the most profound contempt for the sons of rich men, as they circled within his horizon. It would be one of the terms of his will that Magdaléna's first son should be named Yorba, and that the name should be perpetuated in this manner until California should shake herself into the sea.

He had long since determined that Magdaléna should marry no one of the sons of his moneyed friends, nor yet any of the sprouting lawyers or unfledged business youths who made up the masculine half of the younger fashionable set. Nor would he leave his money in trust for trustees to fatten on. Ever since Magdaléna's sixteenth birthday he had been on the look-out for a son-in-law to his pattern. The New Yorker suited him. A wealthy man himself, Trennahan's motives could not be misconstrued. His birth and breeding were all that could be desired, even of a Yorba. He understood the value of money and its management. And he was well past the spendthrift age.

Don Roberto and Mr. Polk had discussed the matter between them; and these two wily old judges of human nature had agreed that Trennahan must become the guardian of their joint millions. Magdaléna was her father's only misgiving. Would a man with an exhaustive experience of beautiful women be attracted into marriage by this ugly duckling? But Trennahan had passed his youth. Perhaps, like himself, he would have come to the conclusion that it was better to have a plain wife and leave beauty to one's mistresses. He had not the slightest objection to Trennahan having a separate establishment; in fact, he thought a man a fool who had not.

Little escaped his sharp eyes. He had noted Trennahan's interest in Magdaléna, the length of the morning ride, his daughter's sparkling eyes at breakfast. Propinquity would do much; and the bait was dazzling, even to a man of fortune.

He became aware that Magdaléna was speaking.

"I have no habit; and Ila says that they intend to have riding parties."

"You can get one habit. Go up to-morrow and order one."

Magdaléna felt a little dazed, and wondered if everything in her life were changing.

"I hear wheels," she said after a moment. They were on the verandah on the right of the house. She stood up and watched the bend of the drive. "It is the Montgomery char-à-banc," she said, "and there are Mrs. Cartright and Tiny and Ila and Rose. Shall you stay?"

"I stay. Bring them here to me. Tiny and Ila beautiful girls. Great Scott! they know what they are about. Rose very pretty, too."

The char-à-banc drew up; and as its occupants did not alight, Magdaléna went down and stood beside it, shading her eyes with her hand.

"We have come to take you for a drive to the hills, 'Léna dear," said Tiny. "Do come."

"Papa has a bad cold. I cannot leave—"

"Poor dear Don Roberto!" exclaimed Mrs. Cartright. "I will get out this minute and speak to him. I know so many remedies for a cold,—blackberry brandy, or currant wine, or inhaling burnt linen and drinking hot water—" But she was halfway down the verandah by this time.

"Do you remember the last time we went to the hills?" asked Ila. "Helena and Rose shrieked with such hilarity that the horses bolted."

"I can answer for myself," said Rose. "I may say that the memory was burnt in with a slipper."

"I never was spanked," murmured Tiny. "That is one of the many things I am grateful for. It must be so humiliating to have been spanked."

"Who can tell what futures may lie in a slipper?" replied Rose, who had a reputation for being clever. "I am sure that my slipperings, for instance, generated a tendency for epigram; something swift and sharp. It destroyed the tendency to bawl continuously,—the equivalent of the great national habit of monologue."

"Rose, you are quite too frightfully clever," said Tiny, with an assumption of languor. "You will be writing a book next."

"I will make 'Léna the heroine," retorted Rose, with a keen glance, "and call it 'The Sphinx of Menlo Park.'"

"Fancy 'Léna being called a sphinx," said Ila, who was looking very bored. "Are you coming, 'Léna, or not? I suppose you don't want to be kept standing in the sun."

"Oh, we're all used to that," said Rose. "I have three new freckles that I owe to Mrs. Washington and Caro Folsom. They called yesterday and kept me standing in the sun exactly three quarters of an hour before they made up their minds to come in and stay ten minutes."

"I'd like to go—"

Mrs. Cartright returned, shaking her head.

"Don Roberto does not want to be left alone," she said. "I fortunately thought of a most wonderful remedy for colds, and I have also been telling him about a terrible cold General Lee had once when he was staying with us. He did look so funny, dear great man, with his head tied up in one of old Aunt Sally's bandannas—"

"Please excuse me for interrupting you, dear Mrs. Cartright," said Tiny, firmly; "but I think we had better get out and talk to Don Roberto, and go to the hills another day when 'Léna can go with us. Don't you think that would be best?" she murmured to the other girls. "We might help to amuse him a little."

"It will be vastly to our credit," said Rose, "for he certainly won't amuse us."

"Has anyone ever been amused here?" asked Ila, looking at Magdaléna, who was politely listening to Mrs. Cartright's anecdote. "Fancy having the biggest house in the smartest county in California and making no more of it than if it were a cottage. The rest of the houses are so cut up; but fancy what dances we could have here."

"I have been thinking over a plan," said Tiny, "and that is to try to manage Don Roberto. 'Léna can't, but I think the rest of us could, and Mrs. Yorba likes to give parties."

"I am told that in early days there was an extra burst of lawlessness after each of her balls,—reaction," said Rose.

"I don't think that it is nice for us to be discussing people at their very doorstep," said Tiny. "I just thought I'd mention my plan. And if it succeeded, and all took charge, as it were, there need be no stiffness in an informal party in the country. Shall we get out?"

"By all means, General Tom Thumb," said Rose, with some ire; "it is very plain who is to be boss in this community, as Mrs. Washington would say."

"Wait till Helena comes," whispered Ila.

XXIV

Don Roberto rose as they approached. He did not take off his skull-cap, but he received them with the courtly grace of the caballero, one of his inheritances which he had not permanently discarded, although he practised what he was pleased to call his American manners in the sanctity of his home.

He bowed low, kissed their finger-tips, and handed them in turn to the chairs which he first arranged in a semi-circle about his own. When he resumed his former half-reclining attitude he had the air of an invalid sultan holding audience.

"We are *so* sorry that you have *such* a dreadful cold," said Tiny, with her sweetest smile and emphasis; "and *so* glad that we happened to drive up. You couldn't come for a drive with us, could you? We should *love* to have you."

Don Roberto rose to the bait at once. He was as susceptible to the blandishments of pretty women as Jack Belmont, although their influence over his purse was an independent matter.

"Very glad I am that I have the cold," he answered gallantly; "for it give me the company of three so beautiful ladies. I no can go for drive, for it blow, perhaps; but I no care, so long as you here with me sit."

"Well, we are going to stay a *long* time; and we are *so* glad we are back in Menlo again,—so many of us together. We used to love so to come here; it seems *ages* ago. And now that we have got 'Léna again, you must expect us to fairly overrun the house."

"It is yours," said Don Roberto, in the old vernacular. "Burn it if you will."

Tiny, who had never heard even an anecdote of the early Californians, gave a quick glance at the whiskey flask, but replied undauntedly,—

"How gallant you are, Don Roberto! The young men say such stupid things. But you *always* were so original!"

"Poor old dear, I feel like wiping it off," whispered Rose to Ila.

But it was evident that Don Roberto's vision was powdered with the golden dust of flattery. He smiled approvingly into Tiny's pretty face. "But I say true, and the young mens do not sometimes. It make me young again to see you here."

"One would think you were *old*," said Tiny. "But do you *really* like to see us here? Should you mind if we came sometimes in the evening? It would be such *fun* to meet at each other's houses and talk on the verandahs."

"Come all the evenings," said Don Roberto, promptly, "si you talk to me sometimes."

"*I* want to do that. Ila plays, and Rose sings *beautifully*. Some evening we will get up charades—to amuse you."

"On Saturday, Sunday, Tuesday, and Thursday nights I am here."

"Those will be our evenings to come here." She gave a peremptory glance to Rose, who responded hurriedly, "Are you fond of music, Don Roberto? It will give me great pleasure to sing for you; and Ila has been learning some of my accompaniments."

Don Roberto did not answer for a moment. His memory had played him a trick: it had leaped back to the days of guitars and gratings. He rarely sought the society of gentlewomen, not, at least, of those whose names were on visiting lists. There was something unexpectedly sweet and fragrant in the company of these three beautiful girls. Don Roberto's memories were hanging in a dusty cupboard, and his heart had shrunken like the meat of a nut too long neglected; but there was life at the core, and the memories came forth, wanting only a breath to dust them. Yes, he should like to have these girls about him. And Magdaléna had lived the life of a hermit. It was time for her to enjoy her girlhood.

"Yes," he said, "alway I like the music. Si the piano need tune, I send one man down. You can dance, too, si you like it. Always I like see the young peoples dance."

Tiny clapped her hands. Ila leaned forward and patted his hand.

"What an inspiration!" she exclaimed. "This will be a simply gorgeous house to dance in. Don Roberto, you certainly are an angel!"

Don Roberto had never been called an angel before, but he smiled approvingly. "Some night this week we have the dance," he said. "My wife write you to-night."

"I am on the verge of nervous prostration," whispered Rose, as his attention was claimed by Mrs. Cartright. "The effort of keeping my countenance—but the way you handle a trowel, Tiny, is a new chapter in diplomacy. Butter and molasses for fifty and after; a vaporiser and *peau d'espagne* for the sharp young things. I was just saying," she added hastily, as Don Roberto reclined suddenly and turned to her, "that young men are a nuisance. I am thinking of writing a book of advice—"

"A book!" cried Don Roberto, his brows rushing together. "You no write the books?"

"Of course she would never publish," interposed Tiny. "She would just write it for our amusement. I think it would be so horrid to publish the *cleverest* book," she said, turning to Magdaléna, unmistakable sincerity in her voice. "It has always seemed to me so—so—*horrid* for women to write things to print—for *anybody* to read."

Magdaléna did not answer her. She was staring at her father, breathless for his next words.

"The ladies never write," announced that grandson of old Spain. "Nor the gentlemens. Always the common peoples write the books."

"Oh, it's better now, really," said Rose. "Some people that write are said to be quite nice. Of course, one doesn't meet them in society,—in San Francisco society, at least,—but that may be the fault of society."

"Of course," said Tiny. "I do not mean that people who write must be horrid. But I think I couldn't know a woman who made her name so public,—I mean if I hadn't been fond of her before; but I should really *hate* to see a friend's name in print. You are not really thinking of writing a book, are you, Rose, dear?"

"I have not the slightest idea of writing a book—for the very good reason that I haven't brains enough. You needn't worry about any of us adding to the glory of California—unless, to be sure, 'Léna should be clever enough."

She spoke at random, and Magdaléna's face did not betray her; but she almost hated the girl who was forcing her to another of her mental crises.

"My daughter write!" shouted Don Roberto. "A Yorba! She make a fool de my name like the play-actor that do the monkey tricks on the stage? Si she do that—"

"Here comes Mr. Trennahan," said Magdaléna, standing up. "Mamma is not here. I must go to meet him."

Trennahan threw the reins to his groom and sprang out of the cart. "I could not wait till evening, you see," he said, as he came up the steps. "What is the matter? Something has gone wrong with you."

She shivered. "Yes. Something. I cannot tell you."

"Can we have our ride to-morrow?"

"Yes, I can ride with you. Don't, d-don't—"

"Yes?"

"Don't talk to me when you get round there."

"I won't; and I won't let them talk to you."

Something *has* gone wrong, he thought. She looks like a condemned criminal.

XXV

The next morning when Trennahan rode up, Magdaléna was already on her horse, and they cantered off at once.

"I must teach you to trot," he said. "This is very old-fashioned. You must not be behind your friends, who would scorn to canter."

"Very well. You can teach me."

The next half-hour was given up to the lesson. Magdaléna did not like the new method, but persevered heroically. A half-hour was all she could endure, and they cantered across the meadows to the back woods.

Magdaléna was as pale as a swarthy person can be. Her eyes were heavy and shadowed.

"You did not sleep last night," said Trennahan, abruptly. "And something had happened yesterday before I came. What was it?"

"I don't think I can tell you. I don't like to talk about things—about myself."

"Then let me tell you that no human being can go through life without help. With all your brain and your natural reticence, you are no exception to the rule. I am much older than you are. I know a great deal of the world. You know nothing of it. I can help you if you will let me."

He was interested, and thought it probable that her trouble came from the depths of her nature. Nevertheless, she was very young, and he prayed that her grief were not the sequence of a rejected manuscript.

Magdaléna flushed, then paled again. She remembered that she had wanted to speak out to him; but face to face with the prospect, the levelling of lifelong barriers appalled her. If she could only tell part and conceal the rest! But she was no artist in words. She drew a deep sigh and opened her lips, but closed them again.

"It will be easier here in the woods," he said, as they rode into the deep shade. "The world always seems quite different to me in a wood." It did not in the least, but he knew that it did to her.

"I should have to go back," she said finally. "I cannot begin with yesterday. And I talk so badly."

"The longer the story, the more interested I shall be. And I like your direct simplicity. Let us walk the horses."

"When I was a child I was very religious,—a Catholic. It was a very great deal to me. When I prayed to the Virgin about my wants and troubles, I felt quite happy and hopeful. I lost it a year or two ago. I had read a great many scientific books; and my religion fell to pieces like—like—There was a beautiful old tree on the edge of the woods once. It looked as if it would stand a century longer. One day there was a terrible wind, and it fell down. Its sap and roots were almost gone. I felt dreadfully—about the religion, I mean. I felt, somehow, as if my backbone had been taken out. I knew that one must have some sort of moral ideal. I thought a great deal, and finally I determined to make my conscience my religion. I made a resolution that I would never do, and try not even to think, what I believed to be wrong. When I was little, I followed Helena into a great many of her naughty escapades,—though nothing so bad as the fire,—and I did not tell my parents, as a rule, because I could not see that it did any good. When my New England conscience, as Helena calls it, got the best of me and I confessed about the fire, the consequences were so terrible that I made up my mind that I would do as I chose and say nothing about it. I kept to that until I lost my religion. Then I was careful about every little thing. It was easy enough for a year. Then—I don't think I can go on."

"Then you wrote a book and your conscience hurts you because you have not told your parents."

Magdaléna dropped her reins and stared at him. Had a voice leapt down from heaven, she could not have been more dumfounded.

"I never told you," she said helplessly. "Can all the others know too?"

"I am positive that no one suspects but myself. Do go on."

"You have guessed something, but not all. I have only begun a book; and I am so ignorant, and my mind is so slow, that I know it will be years before I shall be able to write a book that anybody would read. At first this dismayed me. Now I do not care, so long as I succeed in the end; and it will be a pleasure to see myself improve. I have not thought it wrong not to tell my parents, so long as what I did could not affect them in any way. Do you not think I was right in that?"

"Assuredly."

"I believed that when I had done something excellent, if that time ever came, they would be proud of it. My mother was a school-teacher, you know; and I did not see why my father should care. He hates to hear women talk, but writing is different. At least I thought so. Yesterday, just before you came, the subject came up. Rose said she believed I could write a book, and papa was furious at the mere thought. I knew nothing about old-world prejudices, but it seems that a lady would be thought to have disgraced herself in Spain if she wrote a book: and papa is as Spanish as if he had never learned a word of English, although he would be ready to beat anyone that told him so. He did not have a chance to say much yesterday; but I saw what his ideas were and that nothing could change them.

"I did not go to sleep at all last night. I sat up trying to think what I should do. Of course I need not tell him what I had done; but should I give it up? That was the question. If I continued, I must tell him of my intention to be a writer. He would forbid it. If I refused to obey, which I do not think I have any right to do, he is quite capable of locking me up. But I cannot go on writing in secret. That would be a great wrong; it would be living a lie. I could not make myself believe that I only wrote for the pleasure of writing: I should know that I longed for the time when I should see my book on somebody's shelf. It seems to me that I cannot give it up. I have much less in my life than most girls. In spite of the hard work, I have felt almost happy while writing. And I am afraid that I have as much ambition as pride. But he is my father. My first duty is to him—I cannot make up my mind. I suppose there should be no struggle; but there is, and I feel as if it were killing me."

Trennahan had been the confidant of many women, had listened to many tragic confessions, had seen women in agonies of remorse; but nothing had ever touched him as did this bald statement, abrupt with repressed feeling, of a girl's solitary tragedy. Had her hero been a lover instead of an art, he would have met her confidence with platitudes and a suppressed yawn; but her lonely attitude in the midst of millions and friends, her terrible slavery to an ideal, to a scourging conscience which was at war with all the secretiveness, self-indulgence, and haughty intolerance of restraint which she had inherited with her father's blood, interested him even more profoundly than it appealed to his sympathies. He determined not only to help her, but to watch her development.

"You have honoured me with your confidence," he said. "Don't doubt for a moment that I do not appreciate the magnitude of that honour. I know just how proud and reticent you are, how much it cost you to speak. I believe that I have enough wisdom to help you a little. Go on with your work. If you have a talent, you get it, one way or another, from your parents, and it is as much entitled to your consideration as your health or your riches.

The birthright of every mortal is happiness. Some philosopher has said that happiness is the free exercise of the higher faculties of a man's nature. If that is your instinct, pursue it. Of course we have no right to claim our happiness at the expense of others. But your father is safe for the present. No matter what your talent, you will not know enough, nor have had sufficient bare practice with your pen, to write even a short story of first-rate merit for ten years to come. You may count it a blessing that various causes are preventing you from rushing into print. At the end of that period your father will be ten years older. He will probably be much softened and will look at things differently; or he may be dead. Or you may be—and most likely will be—married. You need only concern yourself with the present. It is possible that you have discovered your only chance of happiness. Do not commit the incredible folly of strangling that chance before it is born. This is not my day for lecturing, but I am going to take your conscience in hand. It needs training. Before you know it, you will be morbid. That means brain rot, and no chance of the commonest sort of enjoyment."

"You are very good; no one has ever been so good. You ought to know far better than I what is right and what is wrong."

"I am afraid I do. Promise me this: that you will do nothing decisive until the end of the summer. Take that time to think it over. There will be little time to write in any case. I shall monopolise a good deal of your time, and I fancy they intend to be rather gay here. Six months from now we will talk it over again. Will you agree to that?"

"I must think it over. My mind is a slow one. But I think you are right."

And several days later, when he was dining at the house, she told him briefly that she should take his advice and write no more until the summer was over.

XXVI

Mrs. Yorba, who did not like to have her plans made for her, decided to give the party on the evening of Saturday week. The floor was to be canvased, and three musicians were engaged. She promised the girls that after this initial party they should dance informally at Fair Oaks as often as they wished.

It was some time before Magdaléna rode alone with Trennahan again. The other girls rode every morning and claimed him. Magdaléna joined these parties as soon as her habit was finished, and met him every afternoon at one or other of the new tennis courts, which consisted merely of chalked lines and a net, — Ila had introduced tennis to Menlo, — but either Ila or Caro possessed him with the tentacles of their kind. Mrs. Yorba had made it understood that her party was to be the first of the season, so the evenings alone were unoccupied. Trennahan dined twice at Fair Oaks, but Don Roberto and Mr. Polk claimed him. Magdaléna wondered if he had forgotten his original programme. But with four handsome girls demanding his attentions, a literary friendship was doubtless a dream of the future. She felt an unaccountable depression, and wondered if she were going to be ill.

By the time the evening of the party arrived, the nervousness which had assailed her when the subject was broached had been tempered by time and constant association with many who would be present. Tiny and the other girls had promised to make "things go." There were to be no ball gowns, and the whole affair was to be as informal as possible. She even harboured pleasurable anticipation. Parties, she had read and heard, were brilliant exhilarating affairs, and she loved dancing as only a Spanish woman can. In this, at least, she should excel her fellows. She had taken lessons once a week for the last two years from a solemn and automatic person who had rarely opened his lips except to complain of the heavy carpets in the cavernous Yorba parlours.

Magdaléna dressed immediately after dinner; the guests were expected by nine. She wore her white organdie, but fastened crimson roses in her hair and belt. She was by no means satisfied with her appearance, — she was too ardent an admirer of beauty for that, — but she knew that she looked far better than she had on the night of her dinner. She shuddered at the memory of that white ribbon about her swarthy throat.

She went downstairs, and thought the big rooms looked very inviting with their white floors; the folding-doors had been rolled back, and the parlour and dining-room made an immense sweep. The vases on the mantels were full of flowers. In the distance she heard the tuning of a fiddle.

The night was hot, and all the windows were open. The dark grounds beyond looked full of mystery, and of infinite depth. She thought at the moment that there was nothing she loved more than the mystery of night in the country. As she stood in the middle of the brilliantly lighted room, the heavy darkness without outlined with trees and great shrubs, the broken spaces above, set with stars, allured her. Almost unconsciously she stepped through one of the windows, crossed the verandah and drive, and entered the long narrow path between the lawns. Here there was more sense of space, for the lawns were very large; but the trees were close along their edge and massed heavily at the end of the perspective. Above was a long banner of night sky. The monotonous chanting of frogs was the only sound.

Certainly, California is a land of beauty and peace, she thought. Mr. Trennahan says he has never known anything like it, and he has been everywhere. Everybody should be happy in it, and I suppose everyone is, mostly. Poets like Tennyson always make weather to suit moods and circumstances. If they are right, one should laugh and be happy for eight months in the year in California, and only sad when it rains. There does not seem much chance for tragedy, although I have heard that there are many murders and suicides; but perhaps that is because the towns are new and excitable. There is nothing in the country itself to make one unhappy, as there must be in other countries where Nature has done so little, and they have so many centuries of tragic past behind them.... Oh, dear, I am struggling toward something, as usual. What is it?

She touched her fingers to her forehead, then drew them lightly back and forth, as if to clear the mist from her brain, the rust from the wheels.... I seem to have seeds in my mind. Why don't they sprout? Why are they for ever knocking at the hard earth over their heads? One would think they were in their graves instead of never having been born.

She sighed and shook her head, but her thoughts ran on. Am I happy? I think so. And all the girls seem happy. Mr. Trennahan says he watched the rest of the world rise into an inverted abyss of smoke when the train slid down the Sierras, and that his memory has been asleep ever since. I have been unhappy here! she continued abruptly. And one night I suffered— suffered horribly—and this last week— —She stopped short, looking at the beauty and peace about her with a feeling of sharp and swift resentment. She had a sense of being betrayed by the country of which she was, far more than her mates, a part. She was of its first blood, the daughter of its Arcadia, the last living representative of all that it had been in the fulness of its power. And she knew California and felt it as no one else did. That sense of betrayal, of personal treachery, passed as swiftly as it had come, but seemed to murmur back that it would come again, and again; and that with each visit she would understand it better.

I have read somewhere that artists must suffer before they can accomplish anything, she thought. Well, I should not mind, I should not—at least, I think I should not.

Some time since she had come to the end of the path and turned to the right and into a long lane running between fields. She sat down on a stump; she had quite forgotten the party. Her brain was full of struggling ideas. But in a few moments she surrendered herself to the spell of the night. There were no trees quite near her, nothing but level fields thick with grain. Far to the left and curving a mile behind her was the black outline of the woods. Far behind them were the towering mountains with their forests of redwoods; those on the crest sharp against the stars. California was a new country. It might have been newer, so vast was its silence, so primeval its peace.

Oh, I am sure I am happy, thought Magdaléna, suddenly. Yes, I am sure. But I wish I might never see anyone again. California is faultless; it is civilisation that has spoilt her.

She was stumbling close upon great truths; but it was part of her inheritance that she had no perception of what she was groping for, and passed almost unheeding the little that came to her.

"Miss Yorba, are you cultivating a reputation for eccentricity?"

She sprang to her feet. Trennahan was approaching her. He was in evening dress, without a hat. His expression was one of extreme amusement, and Magdaléna felt the blood in her face.

"Have they come?" she asked in dismay.

"They are dancing, or were about to begin as your mother sent me to look for you."

"I had forgotten—"

"I was sure you had. Miss Brannan insisted that you were hiding, but I had no doubt that you had wandered off in a reverie." He laughed. "Happy you!" he said. "Happy you!"

"You think I am an idiot."

"Indeed I do not. I feel sorry to think that in a year from now such a thing will no longer be possible. But we must go back, or they will be sending someone to look for us."

"Is papa angry?"

"I don't think he noticed. Miss Montgomery and Miss Brannan were using all their blandishments to make him think the party as interesting as themselves; and I am positive they were succeeding."

When they reached the house, the quadrille which had opened the party was finishing. Don Roberto was making a sweeping bow to Tiny, whose face wore an inscrutable expression. Magdaléna was about to step through the window, but Trennahan guided her to the door, and they entered the room without attracting attention. There were some forty people present. With the exception of the Yorbas, everybody had house guests. Mrs. Yorba sat in a corner with a small group of elderly ladies. Mr. Polk stood before the fireplace in the parlour, his legs well apart, staring absently at the young people, who looked gay and content.

"What am I to do?" asked Magdaléna, helplessly.

"Nothing, just now, as there are no wall-flowers. In a moment one of these youths will ask you to dance, and of course you will consent. It is my misfortune that I no longer dance. I think your fate approaches."

A young man with a rather bright face came toward her. His name was Payne. She had met him at the Montgomerys.

"May I have the pleasure of the first waltz, Miss Yorba?" he asked. "I am told that it will be a unique pleasure,—that you can talk science and waltz in the same breath, as it were."

He did not speak in sarcasm, merely in facetiousness. He was a type of the fresh young San Franciscan whose ways are not as all ways. Magdaléna looked at him in sombre anger and made no reply. He saw that he had made a mistake, and reddened, wondering why on earth she were in society at all, if she could not be like other girls. Magdaléna did not appreciate his natural indignation; but she saw that he was miserable, and relented.

"I will waltz with you if you wish," she said.

Mr. Payne bowed stiffly and offered his arm. They walked the length of the two rooms in utter silence; then the musicians played the opening bars of a waltz. Magdaléna remembered that this would be her first waltz with any man, barring the teacher who had solemnly piloted her up and down the parlours in town. She had hoped much from her first dance; and she was to have it with this silly overgrown boy. It was a minor disappointment, but sharp while it lasted.

"Shall we begin?" he asked formally. He was sulky, and eager to have it over. Two or three of his friends had flashed him glances of ironical sympathy, and he was too young to bear ridicule with fortitude.

Ila was floating down the room with Alan Rush, a young South American, as graceful of foot and bearing as herself. Magdaléna forgot her partner and gazed at them with genuine delight. She had read of the poetry of motion, and this illustration appealed to the passion for beauty which was strong in her nature.

She turned to her partner. "Do they not dance beautifully?" she exclaimed. That much-enduring youth replied that they did, and asked her again if she were ready. She laid her hand on his shoulder and they started. Magdaléna realised at once that her partner was an excellent dancer, and that she was not. She felt that she was heavy, and marvelled at the lightness of Ila and Rose. They seemed barely to touch the floor, and were laughing and chatting as naturally as if they had no feet to guide.

"Could you take a little longer step?" asked Mr. Payne, politely. "I—I—beg pardon for suggesting it, but it's the fashion just now. That's right—a little longer. Oh, I—I—am afraid that your feet are too small. Shall we sit down a moment?"

They sat down in the recess, and Payne wiped his brow. "It is so warm," he muttered apologetically.

"Mr. Rush does not look warm," she said cruelly.

He repressed the obvious reply, but made no other. In a moment he asked her if she cared to finish the waltz.

"No," she said. "I do not. You may go and finish it with someone else, if you like."

He moved off with alacrity, and Magdaléna sat alone for some moments feeling very miserable. What was the matter with her? Could she do nothing well? And she should be a wall-flower for the rest of the evening, of course. That wretched man would tell everybody how badly she danced.

But she had forgotten that she was hostess. A moment after the waltz ended, three young men came over to her and begged for the honour of her hand. They were Rollins, the sharp-faced Fort, and Alan Rush. She gave the dance to follow to Rush, and the others, having inscribed her name on their cuffs, moved off. Rush sat down beside her. He had a frank kind face, and the beauty of his figure and the grace of his carriage had given him a reputation for good looks which had reached even Magdaléna's ears. He was at that time the most popular young man in San Francisco society. Magdaléna decided that she liked him better than anyone she had met except Trennahan. His voice was rich and Southern, although he had no Spanish blood in him.

"I watched you dance," said Magdaléna, abruptly. "I don't dance well enough for you."

"Dancing is all a matter of habit," he said kindly. "This is my third year. You have no idea how awkward I was when I began. I am sure you will be the best dancer in society next winter—with all those Spanish grandmothers."

"Do you think so?" She liked him almost as well as Trennahan for the moment.

He did not, for he had noted that she was lacking in natural grace; but he was chivalrous, and he saw that she was discouraged.

"There's the music," he said. "Suppose we go out in the hall by ourselves, and I will give you a little lesson. No?"

Magdaléna was delighted, but she merely stood up in her unbending dignity and said that she was glad to take advantage of his kindness.

He was a man who danced so well that he compelled some measure of facility in his partner. Magdaléna felt inspired at once, and carefully obeyed every instruction.

"We will have a great many other lessons, no?" he said as the music finished. "By the time that famous coming-out party of yours comes off, you will be in great form."

"Will you open it with me?"

"I shall be delighted, and to help you all I can." They were walking down the hall, and he was bending over her with an air of devotion which she thought very pleasant. His accomplished eyes appealed to the instinct of coquetry, buried deep in the seriousness of her nature, and she smiled upon him and found herself talking with some ease.

She danced with all the young men, but they bored her as much as she felt that she bored them. All the girls danced with her father, and he seemed amiable and pleased, especially when Tiny was smiling upon him. Ila, despite her elegance and refinement, suggested the ladies of his leisure, Rose had too sharp a tongue, and Caro had an exaggerated innocence of manner and eye which experience had led him to distrust. But Tiny, beautiful, cool, and remote, reminded him of the women of his youth, when he was a man of enthusiasms, ideals, and dreams.

Mr. Polk spent the evening wandering about alone or staring from the hearth-rug. One or two of the girls asked him to dance, but he refused brusquely. It was the first dance he had attended since the one given by Thomas Larkin to celebrate the Occupation of California by the United States.

The party broke up a little after twelve, and all assured Magdaléna that the party had been a success with such emphasis that she was convinced that it had been; but when she was in bed and the light out, she cried bitterly.

XXVII

There were no engagements for the following morning, and Magdaléna was sitting idly on the verandah when she saw Trennahan sauntering up the drive. The blood flew through her veins, lifting the weight from her brain. But she repressed the quick smile, and sat still and erect until he reached the carriage block, when she went to the head of the steps to meet him.

"Put on your hat," he said, "and let us hide in the woods before somebody comes to take us for a drive or to invite us to luncheon. I haven't forgotten our private plans, if you have."

"I had not forgotten, but Tiny and Ila manage everything. I don't like to refuse when they are so kind."

"You must develop a faculty—or no, leave it to me. I shall gradually but firmly insist upon having a day or two a week to myself; and Miss Geary informs me that such unprecedented energy can never last in this Vale of Sleep; that before a month is over we shall all have settled down to a chronic state of somnolence from which we shall awaken from Saturday till Monday only. Then, indeed, will Menlo be the ideal spot of which I dreamed while you left me to myself on that long day of my visit."

Her hat was in the hall. She put it on hastily back foremost, and they walked toward the woods. Suddenly she turned into a side path.

"Let us walk through the orchard," she said. "Then we shall not meet anyone."

The cherries were gone; but the yellow apricots, the golden pears, the red peaches and nectarines, the purple plums, hung heavy among the abundant green, or rotted on the ground. Several poor children were stealing frankly, filling sacks almost as large as themselves. Don Roberto had never so far unbent as to give the village people permission to remove the superfluity of his orchard, but he winked at their depredations, as they saved him the expense of having it carted away; his economical graft had never been able to overcome his haughty aversion to selling the produce of his private estate. Magdaléna often came to the orchard to talk to these children: the poor fascinated her, and she liked to feel that she was helping them with words and dimes; but they were not as the poor of whom she had read, nor yet of the fire. They were tow-headed and soiled of face, but they wore stout boots and well-made calico frocks, and they were not without dimes of their own.

"Does California seem a little unreal to you?" she asked. "I mean, there are no great contrasts. The poverty of London must be frightful."

"You ungrateful person, for Heaven's sake reap the advantage of your birthright and forget the countries that are not California."

They passed out of the back gate and entered the middle woods. Magdaléna without hesitation led the way to the retreat hitherto sacred to Art. Trennahan need not have apprehended that she would inflict him with her manuscript, nor with hopes and fears: she was much too shy to mention the subject unless he drew her deliberately; but she liked the idea of associating him with this leafy and sacred temple.

He threw himself on his back at once, clasping his hands under his head and gazing up into the rustling storeys above. About his head was a low persistent hum, a vibration of a sound of many parts. Above were only the intense silences of a hot California morning.

Trennahan forgot Magdaléna for the moment. He felt young again and very content. His restless temperament, fed with the infinite varieties of Europe, had seldom given way to the pleasures of indolence. Even satiety had not meant rest. But California—as distinct from San Francisco—with her traditions of luxurious idleness, the low languid murmur of her woods, her soft voluptuous air, her remoteness from the shrieking nerve centres of the United States, the sublime indifference of her people to the racing hours, drew so many quiet fingers across his tired brain, half obliterating deep and ugly impressions, giving him back something of the sense of youth and future. Perhaps he dimly appreciated that California is a hell for the ambitious; he knew that it was the antechamber of a possible heaven to the man who had lived his life.

He turned suddenly and regarded Magdaléna, wondering how much she had to do with his regeneration, if regeneration it were, and concluded that she was merely a part of California the whole. But she was a part as was no other woman he had met.

She had clasped her hands about her knees and was staring straight before her. Trennahan, in a rare flash of insight, saw the soul of the girl, its potentialities, its beauty, struggling through the deep mists of reserve.

"I could love her," he thought; "and more, and differently, than I have loved any other woman."

He determined in that moment to marry her. As soon as he had made his decision, he had a sense of buoyancy, almost of happiness, but no rejuvenation could destroy his epicureanism; he determined that the slow awakening of her nature, of revealing her to herself, should be a part of the happiness he promised himself. He was proud that he could love the soul of a woman, that he had found his way to that soul through an unbeautiful envelope, that so far there was not a flutter of sense. He was to love in a new way, which should, by exquisite stages, blend with the old. There could be no surprises, no enigmatic delights, but vicariously he could be young again. Then he wondered if he were a vampire feeding on the youth of another. For a moment he faced his soul in horrified wonder, then reasoned that he was little past his meridian in years; that a man's will, if favoured by Circumstance, can do much of razing and rebuilding with the inner life. No, he concluded with healthy disgust, he was not that most sickening tribute to lechery, an old vein yawning for transfusion. He was merely a man ready to begin life again before it was too late. This girl had not the beauty he had demanded as his prerogative in woman, but she had individuality, brains, and all womanliness. Her shyness and pride were her greatest charms to him: he would be the first and the last to get behind the barriers. Such women loved only once.

She turned her head suddenly and met his eyes.

"What are you thinking about?" she asked.

"I have been wondering what that huge pile is behind you."

"That is a wood-rat's nest."

"And you are not afraid of him? Extraordinary woman!"

"He is much more afraid of me. I am very afraid of house-rats."

"And you sit here often? You are not afraid of snakes?"

"There are none in these woods. They always retreat before people — civilisation. Everyone drives through here, but scarcely anyone goes through the back woods; the roads are so bad —"

"Hush!"

The sound of wheels, faint for a moment, grew more distinct; with it mingled the sound of voices. A heavy char-à-banc rolled by, and the words of Tiny and Ila came distinctly to the two in hiding.

"They will have a long and fruitless search," said Trennahan, contentedly. "We are going to stay here and become acquainted."

And they did not move for two hours. For a time Trennahan made her talk, learning almost all there was to know. He even drew forth the tattered shreds of the caballero, who had been little more than a matter of garments, and a confession of her long and passionate desire to be beautiful. The story ended with the lonely and terrible surrender of her religion. He was profoundly interested. Once or twice he was appalled. Did he take this woman, he must assume responsibility for every part of her. She was so wholly without egoism that she would give herself up without reservation and expect him to guide her. That would be all very well with the ordinary woman; but with a nature of high ideals, and possibly of transcendent passions,—was he equal to the task? But in his present mood the prospect fascinated him. One of her slim hands, dark but pretty, lay near his own. He wanted to take it in his, but did not: he wished to keep her unself-conscious as long as possible.

He tried to talk to her about himself, but found it hard to avoid the claptrap with which a man of the world attempts to awaken interest in woman. He had always done it artistically: the weariness, the satiety, the mental grasp of nothingness,—these had been ever revealed in flashing glimpses, in unwilling allusiveness; the hope that he had finally stumbled upon the one woman sketched with a brush dipped in mist. But feeling himself sincere for the first time in incalculable years, he dismissed the tempered weapons of his victories with contempt, and, not knowing what others to substitute, talked of his boyhood and college days. As a result, he felt younger than ever, and closer to the girl who was part of the mystery that had taken him to her heart.

XXVIII

A woman's heart may be said to resemble a subterranean cavern to which communication is had by means of a trap-door. How the lover enters this guarded precinct depends upon the lover and the woman. Sometimes the trap-door is jerked open, and he is hurled down with no by your leave, gobbled up, willing or unwilling. Sometimes there is a desperate fight just over the trap-door, in which he does sometimes, but not always, come off victor. At other times he suddenly finds himself rambling through those labyrinthine passages, to his surprise and that of the woman, who, however, perceives him instantly. There is no such fallacy as that a girl turns in terror or in any other sentiment from the knowledge of this dweller below the trap-door. A woman of experience may, after that first glimpse: she may, in fact, bolt the trap-door yet more tightly and sit herself upon it. But a girl uses it as a frame for her face and watches every movement of the occupant with neither fear nor foreboding until occasion comes,—hanging the halls with the tapestry of dreams, fitting the end of each rose-hued scented gallery with the magic mirror of the future.

Magdaléna, at the end of that morning in the woods, was quite aware that she was in love. She wondered why she had not thought of it before, and concluded that in the prelude she had been merely fascinated by the first enthralling man she had known. The trap-door of her heart was not jealously guarded; nevertheless, it was not yawning for an occupant. Just how and when Trennahan slipped in, she could not have told, but there he certainly was, and there he would stay so long as life was in her.

He went home with her to luncheon, and she longed to have him go, that she might be alone with the thought of him. He left early in the afternoon, and she locked herself in her room and sat for hours staring into the tree-tops swimming in their blue haze. She was not in the least terrified at the beginnings of tumult within her; she rather welcomed them as the birthright of her sex. In this first stage, she hardly cared whether Trennahan were in love with her or not, having none of the instinct of the huntress and her imagination being a slow one. It was enough that she should see him for many hours alone during this dreamy exquisite summer, that she should look constantly into the cold eyes that had their own power to thrill. That he was not the orthodox lover in appearance, manner, nor age pleased her the better. She was not like other girls, therefore it was fitting that she should find her mate among the odd ones of earth. That there might be others like him in the great world whence he came, that he might have loved and been loved by women of the world, never occurred to her. She was content, having found her other part, and wove no histories of the past nor future.

But as the weeks went on and their intimacy grew, she accepted the fact that he loved her before the disposition to speculate had arrived in the wake of love. During the hours that they spent rambling through the woods, or in whatever fashion pleased their mood, although he did not startle her by definite word or act, he managed to convey that their future was assured, that she was his, and that in his own time he should claim her. By the time this dawn broke, her imagination was beating at its flood-gates, and shortly broke loose. Thereafter when she was not with Trennahan in the present, she was his in a future built on the foundations of all she had read and all that instinct taught her. She had no wish that the present should change; it was enough that it suggested the inevitable future. She was happy, and she knew that Trennahan was happy.

Meanwhile they escaped the others and rode together before breakfast, read together after, explored every corner of the woods, and talked of many of the things under heaven. Magdaléna, except for an occasional flutter of eyelid or leap of colour, confessed nothing: her pride was a supple armour that she laced tightly above her heart; but Trennahan's very self lifted the trap-door and looked to him through her eyes, and he had no misgivings. Sometimes he awakened suddenly in the night and gave a quick, short laugh: he was so new to himself. But he knew that he had found something very like true happiness, and he was loving her very deeply. At first he had been pricked by the apprehension that it could not last; that nature had constructed him to move upon the lower planes; that a prolonged tour on the heights would result in disastrous and possibly hideous reaction: his time-worn habits of loving had been of woof and make so different. But as time passed and the light in his spirit spread until it dazzled his eyes and consumed his memories, as the sense of regeneration grew stronger, as the future beckoned alluringly, as he forgot to remember whether Magdaléna were plain or beautiful, as peace and content and happiness possessed him,—he ceased to question his immutability. He had lived in the world for forty years, and it was like an old bottle of scent long uncorked. The ideals of his youth had not changed; they had gone. Beautiful women had turned to gall on his tongue, shrunken to their skeletons in his weary eyes. Fate had steered his bark in the open sea of bachelorhood until he was old enough and wise enough to choose his mate with his soul and his brain, and Fate had steered him to Magdaléna. He was profoundly thankful.

Their intimacy attracted little attention in Menlo Park, for the reason that it was confined within the wooded limits of Fair Oaks. When they rode and drove with the others and attended dinners and dances, they kept apart. As Rose had predicted, gaieties were sporadic, although the young people met somewhere, usually at the Yorbas', every Saturday evening; what others did during the long hot days when there was no company to entertain, concerned no one. Occasionally one of Don Roberto's huge farm waggons, as deep as a tall man's height, was filled with hay, and young Menlo Park jolted slowly to the hills. They ate their luncheon by cool streams dark with meeting willows, and poked at the tadpoles, gathered wild roses, killed, perhaps, a snake or two. Then, toward evening, they jolted home again, hot, dusty, and weary, but supremely content in having lived up to the traditions of Menlo Park. Tiny alone came out triumphant on these trying occasions. Dressed in cool white, she seated her diminutive self in the very middle of the haystack and talked little. The others, undaunted by the sun, started in high spirits, flirted with energy, and changed their positions many times. Upon the return journey, Tiny, again, sat serene and white; the rest dangled over the sides as a last relief for aching limbs and backs, and forgot the very alphabet of flirtation. It is true that Magdaléna did not flirt; but she worked hard to keep her guests pleased and comfortable, and usually went to bed with a headache.

XXIX

It was Tiny who discovered that it was leap year, and invited Menlo to dance at her house one Saturday night and take all advantage of its privileges. Mrs. Yorba consented that Magdaléna should have a new frock, the organdie being in a condition for a maid to sniff at. Magdaléna asserted herself, and ordered a scarlet tarlatan. The frock was smartly made at a good house, and Magdaléna, on the night of the party, was almost pleased with herself. The vivid colour slanted under her swarthy skin. She wore red slippers and red roses in her hair. By this time she knew something of dress,—it was October,—and she had also discovered that red was Trennahan's favourite colour.

She was happy, but a little nervous. There had been more than one sign of late that the pretty comedy of friendship had run its course. The very words they uttered had lost their clear-cut black and white, seemed to grow more full-blooded. His eyes had made her lose her breath more than once, had even sharpened her wits to hasty subterfuge.

The Montgomery parlour was a narrow room at right angles with the dining-room. The two rooms had been thrown into one and canvased.

Tiny invited Don Roberto to open the dance with her, and that platonically enamoured gentleman consented with a grand flourish. Ila exercised her blandishments upon Mr. Polk, but to no purpose. No one could understand his constant attendance at these dances, for he merely stood about with unrelaxing visage, scarcely exchanging a word with even the older men. He wore the suit of evening clothes which had done duty at men's dinners these fifteen years, and had bought a pair of evening shoes and a white necktie. Eugene Fort remarked that he looked like a man whose vital organs had turned to gold and were giving him trouble. Mr. Washington replied that the tight skin which had done such good service was certainly beginning to bag, and that if he didn't knock off and take a vacation in Europe he'd find himself breaking.

"To my knowledge," he added, "he hasn't taken a vacation in thirty years; hasn't even been to Yosemite or the Big Trees. He has always said that work was his tonic; but the truth was that he feared to come home and find a dollar unaccounted for,—neither more nor less. And there comes a time, my dear young man, there comes a time—"

"It comes early in this State."

"It does," Mr. Washington replied, with a sigh and a glance at his young wife. "But the fevers have raged themselves out here, or I am much mistaken. We're in for quiet times. The next generation will live longer, perhaps."

"How old is Polk?"

"Nearly sixty. He's worn better than many, because he's let whiskey alone; never took a drop more than was good for him when Con. Virginia was tumbling from seven hundred to nothing. Neither did Yorba, who is several years older; but he's got the longevity of his race. Jack Belmont is under fifty, and looks older than either,—when you get him in a good light. California is all right, and whiskey is all right, but the two together play the devil and no mistake."

"It is the last place where I should want whiskey," said Trennahan, who had joined them.

"You weren't here half a dozen years ago. While the Virginia City mines were booming, your backbone felt like a streak of lightning; you hadn't a comma in your very thoughts; you woke up every morning in a cold sweat, and your teeth chattered as you opened your newspaper. You believed every man a liar and dreamt that your veins ran liquid gold. The Stock Exchange was Hell let loose. Men went insane. Men committed suicide. No one stopped to remark. Do you wonder that men watered the roots of their nerves with alcohol? I did not, but the fever of that time burnt me out, all the same. I've never been the same man since. Nor has any other San Franciscan. Even Polk and Yorba, although they sold out at the right moment in nine cases out of ten, felt the strain. As for Jack Belmont, he was on one glorious drunk all the time,—and never more of a gentleman. How he pulled through and doubled his pile to boot, the Lord only knows; but he did."

"Miss Belmont will be a great prize," observed Fort, thoughtfully. "The greatest beauty in the State, if she has fulfilled her promise; any amount of go, and one or two cold millions,—the Californian heiress sublimated."

"And mistress of herself and her millions in a few years. I hear that Belmont has not drunk a drop since he has been in Europe with her; he's been gone a year now. That is fatal at his age,—after having been in pickle some thirty years. Poor Jack,—the best fellow that ever lived! I suppose his love for the girl brought him up with a round turn. Doubtless he suddenly realised that she was old enough to understand, and that he must pull himself up if he would keep her respect. There's a good deal of tragedy in

California, Mr. Trennahan, and it's not of the sentimental young folks' sort neither."

"I won't admit it," said Trennahan, who was looking at Magdaléna "Its very air breathes content—now, at any rate. I am glad I did not come earlier."

"California is the Princess Royal of her country," said Fort; "and at her birth all the good fairies came and gave her of every gift in the stores o the immortals. Then a wicked fairy came and turned the skeleton in her beautiful body to gold; and, lo! the princess who had been fashioned to bless mankind carried, hidden from sight by her innocent and beneficent charms a terrible curse. Men came to kiss, and stayed to tear away her flesh with their teeth. When her skeleton has been torn forth, even to the uttermost rib, then the spell of the wicked fairy will be broken, and California be the most gracious mother mankind has ever known."

"Eugene, you like to hear yourself talk, but it must be admitted that you talk well. Will you come out and have a cigar? and you, Mr. Trennahan?"

There was no doubt that the party was a success. Between dances the girls stood together in groups and superciliously regarded the ranks of humble wall-flowers. Suddenly a half-dozen would dash down upon a young man, beg him simultaneously for an eighth of a waltz, and scribble hieroglyphics on their fans. Alan Rush was the belle, and no girl was allowed to have more than a fourth of him at a time. Once the girls left the room in a body, returning, with mumbled excuses, after the music for the next dance had been playing some three minutes. Sometimes a girl would approach a segregated youth, ask him patronisingly if he was enjoying himself, talk to him until the music began, then sidle off with an inaudible remark. Altogether if the young men had sinned during the summer,—and they searched their consciences in vain,—they were punished. The New Woman had not arrived in the Eighties, but the instinct was there, inherited from remotest mother.

The party was a third over when Trennahan approached Magdaléna for the first time. She had taken her partner to his chaperon, Mrs. Geary, and was regarding a group of expectant youths. The spirit of the thing had possessed her and she was enjoying herself. Her shyness had worn off to some extent; she danced rather well, and had learned to make small talk. Being happy, all things seemed easy of accomplishment. She became aware that Trennahan was standing beside her, but did not turn her eyes.

"Will you sit out a dance with me—or rather walk it out in the garden? You must be a little tired, and it is delightful out there."

"I'd rather—I think papa would not like it."

"I am positive that he would not mind."

"I am engaged."

"Let me see your fan."

She delivered it reluctantly.

"You have no one down for the next—nor the next."

"I—I—think I'd rather not go."

"Do you mean that? For if you do, I shall go home. I came for nothing else. I have not seen you alone for three days."

"I am sorry."

"Come."

Her jumping fingers closed about her fan, and the sticks creaked; but she followed him.

As they descended the steps he drew her hand through his arm. The garden looked very wild and dark. The stars were burning overhead. Slanting into the heavy perfume of flowers were the pungent odours of a forest fire.

"You look like a pomegranate flower."

"Do you like my frock?"

"You know that I do."

"Should you like to smoke?"

"I should not."

"It is a beautiful night."

"Very."

"I had a letter from Helena to-day."

"Did you?"

"She described a wonderful experience she had climbing the Alps. Shall I tell you about it?"

"Good God, no! I beg pardon, but the American girl in Europe is interesting to no one but herself."

"She is interesting to me."

"Because you love her. Her letters really bore you, only you won't admit it even to yourself."

"But Helena is really more brilliant than most people."

"Possibly; but I did not come out here to talk about Helena."

Magdaléna's fan was hanging at the end of a chain. She clutched at it missed it, and pressed her hand against her heart, which was hammering.

He saw the motion, and took her hand in his. She glanced about wildly She was in a whirl of terror of everything under heaven. Too dignified to wrest herself away and run, she gave him a swift glance of appeal, then ben her head. He dropped her hand.

"I would not frighten nor bother you for the world, but you know wha I have wanted to say for days past. That, at least, can be no shock: you have known for a long while."

"I'd rather you didn't say it," she gasped.

"I intend to say it, nevertheless, and you will soon get used to it. Wil you marry me?"

"Oh—I—suppose so—that is, if you want me to. Let us go back to the house."

"I have no intention of going back to the house for fully half an hour. Do you love me?"

She hated him at the moment.

"Answer me."

"I—I—thought I did—I don't know."

"Well, we will drop the subject for a moment. There are some other things I want to talk to you about. Shall we walk on?"

She drew a long breath at the respite. He resumed in a moment.

"Of course I am double your age, but I do not think we shall be any less happy on that account. My life, I am going to tell you, has not been an ideal one. After the wildness of youth came the deliberate transgressions of maturity, then the more flagrant, because purposeless sins which followed satiety. I know nothing of the middle classes of the United States,—I have lived little in this country,—but the young men of the upper class are not educated to add to the glory of the American race: they are educated to spend their fathers' millions. It is true that in spite of a rather wild career at college I left it with a half-defined idea of being a scientific explorer, and had taken a special course to that end. But my ambitions crumbled somewhere between the campus and New York. I am not seeking to exculpate myself, to throw the responsibility on my adolescent country: I had something more than the average intelligence, and I pursued my subsequent life deliberately.

Not pursuing an ideal, I had no care to reserve the best that was in me for the woman who should one day be my wife. I entered diplomacy because I liked the life, and because I believed that the day would come when women would mean little more than paper dolls to me, and power would mean everything. I did not reckon on wearying to desperation of the world in general. That time came; with it a desire to live an outdoor existence for the rest of my life. That at least never palled. I determined to come to California. It was an impulse; I hardly speculated upon whether I should remain or not. As the train slid down the Sierras, I knew that I should. Memories jumbled, and I made no effort to pull them apart. For the first time in my life I wanted a home and a wife. The night we met I felt more attracted to you than to the other charming Californians I had met because you seemed more a part of the country. It is singular that a man should love the country first, and the woman as a logical result, but I did. I think that you know I love you; but not how much, nor what it means to me. I am not good enough for you. My soul is old. I see life exactly as it is. I have not an illusion. I am as prosaic as are all men who have made a business of the pleasures of life. I could not make you a perfervid or romantic speech to save my life, and as the selfishness of a lifetime has made me moody and fitful, there will be intervals when I shall be the reverse of lover-like; but on the whole I think you will find me a rather ardent lover. It seems very little to offer a girl who has everything to give. But I love you; never doubt that. What little good was left in me you have coaxed up and trained to something like its original proportions. I want you to understand what my past has been; but I also want you to understand that I am not the same man I was six months ago, and that you have worked the change. When I crossed the continent, it is no exaggeration to say that I had Hell in me,—that ferment of spirit which means mental nausea and the desperate dodging of one's accusing soul. I suppose such a time comes to most men who have persistently violated the original instinct for good. With the lower orders it means crime; with the higher civilisation a legion of imps shrieking in a man's soul. I will not say that my particular band have been silent since I came here, for that would mean moral obtuseness; but they are placated, and have consented to fix a generous eye on the future. I believe, firmly believe, that my future will atone for my past,—morally, I mean; I want you to understand that I have wronged no man but myself, that I have been guilty of no act unbecoming a gentleman. Now look at me and tell me that you do not hate me."

Magdaléna lifted her face. Her lips were dry and parted, her eyes expanded, but not with horror.

"I love you," she said; "I am glad that I can help you."

They were near a huge oak whose limbs shut out the stars. Trennahan drew her into its shadows and took her in his arms and kissed her many times. He lifted her arms about him, and she clasped her hands tightly. He might be business-like, without illusions, but he knew how to make love with energy and grace. Magdaléna from brain to sole was on fire with adoration of him. The words of it surged toward speech, but reserve held her even then. She only clung to him and breathed the passion which his touch had startled. His own pulses were full, and he held her close, glad that the spiritual desires had caught and embraced the human, and that their chances for happiness were all that he could wish and a good deal more than he deserved.

XXX

"Look!" whispered Magdaléna.

They had reached the steps of the verandah, and were about to mount when she laid her hand on his arm. Mr. Polk stood by one of the windows. His head was thrust forward. He was staring into the room with hungry eyes and twitching jaw. The light was full on his white face. In the room Tiny was standing on a chair fanning Alan Rush. Fort was commanding Ila to pick up his handkerchief. The others were laughing and applauding. Lee and Coralie in their obscure corner were wide-eyed with excitement, and happy. Mr. Polk's chest heaved spasmodically. He screwed up his eyes. His face grinned. He looked like a man on the rack. He opened his eyes and glared about; but he saw nothing, for they were blind with tears. He turned and fled.

Magdaléna clung to Trennahan, shaking. "Take me home," she said. "I cannot stand any more to-night."

BOOK II

I

Helena was back.

Magdaléna sat amidst iridescent billows of ballgowns, dinner-gowns, tea-gowns, négligés, demi-toilettes, calling-frocks, street-frocks, yachting-frocks, summer-frocks. She had never seen so many clothes outside of a dry-goods shop, and marvelled that any one woman should want so many. They were on the bed, the chairs, the tables, the divan. Two mammoth trunks were but half unpacked. Others, empty, made the hall impassable.

"I love dress," said Helena, superfluously. "And women forgive your beauty and brains so much more willingly if you divert their attention by the one thing their soul can admire without bitterness."

"You have not grown cynical, Helena?" asked Magdaléna, anxiously.

"A little. It's a phase of extreme youth which must run its course with the down on the peach. I fought against it because I want to be original, but you might as well fight against a desire to sing at the top of your voice when you are happy. But, you darling! I'm so glad to see you again."

She flung herself on her knees beside Magdaléna and demanded to be kissed. Magdaléna, who could hardly realise that she was back, and whose loves were as fixed as the roots of the redwoods, gave her a great hug.

"Tell me, 'Léna, am I improved? Am I beautiful? Am I a great beauty?"

"You are the most beautiful person I have ever seen. Of course I have not seen the great beauties of Europe—"

"They are not a patch to ours. When I was presented, there were eight professionals standing round, and I walked away from the lot of them. Am I more beautiful than Tiny, or Ila, or Caro, or Mrs. Washington?"

"Oh, yes! yes!"

"How? They are really very beautiful."

"I know; but you are—you know I never could express myself."

"I am Helena Belmont," replied that young woman, serenely. "Besides, I've got the will to be beautiful as well as the outside. Tiny hasn't. I have real audacity, and Ila only a make-believe. Caro shows her cards every time she rolls her eyes, and Mrs. Washington never had a particle of dash. I'm going to be the belle. I'm going to turn the head of every man in San Francisco."

"I'm afraid you will, Helena."

"Afraid? You know you want me to. It wouldn't be half such fun if you weren't approving and applauding."

"I don't want you to hurt anybody."

"Hurt?" Helena opened her dark-blue pellucid eyes. "The idea of bothering about a trifle like that. Men expect to get a scratch or two for the privilege of knowing us. It will be something for a man to remember for the rest of his life that I've 'hurt' him."

"I am afraid you're a spoilt beauty already, Helena."

"I've got the world at my feet. That's a lovely sensation. You can't think—it's a wonderful sensation."

"I can imagine it." Magdaléna spoke without bitterness. Helena realised all her old ambitions but one, but she was too happy for envy.

"Describe Mr. Trennahan all over again."

"I am such a bad hand at describing."

"Well, never mind. Fancy your being engaged! Tell me everything. How did you feel the first moment you met him? When did you find yourself going? It must be such a jolly sensation to be in love—for a week or so. Now! Tell me all."

"I'd rather not, Helena. I love you better than anyone besides, but I am not the kind that can talk—"

"Well, perhaps I couldn't talk about it, myself, but I think I could. I can't imagine not talking about anything. But of course you are the same old 'Léna. Will you let me read his letters?"

"Oh, no! no!"

"I'll show you every letter I get. I never could be so stingy."

"I could not do that. I should feel as if I had lost something."

"You were always so romantic. There never was any romance about me. Poor Mr. Trennahan will have something to do to live up to you. An altitude of eleven thousand feet is trying to most masculine constitutions.

But I suppose he likes the variety of it, after twenty years of society girls. Well, let him rest."

A door shut heavily in the hall below. Helena sprang to her feet.

"There's papa. I must go down. I never leave him a minute alone if can help it. That's my only crumpled rose-leaf,—he is so pale and seems so depressed at times. You know how jolly and dashing he used to be. He hasn't a thing to worry him, and I can't think what is the matter. I beg him to tell me, but he says a man at his age can't expect to be well all the time. I can always amuse him, and I like to be with him all I can. He's such a darling. He'd build me a house of gold if I asked for it."

II

When Magdaléna returned home she spread her new garments on the bed and regarded them with much satisfaction. Helena had expended no less thought on these than on her own, and none whatever on the meagreness of Don Roberto's check. There was a brown tweed with a dash of scarlet, a calling-frock of fawn-coloured camel's hair and silk, a dinner-gown of pale blue with bunches of scarlet poppies, and a miraculous coming-out gown of ivory gauze, the deepest shade that could be called white. And besides two charming hats there was a large box of presents: fans, silk stockings, gloves, handkerchiefs, and soft indescribable things for the house toilette. And her trousseau was also to come from Paris! Don Roberto, in his delight at having secured Trennahan, had informed his daughter that she should have a trousseau fit for a princess; or, on second thoughts, for a Yorba.

Magdaléna opened a drawer and took out another of Helena's presents,—a jewelled dagger. While Colonel Belmont and his daughter were in Madrid there was a sale of a spendthrift noble's treasures. They had gone to see the famous collection, and among other things the dagger was shown them.

"It belonged to a lady of the great house of Yorba," they were told. "She always wore it in her hair, and all men worshipped her. The old women said it was the dagger that made men love her, that it was bewitched; there were other women as beautiful. But men died for this one and no other. One day she lost the dagger, and after that men loved her no longer. They ran and threw themselves at the feet of the women that had hated her. She laughed in scorn and said that she wanted no such love, and that when one returned—he had gone as Ambassador to the Court of France—he would show the world that his love did not skulk in the hilt of a dagger. People marvelled at this because she had flouted her very skirts in his face, had not thrown him so much as the humblest flower of hope. When they heard he was coming, they held their breath to see if the magnet had been in the dagger for him too. He arrived in the night, and in the morning she was found in her bed with the dagger to the hilt in her heart. They accused him, and he would not say yes or no, but they could prove nothing and let him go. And when he died the dagger was found among his possessions. No one could ever say how he got it. But it has remained in his family until to-day—and now it goes where?"

"To a Yorba!" announced Helena to Magdaléna, as she repeated this yarn. "I made up my mind to that, double quick! It may or may not be true, and she may or may not have been your ancestress; but it would make a jolly present all the same, so I ordered papa to buy it if all Madrid bid against him. Of course he did what I told him, and I want you to wear it the night of the party."

Magdaléna regarded it with great awe. She was by no means without superstition. Would it bring men to her feet? Not that she wanted them now, but she would like one evening of intoxicating success, just for the sake of her old ambitions: they had been little less than entities at one time; for old friendship's sake she would like to give them their due. She did wish that she felt a thrill as she touched it,—a vibration of the attenuated thread which connected one of her soul's particles with that other soul which, perhaps, had contributed its quota to her making. But she felt nothing, and replaced the dagger with some chagrin.

She put away the clothes and sat down before the fire to think of Trennahan. He had gone East at the summons of his mother, who had invested a large sum of money unwisely,—a habit she had. He might be detained some weeks. Magdaléna, on the whole, was glad to have him gone for a while. She wanted to think about him undisturbed, and she wanted to get used to Helena and her exactions while his demands were abstract: she loved so hard that she must rub the edge off her delight in having Helena again, or the two would tear her in twain.

She found the sadness of missing him very pleasurable,—feeling sure of his return; also the painful thrill every morning when the postman knocked. And to sit in retrospect of the summer was delicious. There may have been flaws in its present; there were none in its past. Her ambition to write was dormant. A woman's brain in love is like a garden planted with one flower. There may be room for a weed or two, but for none other of the floral kingdom.

Trennahan had given her more than one glimpse of his past, and it had appalled without horrifying or repulsing her. Her sympathy had been swift and unerring. She realised that Trennahan had come to California at a critical point in his moral life, and that his complete regeneration depended on his future happiness. He had pointed this out as a weakness, but the fact was all that concerned her. Whatever mists there might be between her perceptions and the great abstractions of life, love had sharpened all that love demanded and pointed them straight at all in Trennahan that he wished her to know. She was awed by the tremendous responsibility, but confident that she was equal to it; for did she not love him wholly, and had he not chosen her, by the light of his great experience, out of all women? She would walk barefooted on Arctic snows or accept any other ordeal that came her way, but she would make him happy.

Suddenly she remembered that she had received a brief dictated note from her aunt that morning, asking her to pack and send to Santa Barbara a painting of the Virgin which hung in her old apartments: she wished to present it to the Mission. Mr. Polk had closed his house a year before and taken up his permanent abode with the Yorbas, but his Chinese major-domo was in charge. Magdaléna reflected that it was not necessary to bother her uncle, who had seemed ill and restless of late; the Chinaman could attend to the matter.

She went downstairs and through the gardens to the adjoining house. The weeds grew high behind it; the windows were dusty; the side door at which she rang needed painting. The Chinaman answered in his own good time. He looked a little sodden; doubtless he employed much of his large leisure with the opium pipe. Magdaléna bade him follow her to her aunt's apartments. As she ascended the imposing staircase she withdrew her hand hastily from the banister.

"Why do you not keep things clean?" she asked disgustedly.

"Whattee difflence? Nobody come," he replied with the philosophy of his kind.

The very air was musty and dusty. The black walnut doors, closed and locked, looked like the sealed entrances to so many vaults. The sound of a rat gnawing echoed through the hollow house. It seemed what it was, this house,—the sarcophagus of a beautiful woman's youth and hopes.

For a year or two after the house was built Mrs. Polk had given magnificent entertainments, scattering her husband's dollars in a manner that made his thin nostrils twitch, and without the formality of his consent. Magdaléna paused at a bend of the stair and tried to conjure up a brilliant throng in the dark hall below, the great doors of the parlours rolled back, the rooms flooded with the soft light of many candles; her aunt, long, willowy, of matchless grace, her marvellous eyes shooting scorn at the Americans crowding about her, standing against the gold-coloured walls in the blood-red satin she had shown once to her small admirers. But the vision would not rise. There was only a black well below, a rat crunching above.

She reached the door of her aunt's private apartments on the second floor and entered. She stepped back amazed. There was no dust here, no musty air, no dimness of window. A fire burned on the hearth. The gas was lit and softly shaded. The vases on the mantel were full of flowers. On one table was a basket of fruit; on another were the illustrated periodicals.

"Mrs. Polk is here?" she said to Ah Sin.

"No, missee."

"She is expected, then? How odd —"

"Donno, missee. Evey day, plenty days, one, two, thlee weeks, me fixee rooms all same this."

"But why?"

"Kin sabbee, missee. Mr. Polk tellee me, and me do allee same whattee he say."

Magdaléna's lips parted, and her breath came short.

She gave the necessary instructions about the picture. The Chinaman followed her down the stairs and opened the door. As she was passing out, she turned suddenly and said to him, —

"It is not necessary to tell Mr. Polk about this, nor that I have been here. He does not like to be bothered about little things."

"Allight, missee."

III

The night of Mrs. Yorba's long-heralded ball had arrived at last. For weeks Society had been keenly expectant, for its greatest heiress and its three most beautiful girls were to come forth from the seclusion in which they were supposed to have been cultivating their minds, into the great world of balls, musicales, and teas, where their success would be in inverse ratio to their erudition.

Rose and Caro had arrived the winter before, and were no longer "buds;" but Magdaléna, Helena, Tiny, and Ila were hardly known by sight outside the Menlo Park set. Magdaléna had never hung over the banisters at her mother's parties. The others had been abroad so long that the most exaggerated stories of their charms prevailed.

The old beaux knotted their white ties with trembling fingers and thought of the city's wild young days when Nina Randolph, Guadalupe Hathaway, Mrs. Hunt Maclean, two of the "Three Macs," and the sinuous wife of Don Pedro Earle had set their pulses humming. They were lonely old bachelors, many of them, living at the Union or the Pacific Club, and they sighed as the memories rose. That was a day when every other woman in society was a great beauty, and as full of fascination as a fig of seeds. To-day beautiful women in San Francisco's aristocracy were rare. In Kearney Street, on a Saturday afternoon, one could hardly walk for the pretty painted shop-girls; and in that second stratum which was led by the wife of a Bonanza king who had been pronounced quite impossible by Mrs. Yorba and other dames of the ancient aristocracy, there were many stunningly handsome girls. They could be met at the fashionable summer resorts; they were effulgent on first nights; they were familiar in Kearney Street on other afternoons than Saturday, and their little world was gay in its way; but Society, that exclusive body which owned its inchoation and later its vitality and coherence to that brilliant and elegant little band of women who came, capable and experienced, to the fevered ragged city of the early Fifties, still struggled in the Eighties to preserve its traditions, and did not admit the existence of these people; feminine curiosity was not even roused to the point of discussion. One day Mrs. Washington met one of the old beaux, Ben Sansome by name, on the summit of California Street hill, which commands one of the finest views of a city swarming over an hundred hills.

Mrs. Washington waved her hand at the large region known as South San Francisco.

"I suppose," she said thoughtfully, "that there are a lot of people in San Francisco whose names we have never heard."

"I suppose so!" he exclaimed.

"I wonder what they are like? How many people are there in San Francisco, anyhow?"

"About three hundred thousand."

"Really? really?" and Mrs. Washington shrugged her pretty shoulders and dismissed the subject from her mind.

Would these new beauties compare with that galaxy of long ago? was the thought that danced between Ben Sansome's faded eyes and his mirror Three to burst forth in a night! That was unwonted measure. Of late years one in three seasons had inspired fervent gratitude. Nelly Washington had been unchallenged for ten years; Caro Folsom was second-rate beside her, and Rose Geary, the favourite of last winter, although piquant and pretty, had not a pretension to beauty. Like the other old beaux, he went only to the balls and dinners of the old-timers, never to the dances and musicales of the youngsters, but he kept a sharp look-out, nevertheless. To-night assumed the proportions of an event in his life.

Several of the young men had met two of these beauties during the summer, but Helena was still to be experienced. The young hands did not tremble, but their eyes were very bright as they wondered if they were "in for it," if they would "get it in the neck," if she were really "a little tin goddess on wheels." Even Rollins, who was madly enamoured of Tiny, and Fort, who had carefully calculated his chances with Rose, were big with curiosity. The former, who had known Helena from childhood, had been refused admittance to the Belmont mansion: Helena had a very distinct intention of making a sensation upon her first appearance in San Francisco; and as all were fish that came to her net, even Rollins must be dazzled with the rest.

Magdaléna's engagement was a closely guarded secret, and more than one hardy youth had made up his mind to storm straight through her intellect to her millions; but even these thought only of Helena as they dressed for the ball.

Meanwhile the girls were thinking more of their toilettes than of the men who would admire them. All were to wear white, but each gown had been made at a different Paris house, that there should be no monotony of touch and cut, and each was of different shade and material: Magdaléna's of ivory gauze, Tiny's of pearl-white silk, Ila's of cream-white embroidered *mousseline de soie*, Helena's of pure white tulle.

What little of Magdaléna's neck the gown exposed, she concealed with a broad band of cherry-coloured velvet, and a deep necklace of Turkish coins, a gift from Ila. She revolved before the mirror several times in succession after the maid had left the room. She was laced so tightly that she could scarcely breathe, but she rejoiced in her likeness to a French fashion-plate, and vowed never to wear a home-made gown again. In her hair was a string of pearls that Trennahan had given her; and the dagger. Would it work the spell?

She gave a final shake to her skirts and went downstairs.

There was no lack of gas to-night; the lower part of the house was one merciless glare. No flowers graced the square ugly rooms, no decorations of any sort; but the parlours were canvased, the best band in town was tuning up, and the supper would be irreproachable. The dark-brown paper of the hall looked very old and dingy, the carpet was threadbare in places, the big teak-wood tables were in everybody's way and looked as if they were meant for the dead to rest on; but when gay gowns were billowing one would not notice these things.

Mrs. Yorba was in the green reception-room at the end of the hall. She wore black velvet and a few diamonds, and looked impressively null. Tiny and Ila arrived almost immediately. They looked, the one an angel with a sense of humour, the other Circean with an eye to the conventions, both as smart as Paris could make them. It was nearly ten o'clock, and there was a rush just after.

Magdaléna waited a half-hour for Helena, then opened the ball in a brief waltz with Alan Rush instead of the quadrille in which the four débutantes were to dance. She sent a message to Helena, and Mrs. Cartright scribbled back that the poor dear child had altered the trimming on her bodice at the last moment, and would not be ready for an hour yet. Caro took her place in the quadrille, as she also wore white.

The ball promised to be a success. There were more young people than was usual at Mrs. Yorba's parties, and more men than girls. They danced and chatted with untiring energy, and between the dances they flirted on the stairs and in every possible nook and corner. Magdaléna frolicked little, having her guests to look after; but whenever she rested for a moment there was an obsequious backbone before her. Tiny and Ila were besieged for dances, and divided each.

The older women sat against the wall, a dado of fat and diamonds, and indulged in much caustic criticism.

The old beaux stood in a group and exchanged opinions on the relative pretensions of the old and the new.

"Take it all in all, not to compare," said Ben Sansome. "Miss Montgomery is excessively pretty, but no figure and no style. Miss Brannan looks like a Parisian cocotte. Miss Folsom has eyes, but nothing else—and when you think of 'Lupie Hathaway's eyes! And not one has the beginnings of the polished charm of manner, the fire of glance, the *je ne sais quoi* of Mrs. Hunt Maclean. Just look at her in her silver brocade, her white hair *à la marquise*. She's handsomer than the whole lot of them—"

At that moment Helena entered the room.

The white tulle gown, made with a half-dozen skirts, floated about her so lightly that she seemed rising from, suspended above it. Even beside her father she looked tall; and her neck and arms, the rise of her girlish bust, were more dazzlingly white than the diaphanous substance about her. Her haughty little head was set well back on a full firm throat, not too long. Her cheeks were touched with pink; her lips were full of it. Her long lashes and low straight brows were many shades darker than the unruly mane of glittering coppery hair. And she carried herself with a swing, with an imperious pride, with a nonchalant command of immediate and unmeasured admiration which sent every maiden's heart down with a drop and every man's pulses jumping.

"I give in!" gasped Ben Sansome. "We never had anything like that— never! Gad! the girl's got everything. It's almost unfair."

Alan Rush turned white, but he did not lose his presence of mind. He asked Don Roberto to present him at once, and secured the next dance. It was a waltz; and as the admirably mated couple floated down the room, many others paused to watch them. Helena's limpid eyes, raised to the eager ones above her, did all the execution of which they were capable. During the next entre-dance she was mobbed. Twenty men pressed about her, introduced by Don Roberto and Rollins, until she finally commanded them to "go away and give her air," then walked off with Eugene Fort, finishing his first epigram and mocking at his second. He had only a fourth of the next dance; but as Helena had refused to permit her admirers to write their names on her card, and as she was at no pains to remember which fourth was whose, giving her scraps to the first comer, Rush and Fort, who had had the forethought not to pre-engage themselves, and were constantly in her wake, secured more than their share. But the other men had time and energy to fight for their own: Helena was constantly stopped in the middle of the room with a firm demand that she should keep her word. Between the dances the men crowded about her, eager for a glance, and at supper the small table before her looked like an offering at a Chinese funeral.

"Well," exclaimed Mrs. Washington, "I always said that no girl could be a belle in this town nowadays, that the men didn't have gumption enough; but I reckon it's because the rest of us haven't come up to the mark. This looks like the stories they tell of old times."

"It makes me think of old times," said Mr. Sansome. "Makes me feel young again; or older than ever. I can't decide which."

Tiny took her eclipse with unruffled philosophy, and divided her smiles between two or three faithful suppliants. Ila had a very high colour, and her primal fascination was less reserved than usual. Rose admired Helena too extravagantly for jealousy, and what Caro felt no man ever knew.

Colonel Belmont renewed his acquaintance with many of the women of his youth, long neglected, although he had loved more than one of them in his day. They filled his ears with praises of his beautiful daughter. Helena's beauty was of that rare order which compels the willing admiration of her own sex: it was not only indisputable, but it warmed and irradiated. When Colonel Belmont was not talking, he stood against the wall and followed her with adoring eyes. If she had been a failure—admitting the possibility—his disappointment would have been far keener than hers.

"You've cause to be proud, as proud as Lucifer," said Mr. Polk to him. "But you ain't looking well, Jack. What's the matter?"

"I'm well enough. I shall live long enough to give her to someone who's good enough for her, and that's all I care about—although I'm in no hurry for that, either. But I'm *not* feeling right smart, Hi; I don't just know what's the matter."

"We're both getting old. I feel like a worked-out old cart-horse. But you've got ten years the best of me, and I'll tell you what's the matter with you: you can't switch off drink at your age after being two thirds full for twenty-five years. We all need whiskey as we grow older, and the more we've had, the more we need. I'd advise you to take it up again in moderation."

"Not if it's the death of me! It's nothing or everything with me. The first cocktail, and I'd be off on a jamboree. Then she'd know, and I'd blow out my brains with the shame of it. She thinks I'm the finest fellow in the world now, and so she shall if I suffer the tortures of the damned."

"Well, I guess you're right. The young fellows talk about dying for th girls, but I guess we're the ones that would do that for our own if it came t the scratch."

"It's too bad you have none," said Colonel Belmont, with the sympath of his own full measure. And then, although Mr. Polk's iron features did no move, he looked away hastily.

"I guess I didn't deserve any," Mr. Polk answered harshly. "I don't know that you did, for that matter, but I certainly didn't. Look at Don cavorting round with those girls," he added viciously. "It's positively sickening."

"Not a bit of it. He's making up for what he's missed. And a little of i would do you good, old fellow. You've never had half enough fun, and you ought to take a little before it's too late. You haven't a pound of flesh on you and are as spry as any of them. Go and make yourself agreeable to the girls Even a smile from them goes a long way, I assure you."

Mr. Polk shook his head. "I couldn't think of a thing to say to them. didn't learn when I was young."

IV

When Magdaléna drew the dagger out of her hair that night, she laughed a little and tossed it into her handkerchief box. She had seen men carried off their feet for the first time, not caring whether the world laughed or not. She had also noted the exact order of homage that she was to expect from men. Helena infatuated. The other girls inspired admiration in varying measure. Respect for her father's millions was her portion. She had watched and compared all the evening. It would have distressed and appalled her had she made her début last winter. As it was, it mattered little.

Occasionally there is a lively winter in San Francisco. This promised to be almost brilliant. There were six balls in the next two weeks. At each Helena's triumphs were reiterated. The men waited in a solid body between the front door and the staircase, and she had promised, divided, and subdivided every dance before she had set foot on the lowest step. It was almost impossible to begin a party until her arrival. Kettledrums had been inaugurated the previous winter, and hardly a man been got to them. Now the men would have begged for invitations. They even began to attend church; and Helena's "evening" was so crowded that she was obliged to ask five or six of her girl friends to help her. Alan Rush, Eugene Fort, Carter Howard, a Southerner of charming manners, infinite tact, and little conversation, and "Dolly" Webster, a fledgeling of enormous length and well-proportioned brain, were her shadows, her serfs, her determined, trembling adorers. They barely hated one another, so devoured were they by the sovereign passion; and as they were treated with exasperating similitude, there was nothing to set them at one another's throats.

Helena had all the gifts and arts of the supreme coquette. She allured and mocked, appealed and commanded; adapted herself with the suppleness of bronze to mould, with enchanting flashes of egotism; discarded all perception of man's existence in the abstract, when she had surrendered her attention to one, to jerk him out of his heaven by ordering him to go and send her his rival; possessed a quickness of intuition which finished a man's sentences with her eyes, an exquisite sympathy which made a man feel that here at last he was understood (as he would wish himself understood, rather than as he understood himself); an audacity which never failed to surprise, and never shocked; a fund of talk which never wore itself into platitudes, and a willing ear; and an absolute confidence in herself and her destiny. In addition she had great beauty, the high light spirits of her mercurial temperament, a charming and equable manner (when not engaged in judiciously tormenting her slaves), and a shrewd brain. What wonder that her sovereignty was something for the men who worshipped her to remember when they too were old beaux, and that their present condition was abject? The wonder was that the women did not hate her; but so impulsive and unaffected a creature disarms her own sex, particularly when her gowns are faultless, and she is not lifeless in their company, to scintillate the moment a man enters the room.

And they forbore to criticise the dictates of her royal fancy. It is true that she deferred to no one's opinion, but she escaped criticism nevertheless. If she capriciously refused to dance at a party, but sat the night through with one man, not recognising the existence of her lowering train, people merely smiled and shrugged their shoulders, saving their scowls for those who were not the fashion. Sometimes these flirtations took place in the open ball-room, sometimes in the conservatory; it was all one to Helena, whose powers of concentration amounted to genius. At one of the Presidio hops she spent the evening—it was moonlight—in a boat on the bay with an officer who was as accomplished a flirt as herself. The appearance of Rush, Fort, Howard, and Webster upon this occasion was pitiable. On her evening, if she tired of her admirers before they could reasonably be expected to leave, she walked out of the room without excuse and went to bed. She not only ran to fires when the humour seized her, but she commanded her quartette to rush every time the alarm sounded, that they might be at her beck in the event of officious policemen. As fires are frequent in San Francisco, these enamoured young men were profoundly thankful when they occurred at such times as they happened to be in their tyrant's presence: they were willing to bundle into their clothes at two in the morning, or to leave their duties at midday, were they sure of meeting her; but as she was as capricious about fires as about everything else, their chances were as one in ten. They hinted once that she might advise them of her pleasure by telephone, but were peremptorily snubbed. Helena never made concessions.

It was at the end of the second month that her father imported a coach from New York. She had driven since her baby days, and could handle four horses as scientifically as one. Thereafter, one of the sights of Golden Gate Park on fine afternoons was Helena on the box of the huge black and yellow structure, tooling a party of her delighted friends, her father beside her, one of her admirers crouched at her indifferent shoulder. It was the only gentleman's coach in California, for in the Eighties the youth of the city had not turned their wits and prowess to sport. Few of them could drive with either grace or assurance, and Helena's accomplishment was the more renowned. Occasionally Colonel Belmont was allowed to drive, a favour which he enjoyed with all the keenness of his dashing youth.

"I told you how it would be," said Ila to Rose. "She is not only belle, but leader. That's the real reason Caro's gone to New York. We are nowhere. I'd turn eccentric, regularly shock people, if I had the good luck to be the fashion. But I've got to marry well. When I have—you'll see."

"We can't all be raving belles," said Rose. "If Helena were so much as doubled, the men would be gibbering idiots. I don't care, so long as I have a good time; and I hold my own. So do you. As for Tiny, she may not be mobbed, but she has one man in love with her after another. As soon as poor Charley Rollins got his congé, Bob Payne took the vacant seat, and I see a third climbing over the horizon with business in his eye. There can be only one sun, but we're all stars of the first magnitude."

"But we'd each like to be the sun, all the same."

V

Magdaléna, although much interested in Helena's performances, felt at times as if dream-walking, half expecting to awaken at the foot of her little altar. In the days when she had prayed, full of faith, for beauty and its triumphs, although ignorance had handled the brush of her imagination, yet the vigorous outline sketch had closely resembled all that was now the portion of her friend. She pondered on the fancy she had had as a child that Helena realised all her own little ambitions. She certainly had realised all her larger, but one. She dreaded to ask Helena if she had ever cared to write, fearing to surprise a confession to the authorship of the novel of the day. This, she concluded, after due reflection, was exaggeration; for if Helena had written, even without publication, she certainly would have talked about it, reticence being no vice of hers. But the suggestion might prick a latent talent into action. This was just the one thing Magdaléna could not endure, and she decided to let the talent sleep. The rest mattered little, aside from the sense of failure which the vicarious accomplishment of ambition must always induce; for she had her advantage of Helena, the greatest one woman can have of another. She was happy, but Helena was only satisfied for the moment; so restless and passionate a heart would not long remain content with the husks. It was true that Trennahan had not gone mad over herself as other men over Helena; but what of that? It was a question of years alone.

It was now three months since he had left California. He had found his mother's affairs in a serious condition, but had managed to gather up the threads, and the knot would be tied before long. There was no doubt about his desire to return. In fact, as the time waned, his ardour waxed. Sometimes Magdaléna was driven to wonder if his yearning for California or herself were the greater; but on the whole she was satisfied, for she liked to accept his fancy that the two were indissoluble. He wrote delightful letters, witty and graceful, full of interesting gossip, and with many personal and tender pages. But the novelty of his absence had worn off some time since, and she longed impatiently for his return. She was caught in the whirl of social activity, and was the restless Helena's constant companion; nevertheless, there were lonely hours, when the future with its imperious demands routed the past.

The engagement was still a profound secret; Magdaléna had told Helena at once, but it was unguessed by anyone else. Mrs. Yorba had insisted that her daughter should have one brilliant girl season. The truth was that she was delighted at Don Roberto's sudden interest in the world of fashion, and was determined to make the most of it. He developed, indeed, into an untiring seeker after the innocent amusements of his wife's exclusive kingdom, and had given a fashionable tailor permission to bring his wardrobe down to date; he had hitherto worn clothes of the same cut for twenty years. The girls always gave him a square dance; during the round dances he stood against the wall with Mr. Polk and Colonel Belmont, and fairly beamed with good-will. The Yorbas seldom spent an evening at home unless their own doors were open, and Don Roberto consented to two parties and several large dinners. Mrs. Yorba shuddered sometimes at the weakening of her inborn and long-nurtured economical faculty, but thoroughly enjoyed herself—forming an important item of the dado—and hoped that her husband's enthusiasm would endure.

VI

"I'm not a bit blasé," remarked Helena, "but I'd like to be engaged for a change—not to last, of course. Only I can't make up my mind which of the four; and whichever I choose the other three will be so disagreeable. If I could only let them know I didn't mean it,—at least wouldn't later,—but that would never do, because I shouldn't enjoy myself unless I really thought I was in earnest. Besides, I haven't been able to fall in love with any of them yet."

"You don't really mean what you say when you talk that way, do you, Helena?" asked Magdaléna, with much concern. "It would be so—so unprincipled; and I can't bear to think that of you."

"But, 'Léna dearest, I should be in earnest for the time being; I'm just talking from the outside, as it were. At the time I should think I really meant it. Otherwise I'd be bored to death, and the engagement wouldn't last five minutes after I was. I'm simply wild to fall in love, if only to see what it's like. You won't tell me; anyhow, I don't think that would satisfy all my curiosity if you did. I wish some new man would come along."

"Alan Rush is charming."

"He's too much in love with me."

"Mr. Fort keeps your wits on the jump."

"My wits are in my brain, not my heart."

"Mr. Howard?"

"He has so much tact that he has no sincerity."

"There is still Mr. Webster."

"Poor Dolly!"

"What *do* you want?"

Helena was moving restlessly about her boudoir,—a bower of pearl-grey embroidered with wild roses, in which she reclined luxuriously when free from social duties, and improved her mind. A volume of Motley lay on the floor. Walter Pater's "Imaginary Portraits" was slipping off the divan, and there was a pile of Reviews on the table. She was biting the corner of a volume of Herrick.

"I haven't any ideal, if that's what you mean. I think it would have to be a man of the world, for conversation so soon gives out with the men of this village. Mr. Fort takes refuge in epigrams. If I married—became engaged to him—I should feel as if I were living on pickles. I think that one reason why Alan Rush and Mr. Howard are so determined to make love to me is because they have nothing left to talk about."

"You've told me twice what you don't want, but you don't seem to know what you do. 'A man of the world' is not very definite."

"No; he must be capable of falling violently in love with me, and at the same time not make himself ridiculous; to keep his head except when I particularly want him to lose it. Of course I want to inspire a grand passion as well as to feel one, but I don't want to be surrounded by it; and the first time he looked ridiculous would be the last of him as far as I was concerned. I might be in the highest stages of the divine passion, and that would cure me."

"Well! is that all? Some men could not be ridiculous if they tried."

"You are thinking of Mr. Trennahan, of course. If he did, I do believe you wouldn't see it. But I should; I have a hideous sense of the ridiculous. Well, lemme see. He must have read and travelled and thought a lot, so that he would know more than I, and I could look up to him; also that subjects of conversation would not give out. The platitudes of love! That would be fatal."

"I don't believe they ever sound like platitudes."

"Hm! I won't undertake to discuss that point, knowing my limitations. What next? He must have suffered. That gives a man weight, as the sculptors say. My quartette will be much more interesting to the next divinity than they are to me. Then of course he must have charming manners and an agreeable voice: I could not stand the brain of a Bismark in the skull of an Apollo if he had a nasal American voice. I believe that's all. I'm not so particular about looks, so long as he's neither small nor fat."

"And if you found all that wouldn't you marry it?"

"N-o-o—I don't know—but I'd be engaged a good long time. You see I want to be a belle for years and years."

"And what is to become of the poor men when you are through with them?"

"Oh, they'll get over it. I shall. Why shouldn't they?"

"I thought you said once you wanted to marry a statesman."

"Sometimes I do, and sometimes I don't. I'll consider that question ten years hence. I want to be a perfectly famous belle first."

"You are that already."

"Oh, I must have a season in New York, and another in Washington, and another in London. The gods have given me all the gifts, and I intend to make the most of them. Now let's read a chapter of Motley out loud, and if I jump off to other things you jerk me back. Let's finish Pater, though. It's like lying under a cascade of bubbles on a hot summer's day. My brains are addled between trying to be well read and trying to keep four men from proposing. You read aloud, and I'll brush my hair. No, I'll embroider on papa's mouchoir case; I've been at it for thirteen months. Oh, by the bye, I didn't tell you that I had a brilliant idea. It darted into my head just as I was dropping off last night. I forgot to speak about it to papa this morning, but I will to-night. It's this: I'm going to give a ball at Del Monte. Take everybody down on a special train. Don't you think it will be a change? The spring has come so early that we can have the grounds lit up with Chinese lanterns; and there may be some Eastern men there. There often are. So much the better for my ball—and me. Now read."

VII

Trennahan arrived late in the evening, and went directly to the Yorbas' to dinner. He saw Magdaléna alone for a moment before the others came downstairs, and his delight at meeting her again was so boyish that she could hardly have recalled his eventful forty years had she tried. He was one of those men, who, having a great deal of nervous energy, are possessed briefly by the high animal spirits of youth when in unusual mental and physical tenor, — with coincident obliteration of the bills of time. Trennahan was in the highest spirits this evening. He was delighted to get back to California, delighted to see Magdaléna, whom he thought improved and almost pretty in her smart frock. Moreover, no woman had ever seemed to him half so sincere, half so well worth the loving, as this girl who said so little and breathed so much.

Don Roberto and Mr. Polk detained him some time after dinner, and Magdaléna, who thought them most inconsiderate, awaited him in the green-and-brown reception-room. She knew the ugliness of these rooms now, and wondered, as Trennahan finally entered, if it clashed with his sentiment. But he gave no sign. He pushed a small sofa before the fire, drew her beside him, and demanded the history of the past four months. He held her hand and looked at her with boyish delight. Even the lines had left his face for the moment, the grimness his mouth. He looked twenty-six.

"Your trip has done you more good than California did. You never looked so well here."

"I have been funereal since the day I left. This is pure reaction. I never felt so happy in my life. Couldn't we have a walk or ride somewhere to-morrow early — out to the Presidio? I want to be in the open air with you."

"I am afraid we couldn't. Nobody does such things, you know — except Helena. Someone would be sure to see us, and it would be all over town before night. Then we should have to announce — I'd rather not do that until just before — I should hate being discussed."

"Well, but I must have you to myself in my own way. I wonder if your mother would bring you down to my house for a few days. Don Roberto and Mr. Polk could come down every evening."

"I think they would like it."

"And you?"

"Oh, I should like it. The woods must be lovely in winter."

"Who has been teaching you coquetry? Who has fallen in love with you since I left?"

"With me? No one. No one would ever think of such a thing but you—"

"I love you with an unerring instinct."

"They are all in love with Helena. I suppose you heard of her in New York."

"It certainly was not your fault if I did not."

"But surely you must have heard otherwise. She is a great, great belle."

"My dearest girl, you do not hear California mentioned in New York once a month. It might be on Mars. The East remembers California's existence about as often as Europe remembers America's. They don't know what they miss. When am I to see your Helena?"

"A week from to-night; she gives a ball then at Del Monte. She and her father have already gone, because each thought the other needed rest."

"Monterey,—that is the scene of your Ysabel's tragedy. We will explore the old part of the town together."

She moved closer to him, her eyes glistening. "That has been one of my dreams,—to be there with you—for the first time. We can guess where they all lived—and go to the cemetery on the hill where so many are buried— and there is the Custom House on the rocks, where the ball was and where Ysabel jumped off—it will be heaven!"

He laughed and caught her in his arms, kissing her fondly. "You dear little Spanish maid," he said. "You don't belong to the present at all. No wonder you bewitched me. I am beginning to feel quite out of place in the present, myself. It is a novel and delightful sensation."

VIII

Mrs. Yorba decided that it would be wiser for them all to go to Fair Oaks; no one would know whether Trennahan were their guest or not. This was her first really gay winter, and could she have thought of a plausible excuse she would have delayed the marriage for a year or two. But both Don Roberto and Trennahan were determined that the wedding should not take place later than June.

They were to spend five days at Fair Oaks. Then Don Roberto, Mrs. Yorba, and Magdaléna would go to Monterey, Trennahan to follow on the evening of the ball.

The winter woods were wet and glistening. Thick in the brush were the vivid red berries and the firm little snowballs. The air was of a wonderful freshness and fragrance, cool on the cheek, but striking no chill to the blood. The grass tips in the meadows were close and green. There was no haze on the distant mountains: the redwoods stood out sharply; one could almost see the sun baldes crossing in their gloomy aisles. Close to the ground was a low, restless, continuous mutter, — the voluntary of Spring.

Trennahan and Magdaléna rode or strolled in the woods during most of the hours of light. They could not sit on the damp ground, but they swung hammocks by the path-side to sit in when tired. Trennahan would have slept on the verandah had not his enthusiasm for outdoor delights been controlled by his matter-of-fact brain, but he grudged the hours at table, and persuaded Magdaléna to go early to bed that she might rise and go forth at five in the evening of night. After four months of snow and nipping winds and furnace heat, small wonder that he was as happy as a boy out of school, and that he made Magdaléna the most wonderingly happy of women. He did little love-making; he treated her more as a comrade upon whose constant companionship he was dependent for happiness, — his other part, with which he was far better satisfied than with the original measure.

"We will camp out up there during all of July and August," he said to her one morning, as they stood on the edge of the woods and watched the rising sun pick out the redwoods one by one from the black mass on the mountain. "I can't imagine a more enchanting place for a honeymoon than a redwood forest. We'll take a servant, and a lot of books; but I doubt if we shall read much,—we'll shoot and fish all day. If we like it as much as I am sure we shall, we'll build a house there. Do you think you should like it?"

"Oh, I should! I should!"

"You are so sympathetic in your own particular way; not temperamentally so, which is pleasant but means little, but with a slow, sure understanding which goes forth to few people, but is unerring and permanent."

"I love no one but you and Helena. I have never cared to understand anyone else."

"We all have great weaknesses in us. I wonder if mine were ever revealed to you—which God forbid!—if you have sympathy enough to cover those, too."

"I am sure that I have. I am neither quick nor generally affectionate, but I do nothing by halves."

"I believe you. You are the one person on whose mercy I would throw myself. However,—it is a long time since we have spoken of another subject. Do you think no further of writing?"

"I haven't lately. There has been no time. Some day—Oh, yes, I think I should never wholly give it up. Should—should you object?"

"Not in the least. But I am afraid I sha'n't give you much time, either. What were you writing,—your Old-California tales?"

"No,—an—an historical novel—English."

"Of course! And with fresh and fascinating material begging for its turn. I arrived in the nick of time. When you have transcribed those stories into correct and distinguished English, you will have taken your place among the immortals. But style alone will give you a place in letters worth having. Always remember that. The theme determines popular success, the manner rank. Don't misunderstand me; there is no greater fraud or bore than the writer who has acquired the art of saying nothing brilliantly. You must have both. And you are too ambitious, too intellectual, as distinguished from clever, too serious and logical, to be contented with anything short of perfection. I shall be your severest critic; but you yourself will work for years before you produce a line with which you are wholly satisfied. Is not this true?"

"Yes; I should always be my severest critic."

He drew a long breath of relief. He had no desire for a literary wife; nor to be known as the husband of one. Magdaléna should be as happy as he could make her, but the sooner she realised that genius was not her portion, the better.

IX

"Never I think I come to Monterey again," said Don Roberto, as the 'bus which contained his party only drove from the little toy station to the big toy hotel. "Once I hate all the Spanish towns, because so extravagant I am before that I feel 'fraid, si I return, I am all the same like then; but now I am old and the habits fixit; and now I know my moneys go to be safe with Trennahan, I feel more easy in the mind and can enjoy. But I no go to the town, for all is change, I suppose: all the womens grown old and poor, and all the mens dead—by the drink, generalmente. Very fortunate I am I no stay there; meeting Eeram in time. Ay, yi! What kind de house is this? Look like paper, and the grounds so artifeecial. No like much."

Magdaléna hardly knew her father these last months. From the day that he found a reminiscent pleasure in the mild diversions of Menlo he had visibly softened. From the day he was assured of Trennahan he had become almost expansive, and at times was moved to generosity. Upon one occasion he had doubled Magdaléna's allowance, and at Christmas he had given her a hundred dollars; and he had paid the bills of the season without a murmur. The fear which had haunted him during the last thirty years,— that he should suddenly relapse into his native extravagance and squander his patrimony and his accumulated millions, dying as the comparions of his youth had died,—he dismissed after he met Trennahan. Polk had been the iron mine to the voracious magnet in his character. In the natural course of things Polk would outlive him; but the possibility of Polk's extermination by railroad accident or small-pox had been a second devil of torment, and during the past year he had visibly failed. Now, however, there was Trennahan to take his place. Don Roberto would enjoy life once more, a second youth. He was almost happy. If he felt his will rotting, he would transfer all his vast interests to Trennahan in trust for his wife and daughter, retaining a large income. He did not believe, at this optimistic period, that there was any real danger, after an inflexible resistance of thirty years; but he also realised for the first time what the strain of those thirty years had been.

Helena, dazzlingly fair in a frock of forest green, and surrounded by five new admirers, three Eastern and two English tourists, awaited Magdaléna on the verandah. The strangers gave Magdaléna a faint shock: being the only well-dressed men she had ever seen except Trennahan, they assumed a family likeness to him, and seemed to steal something of his preeminence among men. She commented distantly on this fact as she went up the stair with Helena.

"Oh, your little tin god on wheels is not the only one," replied Helena, the astute. "There are five here with possibilities besides dress, and more coming to-morrow. They *are* such a relief! If I feel real wicked to-morrow night—well, never mind!"

"Helena! You will not make those four young men any more miserable than they are now?"

Helena shook her head. She was looking very naughty. "Four months, my dear! I didn't realise what I had endured until I had this sudden vacation. Two days of blissful rest, and then the variations for which I was born."

They were in Helena's room, and Magdaléna sat down by the open window, where she could smell the cypresses, and regarded her beloved friend more critically than was her habit.

"I wonder if you will ever mature,—get any heart?" she said.

"'Léna! What do you mean! Heart? Don't I love you and my father; and the other girls—some?"

"I don't mean that kind. Nor falling in love, either. I never expressed myself very well, but you know what I mean."

"Oh, bother. What were men and women made for but to amuse each other?"

"Life isn't all play."

"It is for a time—when you're young. I am sūre that that is what Nature intended, and that the people who don't see it are those who make the mistakes with their lives. Otherwise life would be simply outrageous,—no balance, no compensation. After a certain age even fools become serious: they can't help it, for life begins to take its revenge for permitting them to be young at all, and to hope, and all that sort of thing. Therefore those that don't make the most of youth and all that goes with it are something more than fools."

Magdaléna looked at her in dismay. "How do you realise that, at your age? I have lived alone, thought more—had more time to think and to read—but I never should—"

"I have intuitions. And I've seen more of the world than you have. I see everything that goes on—you can bet your life on that. Talk about my powers of concentration! They're nothing to my antennae."

"But have you no principles of right and wrong? No morality? You would not deliberately sacrifice others to your own pleasure, would you?"

"Wouldn't I? I don't take the least pleasure in cruelty, like some women. If I could give people oblivion draughts, I'd do it in a minute—for my vanity has nothing to do with it, either. But the world is at my feet, and there it shall stay, no matter who pays the piper. I love life. I love everything about it. I've never seen anything in the world I thought ugly. I don't think anything is ugly. If it was, I should hate it. I've never been through a slum,—a horrid slum, that is,—and I don't want to. The beauty of the earth intoxicates me. When I even think about it, much less look at it, I feel perfectly wild with delight to think that I am alive. And my senses are so keen. I see so far. I can hear miles. I believe I can hear the grass grow. I eat and drink little, but that little gives me delight. A glass of cold spring water intoxicates me. And, above all, I enjoy being loved. I never forget how much you and papa love me. I couldn't exist without either of you. Papa is looking much better since he came down. Don't you think so? And I like to see love in the eyes of men I don't care a rap about. Their eyes are like impersonal mirrors for me to read the secrets of the future in. And I don't really hurt them. Most men have a lot of superfluous love in them. I may as well have it as another. It won't interfere with the destination of the reserve in the least."

"Helena!" exclaimed Magdaléna, with a sinking heart. "I believe you are a genius."

"I have the genius of personality, but I couldn't do a thing to save my life."

Magdaléna breathed freely again.

X

Trennahan, who was to have arrived in time to dine with the Belmonts and Yorbas, missed his train and took his dinner alone. Afterward, he saw Magdaléna for a few moments in the Yorbas' private parlour, but she had to dress, and he went off to smoke in the grounds with Don Roberto, Mr. Polk, Mr. Washington, and Colonel Belmont. They subsequently had a game of bowls, and—excepting Colonel Belmont—several cocktails. When they suddenly remembered that a ball was in progress to which they were expected, it was eleven o'clock, and Trennahan was not dressed.

It was Helena's ball, but she had made every man promise to look after the wall-flowers, that she might be at liberty to enjoy herself. Her aunt, Mrs. Yorba, and Magdaléna received with her; and as all the guests had arrived by the same train, and had dressed at about the same time, the arduous duty of receiving was soon over. Helena left the stragglers to her chaperons and prepared to amuse herself. As usual, she had refused to engage herself for any dances, but she gave the first two to her devoted four, then announced her intention to dance no more for the present. The truth was that one of her minute high-heeled slippers pinched, but this she had no intention of acknowledging; if men wished to think her an angel, so they should. She was a sensible person, far too practical to reduce the sum of her happiness by physical discomfort; but the slippers, which she had never tried on, matched her gown, and she had no others with her that did. But the one rift in her lute induced a sympathetic rift in her temper.

The party was very gay and pretty. The rooms had been fantastically decorated with red berries and snowballs, pine, and cedar. The leader of the band was in that stage of intoxication which promised music to make the soles of the dado tingle. All the girls had brought their prettiest frocks, and all the matrons their diamonds. There were no tiaras in the Eighties, but there were a few necklaces, stars, and ear-rings—of the vulgar variety known as "solitaires." It is true that certain of the Fungi looked like crystal chandeliers upon occasion; but Helena would have none of them.

Herself had rarely been more lovely,—in floating clouds of pale pink tulle, which looked like a shower of almond blossoms. Her hair was roped up with pearls, hinting the head-dress of Juliet, but stopping short of eccentric effect. She wore nothing to break the lines of her throat and neck, but on her arms were quantities of odd and beautiful "bangles," many made from her own suggestions, others picked up in different parts of the world.

She was standing opposite the door in the middle of the room as Trennahan entered, leaning lightly upon a little table to rest her mischievous foot. Only one man was beside her at the moment, and Trennahan's view of her was uninterrupted. He knew at once who she was. His second impression was that he had seen few girls so beautiful. His third, that she possessed something more potent than beauty, and that he was responding to it with a certain wild flurry of the senses, and a certain glad exultation in youth and danger which had not been his portion for many a long year. The instinct of the hunter leaped from its tomb, shocked into the eager quivering life of its youth. Trennahan was appalled to hear the fine web he had spun between his senses and his spirit rent in a second, then gratified at the youthful singing in his blood. The old joy in recklessness, in surrender to the delirium of the senses, came back to him. He pushed them roughly aside, and looked about for Magdaléna. She was listening to the rapid delivery of Mr. Rollins. He thought she looked ill, and was about to go to her when Colonel Belmont took him by the arm.

"You must meet my daughter," he said. "Oh, bother! There go half a dozen."

When Trennahan reached Helena, he was presented in the same breath with two other new arrivals, and her slipper was fairly biting. She did not even hear his name. She was in a mood to make her swains unhappy; and she liked Trennahan's face, and what she saw there. There was eager admiration in his eyes and nostrils, and on his face the record of a man who might possibly be her match. Of man's deeper and more personal life she never thought. She had heard that men sometimes loved married women, and others whose like she had never seen; but she hated the mere fact of vice as she did all forms of ugliness, and dismissed it from her mind. She read in Trennahan's face that he had had many flirtations, nothing more.

"I am not going to dance any more to-night," she announced. She placed her hand in Trennahan's arm. "Take me to the conservatory," she said.

There was really nothing for him to do but take her. But it was three hours before either was seen again.

XI

"You are not looking well this morning," said Trennahan, solicitously about twelve hours after he had appeared in the ball-room. He had just entered the Yorbas' private parlour.

"Neither do you," replied Magdaléna.

"I sat up late with some of the men, and slept ill after."

Magdaléna raised her eyes and looked at him steadily. "You have fallen in love with Helena," she said.

"What nonsense! My dear child, what are you talking about? Miss Belmont asked me to take her to the conservatory; and as I do not dance, and as you do, and as she announced her intention of not dancing again, and is a very entertaining young woman, I decided to remain there. If our engagement had been made known, of course I should have done nothing of the sort. But as it was—"

"You turned white when you first saw her. Alan Rush looked just like that. Now he is mad about her."

"I am not Alan Rush, nor any other boy of twenty-five. The man you have elected to marry, and who is not half good enough for you, as I have told you many times, is a seasoned person past middle age, my dearest. I could not go off my head over a pretty face if I tried. My day for that is long past."

He spoke vehemently.

"You never looked at me like that."

"Doubtless my pallor was due to some such unromantic cause as an extremely bad dinner."

"I have seen that look several times. Alan Rush is not the only one. And Helena is no doll. She has every fascination."

"Possibly. Shall we go for our walk? I am most anxious to see those old houses and graves."

He did not offer to kiss her. She was too proud to take up woman's usual refrain. She put on her hat, and they left the hotel, and walked toward the town.

"I believe the cemetery comes first," she said. "I have made inquiries. We can see the town from there, and go on afterward—if you like."

"Of course I like. How good of you to wait for me! I know you have been longing for the town which I am convinced is a part of your very personality."

"Yes, I have been longing. I don't care much about it this morning."

"Which of your heroines is buried in the cemetery?"

"Benicia Ortega, La Tulita, and some of aunt's old friends."

"You must certainly write those old stories. I often think of them."

"Nothing that you say this morning sounds like the truth."

"My dear girl! I am dull and stupid after a sleepless night. And the night after you left I sat up until two in the morning writing important letters."

"I think it was disloyal of Helena."

"I must rush to her defence. She did not know until the end of the evening who I was. She took me for one of the several Easterners who arrived to-day. Two of them brought letters to her father from Mr. Forbes. One was the son of an old friend. As her father presented me—"

Magdaléna faced about. "And you did not tell her? You did not speak of me?"

"I am going to be perfectly frank, knowing how sensible you are. I had a desperate flirtation with your friend, as desperate and meaningless as those things always are; for it is merely an invention to pass the idler hours of society. There was nothing else to do, so we flirted. It added to the zest to keep her in ignorance of my identity. It was a silly pastime, but better than nothing. I should far rather have been in bed. If I could have talked to you, it would have been quite another matter."

Magdaléna hurried on ahead. He had the tact not to accelerate his own steps. After a time she fell back. She said,—

"What is this 'flirtation,' anyhow? I have heard nothing but 'flirtation' all winter, and I heard a good deal of it last summer. But I have not the slightest idea what it means. What do you do?"

"Do? Oh—I—it is impossible to define flirtation. You must have the instinct to understand. Then you wouldn't ask. Thank Heaven you never will understand. Flirtation is to love-making what soda-water is to champagne. I can think of no better definition than that."

"Did you kiss Helena?"

"Good God, no! That's not flirtation. She is not the sort that would le me if I wished."

"Did you hold her hand?"

"I have held no woman's hand but yours for an incalculable time."

"Did you tell her that you loved her?"

"Certainly not!"

"I must say I can't see how a flirtation differs from an ordinary conversation."

"It only does in that subtle something which cannot be explained."

Magdaléna had an inspiration. "Perhaps you talk with your eyes some."

"Well, you are not altogether wrong. Did you ever see a fencing match? Imagine two invisible personalities dodging and doubling, springing and darting. That will give you some idea. And all without a flutter of passion or real interest. It is good exercise for the lighter wits, but stupid at best." He did not add that the very essence of flirtation is its promise of more to come.

It was some time before Magdaléna spoke again. Then she asked, —

"What did Helena say when you told her your name?"

"I believe she said, 'Great Heaven!'"

"I think this must be the cemetery."

They ascended the rough hill, and pushed their way through weeds and thistles and wild oats to the dilapidated stones under the oaks. Magdaléna had imagined her conflicting emotions when she visited the graves of her youthful heroines; among other things the delightful sense of unreality. But the unreality was of another sort to-day. They were a part of an insignificant past. Trennahan elevated one foot to a massive stone and plucked the "stickers" from his trousers.

"This is all very romantic," he said, "but these confounded things are uncomfortable. Have you found your graves?"

"I think this is Benicia's. We can go if you like."

"By no means." He went and leaned over the sunken grey stone which recorded the legend of Benicia Ortega's brief life and tragic death, then insisted upon finding the others.

"You don't take any interest," said Magdaléna. "Why do you pretend?"

He caught her in his arms and seated her on the highest and driest of the tombs, then sat beside her. He kept his arm about her, but he did not kiss her. "Come now," he said, "let us have it out. We must not quarrel. I humble myself to the dust. I vow to be a saint. I will not exchange two consecutive sentences with your friend in the future. Make me promise all sorts of things."

"If you love her, you can't help yourself."

"I have no intention of loving her. Perhaps you will be as sweet and sensible as you always are, and not say anything so absurd again. I am deeply sorry that I have offended you. Will you believe that? And will you forgive me?"

"Do you mean that you still wish to marry me?"

"Great Heaven, 'Léna! Even if my head were turned, do you think that I have not brains enough to remember that that sort of thing is a matter of the hour only, and that I am a man of honour? I have no less intention of marrying you to-day than I had yesterday. Does that satisfy you? And — since you take it so hardly — I wish I might never see Miss Belmont again."

Magdaléna raised her eyes; they were full of tears. Her hat was pushed back, her soft hair ruffled. In the deep shade of the oaks and with the passion in her face she looked prettier than he had ever seen her. A kiss sprang to her lips. He bent his head swiftly and caught it; and then he was delighted at the depth of his penitence.

"'Léna, you ought to hate me, but I didn't know! I swear I didn't!"

"I know you did not. He told me that it was entirely his fault, and I have forgiven him; so don't let us say any more about it."

"Well, I am glad he admitted that. I'm pretty selfish, as I've never denied, but I'd never be disloyal. Not to you, anyhow," she added on second thoughts. "I shouldn't mind Ila so much, nor Caro."

"You don't mean to say you would take any girl's lover away from her, Helena?"

"Yes, I would if I wanted him badly. But I'd do it right out before her face. I'd never be underhand about it. I loathe deceit. I was furious for a time with Mr. Trennahan last night, but I really believe I was more furious because he was the most interesting man I had ever met and I couldn't have him, than because he hadn't behaved quite properly."

Magdaléna reached her right hand to a bow on her left shoulder, that Helena should not see the sudden leap of her heart. "Do you mean to say that you had—had intended to—to—add him to the quartette?"

"I had had a very definite idea of turning the entire quartette out in his favour. I don't mind telling you that, because wild horses couldn't make me so much as flirt an eyelash at him again; and of course it was only one of my passing fancies. Nothing goes very deep with me. I'm made on a magnificent plan. So is he. We'll both have forgotten last evening before the end of the week. I hate the morning after a ball, don't you? One always feels so devitalised. Wasn't Ila's gown disgracefully low? And the way some girls roll their eyes is positively sickening. Let's go out and get a breath of air."

XII

Two nights later Tiny had a large dinner. A place had been kept for Trennahan. He had expected to be sent in with Magdaléna,—somewhat illogically, as no one suspected his engagement. He was sent in with Helena.

The long low dining-room of the old house on Rincon Hill had never been double-dated with gas fixtures. There was a large candelabra against the dark wainscot at each end of the room, and little clusters of flame on the table. The girls never looked so pretty, so guileless, never planted their arrows so surely, as in this room, in the soft radiance of its wax candles.

On Helena's other side sat Rollins, whom she honoured by regarding as a brother. On Trennahan's left Ila was intent upon the subjugation of a younger brother of Mr. Washington, who had recently returned to San Francisco after six years in Europe, and had knelt at her shrine at once. He was wealthy, and she had made up her mind to marry him. Trennahan she had given up during the summer. Had she not, she would have known better than to pit her charms against Helena's. Magdaléna was on the same side of the table.

Helena wore white, in which she looked her best; the silk softened with much lace on the bust. She raised her eyes defiantly to Trennahan's. Their coquetry had been ordered to the rear.

"We've got to talk, or look like idiots," she said. "I had made up my mind never to speak to you again. I think you were quite too horrid the other night."

"I certainly was."

"Was it your fault or mine?"

"Wholly mine—despite your fascinations."

"I wouldn't have been fascinating if I had known. I am glad you admit that it was all your fault. It makes me believe that it was. What made you keep it up for three hours?"

"The weakness of man."

"Is that what you told 'Léna?"

"No; it is not."

"What did you tell her—Oh, how horrid of me to ask! Let's talk about something else. Do you like California better than New York?"

"It will take exactly eight minutes to exhaust that subject; I am an old hand at it. So while I assure you that I do, and am giving my reasons, please cast about for a subject to follow."

"My thinker is not good to-night. I expect you to take care of me."

"What greater delight! You are paler than you were. Are you not well?"

Trennahan's voice became tender from long habit. The softness and fire sprang to Helena's eyes. The pink tide poured into her cheeks. A sudden intense light sprang into Trennahan's eyes. It held hers for the fraction of a moment, then both looked away; and ate their oysters.

It was Helena who spoke first. "Another moment, and we should have been launched into the second chapter. But we are not to flirt; we understand that thoroughly. I don't think, on second thoughts, that I should like you at all. You have yourself too well in hand; you look as if you had been through it all too many times; there isn't a bit of freshness about you—Oh, bother, I hate lying! I'll tell you plainly and have done with it,—I should be in love with you by this time if it were not for 'Léna. That's not the way of older climes, but it's mine: I've got to talk out or die. I've always said everything that occurred to me. Let's talk this out, and then we'll never talk for two minutes alone again. If you had not been in love with 'Léna, should you be in love with me by this time?"

He put his fork down abruptly and turned to her. She shrank a little. "I think we had better let that subject alone. As a product of older climes, I am competent to judge."

"I must know. I will know. Tell me."

"Well, then, I should."

"As much as you are with 'Léna?"

"I should have been madder about you than I have been about any woman for fifteen years."

"If you know that, how can you help it now?"

"There is such a thing as honour in men."

"That means that there is none in women? Well, I don't believe there is. But honour does not keep a man from loving a woman."

He made no reply.

"Does it?"

"Are you mad about fire? Or is it your vanity that is insatiable?"

Again he met her eyes. And this time her face was as white as her gown. Her bosom was heaving. Her skin was translucent. To Trennahan's suffused vision she seemed bathed in white fire.

"I love you," he said hoarsely; "and I would give all the soul I've got to have met you a year ago."

XIII

Talk about the complex heart of a woman. It is nothing to that of a man

Trennahan had loved a good many women in a good many ways Perhaps he understood women as well as any man of his day: he had been bred by women of the world, and his errant fancy had occasionally sent him into other strata. He also thought that he knew himself. His mind, his heart, his senses, the best and the worst in him, had been engaged so often and so actively that he could have drawn diagrams of each, alone or in combination, with accommodating types of woman. He also, without generalising too freely, knew men, and he had spent ten years of his life in diplomacy. But he now stood before himself as puzzled as he was aghast.

If his grip upon himself had suddenly relaxed, and he had spent a wild night with the wild young men of San Francisco, he should not have been particularly surprised: he had been living on an exalted plane for the last ten months. But that he loved Magdaléna with the love of his life, that he realised in her some vague youthful ideal, that she was the woman created for the better part of him, that his highest happiness was to be found in her, he had never doubted from the minute he had finished his long communion with himself and determined to marry her. And every moment he had spent with her had strengthened the tie. Nothing about her but had pleased him: her intellect, her pride, her reticence, her difference from other women; even, after the first shock to his taste was over, her lack of beauty. It was true that she had no great power over his pulses, but he was tired of his pulses. She appealed to his tenderness and deeper affections as no woman had done. Above all, she had given him peace of mind; and she held his future in her hands.

And now?

Helena Belmont was that most dangerous rival of other women,—a girl whom men loved desperately with no attendant loss of self-respect. Whatever their passion, they felt a keen personal delight in the purity of her mind; and they admired themselves the more that they appreciated her cleverness. She was not only a woman to love but to idolise; she gave even these prosaic San Francisco youths vague promptings to distinguish themselves by some great and noble action, sending her shafts straight through the American brain to those dumb inherited instincts which had straggled down through the centuries from mediæval ancestors. Her very selfishness—which she was pleased to call Paganism—charmed them: it was one of the divine rights of the woman born to rule men and to create a happiness for one unimagined by lesser women. No man but idealised her, unfanciful as he might be, not so much for her beauty or gifts, or for all combined, as because when she gave herself it would be for the last as it was for the first time. As the reader knows, there was nothing ideal about Helena. Even her fastidiousness was natural in view of her upbringing. She was a most practical young flirt, with a very distinct intention of having her own way as long as she lived. The wealth and petting and adulation which had surrounded her from birth had made a thorough-going egoist of her, albeit a most charming one; for she was warm-hearted, impulsive, generous, and kind—in her own way. Naturally the men for whom her lovely eyes beamed welcome, for whom her tantalising mouth pouted into smiles, thought her nothing short of a goddess, and were moved to inarticulate rhyme.

Trennahan had met many more women who were beautiful, seductive, dashing, and withal fastidious, than had these young men of a cosmopolitan and still chaotic State; nevertheless, he might have been Adam ranging the dreary solitudes of Paradise, facing about for the first time upon the first woman. Helena was the type of woman for whom such men as meet her have the strongest passion of their lives, if for no other reason than because she induces an exaggeration of their best faculties and a consequent exaltation of self-appreciation, as distinguished from mere masculine self-sufficiency. Never is the briefly favoured one so much of a man apart from a type, looking down upon that type with pitying scorn. This is a mere matter of fascination, too subtle, and composed of too many parts for man's analysis, but it is the most telling force in the clashing of the sexes.

Trennahan was an extremely practical man. He called things by their right names, and scorned to turn his head aside when life or himself was to be looked squarely in the eye. It is true that he cursed himself for a fool. He was neither in his youth nor in his dotage; he was in that long intermediate period where a man may hope that his will and sound common-sense are in their prime,—the interval of the minimum of mistakes. Nevertheless, he was as madly in love with Helena Belmont as was the first man with the first woman, as a boy with his first mistress, an old man with his last. He admitted the fact and ordered his brain to make the best of the situation.

He was not conscious of any change in his feelings for Magdaléna except that he no longer desired to marry her. The sense of rest, of comradeship, the tenderness and affection, had not abated. He was just as sure that she was the woman for him to marry as he had been two weeks ago; and he knew that he could not make a greater mistake than to marry Helena Belmont. He believed that it would be years before she would be capable of loving any man for any length of time. Such women not only develop slowly, but they have too much to give, men too little. The clever woman is abnormal in any case, being a divergence from the original destiny of her sex. The woman who is beautiful, fascinating, passionate, and clever is a development with which man has not kept pace.

He spent the greater part of the three days following the dinner, on the cliffs beyond the Golden Gate. There was no great moral battle going on in his mind; he intended to marry Magdaléna. One of his pet theories was that one secret of the rottenness underlying the social, and in natural sequence, the political structure of the United States was the absence of a convention. Men were on their knees to women so long as their pleasure was materially abetted by the attitude; but the moment the motive ceased to exist, any display of chivalry toward her would be as useless and wasted as toward the ordinary run of women. It is always the woman of the moment, never woman in general. The so-called chivalry of American men does not exist; the misconception has arisen out of the multitudinous examples of American subserviency to the individual woman,—which is part of a habit of exaggeration natural to a youthful nation. There is an utter absence of all responsibility that is not the concomitant of personal desire.

The new country is full of good impulses with little to bind them together. Children respect their parents if they feel like it, just as they are polite when in a responsive mood, not through any sense of convention. The American press is an exemplification of this absence of *noblesse oblige*, and more particularly in its treatment of women. Even when not moved by personal jealousy or spite, the total lack of respect with which the American press treats women who have not in any way challenged public opinion— society women with whom the public has no concern, women upon whom either the misfortune of circumstances or of a powerful individuality has fallen—is the most significant foreboding of the degeneration of a national character while yet half grown. It is individualism, which is a polite term for rampant selfishness, run mad, a fussy contempt and hatred for the traditions of older nations.

Fifty years ago, when the United States was still so old-fashioned as to be hardly "American," it was more or less bound together by the conventions it had inherited from the great civilisations that begat it. These conventions exist to-day only in men of the highest breeding, those with six or eight generations behind them of refinement, consequence, and fastidiousness in association. In these men, the representatives of an aristocracy that is in danger of being crippled and perhaps swamped by plutocracy, exists the convention which forces the most deplorable degenerate of old-world aristocracy to manifest himself a gentleman in every crucial test. So thoroughly did Trennahan comprehend these facts, so profound was his contempt for the second-rate men of his country, that he was almost self-conscious about his honour. He would no more have asked Magdaléna to release him, nor have adopted the still more contemptible method of forcing her to break the engagement, than he would have been the ruin of an ignorant girl. But he would have sacrificed every green blade in his soul to have met Helena Belmont a year ago, and would have taken the chances with defiance and the consequences without a murmur.

To marry Magdaléna in June was impossible. That he should ever cease to desire Helena Belmont, to regret the very complete happiness which might have been his for a few years, was a matter of doubt,—with even possibilities. But there must be a long intermission before he could marry another woman. His determination to leave California for a year was fixed, but what excuse to offer Don Roberto and Magdaléna was the question which beset him in all his waking hours and amid all his torments.

During these three days he avoided seeing Magdaléna alone. On the afternoon of the fourth day he came face to face with Helena Belmont in the Mercantile Library.

She was leaving as he entered. They looked at each other for a moment, then without a word both walked toward a room at the right of the door.

This was a long narrow apartment leading off the great room, and was darker, dustier, gloomier, grimmer. As the building stood almost against another of equal height, its side windows looked upon blank walls; but some measure of grey light was coaxed down from the narrow strip above by means of reflectors. The walls were lined with old books bound in calf black with age, and in the centre was a long narrow table which looked as if ¬ it should have a coffin on it. This room had depressed many cheerful lovers in its time; it was enough to drive tormented souls to suicide.

Trennahan and Helena sat down in an angle where they were least likely to be seen.

"What are you going to do?" asked Helena.

"I am going away for a year as soon as I can invent a decent excuse."

"Then shall you come back and marry 'Léna?"

"Yes."

"Suppose you still love me?"

"It will make no difference. And Time works wonders. You will have quite forgotten me."

"I sincerely hope I shall." Her voice shook. There was agitation in every curve of her figure. But had anyone entered, their faces could not have been distinguished two feet away. The sky was grey. There was no light to reflect

"It is the first time I haven't got what I wanted," she said ingenuously.

"It will make your next triumph the keener. I shall be glad to serve as a shadow for the high lights."

"I have suffered horribly in the last week."

"So have I, if that consoles you. But I have had a good deal of suffering in my life, one way and another, and I shall weather it. I wish I could take your share."

"Shouldn't you like to marry me?"

"Of course I should. Why do you ask such foolish questions?"

"I want to talk it all out. I love 'Léna, but I don't love her better than I do myself, and I don't see why I should suffer instead of she. Don't you think that if we told her she would release you?"

"Undoubtedly; but I shall not ask her. Nor must you think of such a thing. Why two young and exceptionally fortunate girls should want what is left of me God only knows; but if they do the prior rights must win the day. If I don't marry 'Léna, I shall marry no woman, — not even you."

She gave him a swift glance. His face was not as stern as his words. "You know that you would," she said with decision. "You are too honourable to break the engagement, but you would marry me if it were broken for you."

He drew his brows together and bent his face to hers. "Listen to me," he said. "I mean what I say. I love you, — how much you have not the vaguest idea; but I will not have her happiness ruined. If you ask her to break the engagement, I shall never see you again. Will you remember that?"

"I suppose you are right. I had not really thought of asking her. But I've got to tell her that I love you. I feel like a hideous hypocrite. I can hardly look her in the face. I'll promise not to betray you, but I must tell her that. She has been so sweet to me this last week, ever since that night at Monterey. She's the very best creature that ever lived. Then I'll ask papa to take me away. You need not go."

"I shall go. Can't you go away without saying anything to her about it? I don't see why her peace of mind should be disturbed."

"I should feel just as guilty when I came back."

"You would have forgotten it by that time."

"Oh, no; I shouldn't! I shouldn't!"

There was no mistaking the passion in her voice. Trennahan half rose, but sat down again. "I would rather you wrote it to her after you left," he said. "Then there would be no danger of saying too much. If you want to go to Europe, I will go to the South Sea Islands."

"Well, I will arrange it that way, if you like."

Her head was lowered. She spoke dejectedly. There was little of the old Helena manifest. In truth, she had been making a mighty effort to control herself for the first time in her life. She hardly knew whether she wished to do what was right or not; for the moment she was dominated by a stronger will than her own. She drew a deep sigh. "I wish I could take it as coolly as you do," she said.

"I take it less coolly. But I am older and used to self-control."

"I hate self-control."

"So do I."

"I feel as if life were quite over. I would a great deal rather die than not. I wish I were older. I don't know what to do. I feel that it cannot be right to throw away the happiness of one's life, but I don't know how to hold you, and, above all, I don't want to hurt 'Léna. I thought that I knew so much; but I know nothing at all—nothing."

"If you do what is right, you will be very glad a year hence."

"A year is such a long time." Her head dropped lower. She looked utterly dejected. In a moment she put her handkerchief to her face and cried silently. The undemonstrativeness of the act, so unlike her usual volcanic energy, touched him out of prudence. He put his arm about her and pressed her head against his shoulder. In a moment he laid his face against hers and closed his eyes to crowd back the tears that sprang from the depths of his soul. When he opened his eyes, it was to meet those of Magdaléna.

XIV

She had left them without a word, and Trennahan did not see her until the following evening, when she sent for him.

She received him in the room at the end of the hall, where they were sure not to be interrupted. As he entered he averted his face hastily, and cursed himself for a scoundrel. But he went straight to the point.

"I have made you suffer," he said, "and as only you can suffer. I have no excuse to offer except my own weakness. Do you remember that I asked you once if you thought you could love me did you come to understand all the weakness of my nature, and that you replied you could? Will you forgive me this display of it? I have no desire—no intention of marrying any other woman."

"I have not doubted your honour. But I shall not marry you. I do not want you without your love. I see now that I never had it."

"You did, and you have it still. It is impossible for a man to explain himself to a woman. Will you let me decide for both? I am going away for a time. When I return I want you to marry me."

She shook her head. "There would be three people miserable instead of one. If I had not gone there yesterday, perhaps I should never have known: I simply made up my mind after that night at Monterey that I would think no more about it. By and by you might have got over it and we might have been happy in a way—I don't know. It is not your fault that I found out. And I went to the Library by the merest chance yesterday. It seems like fate, and I shall recognise it. If Helena did not love you, it would be different; but I had a terrible scene with her last night. I never thought even she could feel so. For the time I felt much sorrier for her than for myself—I felt rather dull, for that matter. After she went I thought all night. It was a terrible night." She stopped and shivered.

He took her hand, but she withdrew it. "I thought of everything. You know I once told you that my only religion was to do what I believed to be right. If love means anything, it means that one should make the other person happy, not oneself. I thought and thought. You two were more to me than any people living. I have not ever really loved anyone else, except my aunt, and her not half so much as Helena. Therefore my love would not be worth much if I did not consider you two before myself. If Helena did not love you, it would be different. I would try to forget that she had fascinated you, and I should see no reason why I should not marry you if you still wished me to. But she loves you. I never expected to see such tragedy. But even if I did not believe she would make you happy, I would not give you to her, for I vowed to live for that—long before the night at Tiny's—in the garden. But Helena could make any man happy. She has everything."

She paused again. He made no reply for a moment. He was staring at the carpet, at a hideous green-and-yellow dragon. The comedy which cuts every black cloud in thin staccato blades was suggesting that he had something to be grateful for, inasmuch as the scene with Helena had been spared himself.

"You are far more suited to me than she is," he said finally. "I am too old for her. I am not for you. If we have souls, yours and mine were made for each other. Years have nothing to do with us. They would mean everything between Helena and myself."

She leaned forward and fixed her eyes on his, compelling his gaze.

"If you had never met me, would you not be engaged to Helena by this time?"

"Doubtless, but that proves nothing."

"Will you give me your word of honour that you do not wish you were free, that you would not gladly marry her now?"

He drew a long breath. He felt like a prisoner on the witness stand driven to save himself by incrimination of another. But he was in that state of mind when only the truth is possible.

"I will put it in another way. Do you want anything in the world as much as Helena?"

"No," he said; "I do not."

She got up and walked to the window, and drew aside the curtains. The sky was brilliant with moon and stars; the bay and hills lovely with the mystery of night. California had never been more unsympathetically beautiful. She jerked the curtains together and went back to him. As she did not sit down, he rose.

"That is all," she said, "except that you must let me explain to my father."

"And let you bear the whole brunt of it. Not if I know myself."

"You must. I understand him, and you do not. Besides, if he knew that you and Helena had anything to do with the breaking of the engagement he would never let me speak to either of you again, and I have no other friends. I shall tell him that I no longer wish to marry you, and he cannot compel me to give reasons. If he speaks to you about it, you must tell him that you will marry no woman against her will, and let him see that you mean it."

"Magdaléna, you are a grand woman."

"I am a very dull and stupid person who has made up her mind that the only chance of making life bearable is to do what is right. I am terribly commonplace. I wonder you stood me as long as you did."

"You are the reverse of stupid and commonplace; and I am by no means sure that you are doing right. I, too, have thought over this matter, for nearly as many days as you have hours. I have tried to get outside myself, to view the case quite dispassionately; and I honestly believe that—as you insist upon putting me before yourself—it would be better for me to marry you than Helena."

"I do not believe it. Nor could I marry you after what you just acknowledged. I have never had much pride with you, but I have that much. Marry you when you said that you wanted nothing so much in the world as to marry Helena Belmont? That was the end of everything."

He left the room and the house. Magdaléna went up the stair slowly, assisting herself with the banister. Her limbs felt as if their muscles had fallen to dust. Her heart seemed to have taken it outside of herself altogether, there was no sensation where sensation was supposed to sit, unless it were that of vacancy. Her brain was not confused; she did not feel in the least as if she were going to be ill. She knew what she had done, what she had to do in the future; and she wished that her heavy limbs were as dead as that something within her for which she had no name.

XV

The next morning she received a note from Trennahan.

> I am sailing for Honolulu. Do nothing until my return.
> I shall be gone six weeks. Until your final decision I shall
> consider myself bound to you. And, I repeat, I think it best
> that we should marry. You have acted on impulse, and your
> mind and judgment were constructed to work slowly. And
> God knows this is not a matter to be decided in haste. I shall
> have sailed before even a telegram from you could reach me.
> Don Roberto knows that I have thought more than once of a
> trip to the Islands. Tell him when he returns that I suddenly
> decided to go. J. T.

But Magdaléna wanted no respite. It was her temper to die once rather than a thousand times. Her father was in Sacramento on business. He would return the following day. She was too dull and listless to feel fear of him, but she wanted it over.

She wrote at once to Helena, enclosing Trennahan's letter: "I have made up my mind, and that is the end of it. As far as I am concerned, he now belongs to you. I shall speak to papa to-morrow night. Immediately after I shall write to Mr. Trennahan, and that will put an end to my part in the matter."

Helena ordered her devoted parent to take her to Southern California at once. To pick up the old routine, to show herself daily and nightly in the studied simulacrum of her former self, was no part of her code. She felt she should tell every man that came near her that she hated him, and the reason why. Nor was hers the temperament for suspense without diversion. She could live through the next six weeks with change of scene, but not otherwise. She made a full confession to her father and received the severest reprimand of her life; but Colonel Belmont took her to Southern California.

Magdaléna went to a lunch-party on the day following Trennahan's departure and paid calls during the afternoon. The small details diverted her, and she found herself able to make conversation, despite the sluggish current of misery beneath. She had told her mother of her determination not to marry Trennahan; and although Mrs. Yorba had paced the room in apprehension of her husband's wrath, she was secretly pleased. A daughter particularly one that gave no trouble, was companionable and useful, and she saw no reason why she should be asked to give her to any man for years to come. Although meagre, she was not heartless, and was much relieved that Magdaléna appeared indifferent to the sudden break. She was dimly conscious that she did not understand her daughter, but she had no desire to plumb the depths; she had a substantial distaste for the Spanish nature when roused.

Her husband was expected to return in time for dinner. She went to bed with an attack of neuralgia a little after six.

Magdaléna did not see her father until he entered the dining-room with her uncle. He inquired immediately for Trennahan, who usually dined with him when there were no engagements elsewhere.

"He decided suddenly to go to the Sandwich Islands and sailed yesterday."

"Very sorry he no wait until I come back. I think I gone with him Always I want to see the Islands. I work long enough now: go to travel some and see the world. So queer to think is so much world outside California When you go to Europe, I go too. And you, too, Eeram. You no can go with us, for both cannot leave the bank, but when we coming back you take the vacation, too."

"I never expect to see the outside of California again," said Mr. Polk, shortly.

Magdaléna's nerves shook for the first time in seventy-two hours. She appreciated the ordeal she had to face within the next. The dull ache in every nerve of her gave place to a certain keenness of apprehension. What would that terrible little man do? She had absorbed something of her father's personality as a child. During the last year she had talked much with him and had discovered the strange weaknesses and fears which lurked in that manufactured character. She fully realised what a son-in-law like Trennahan meant to him. He was quite capable of killing her. And during the last three or four weeks he had flown into more than one violent passion, prompted by a liver disordered by too much dining out.

While the two men were drinking their coffee, she left the room and went to the office. The riding-whip was in its old place; on a shelf in the cupboard was a brace of pistols. Magdaléna threw the whip into the cupboard, locked the door, and slipped the key behind a book on the mantel. Her father came in a moment later. She handed him a cigar and a match. He drew his heavy brows together and puckered his eyelids.

"What the matter?" he demanded drily. "So white you are, and the hand tremble."

Magdaléna sat down and took control of herself.

"I am not going to marry Mr. Trennahan," she said.

She held her breath for the expected outburst; but Don Roberto only stared at her, his eyes slowly expanding. The cigar dropped from his fingers.

"He no want marry you?" he ejaculated finally.

"I told him that I did not wish to marry him,—I never wish to marry any man,—and he is too proud to insist upon marrying a woman who does not want him. We had a long conversation. We quite understand each other. He will never ask me again."

"*Dios!*" gasped Don Roberto. "*Dios!*" But there was no anger in his voice. His eyes rolled from Magdaléna to the window and back again. Finally he said,—

"He no come back, then?"

"He is coming back in six weeks."

Don Roberto drew a long breath and seemed to recover himself.

"Then si he no break the engagement, he feel glad si it is make again. You marry him the day after he come back. I fixit that."

"No power on earth can make me marry him."

Her father searched her countenance. He knew her character. Did it not have that iron of New England in it for which he would have sold his birthright? He might turn her into the street, and it would avail him nothing. Again his features relaxed, this time not with surprise and consternation, but with abject fear. He shuddered from head to foot; then his hands shot up to receive his face. He groaned and rocked from side to side.

Magdaléna was aghast. What feeling was alive in her united in filial tenderness. She went to him and put her hands uncertainly about his head, then stroked his hair awkwardly: she was little used to endearments.

"I never thought—" she stammered. "I never thought—"

"Thirty years I work like the slave, and now all going! Eeram, he have the death-tick in him: I hear! And now I no go to have the son, and I go to die in the streets like the others; with no one cents! *Ay! yi! ay! yi!*"

Magdaléna was pricked with a new fear: Was her father insane? She had heard of the "fixed idea." This weevil had been burrowing in his brain for more than a quarter of a century. She went back to her chair and said assertively, —

"You are one of the ablest financiers in California: everybody says so. Nothing can change that, whether uncle dies or not. This is all a fancy of yours. You don't half appreciate yourself. And you are tired out to-night, and have not been well lately—"

"All going! All going! *Ay de mi! Ay de mi!* Why I no dying with the wife and the little boy? Make myself over, and now the screws go to drop out my character, and I am like before."

Magdaléna had an inspiration. "Take me into the bank," she said eagerly. "Teach me everything. I am sure I can learn. Then I will look after everything when uncle dies. I want to work—"

Don Roberto dropped his hands and gave a low roar. "The women all fools, and you the more big fool I never see. You throw way the clever man like he is old hat, and think you can manage the bank! *Madre de Dios!* Si I no feel like old clothes, no more, I beating you. To-morrow I do it." His eyes kindled at the prospect. "To-morrow si you no say you marry Trennahan, I beating you till you are black like my hat."

What remained of Magdaléna's apathy left her then. She stood up and faced him, drawing her heavy brows together after his own fashion. "You will never beat me again," she said. "Let us have an understanding on that subject before we go to bed to-night. I am your daughter, and I shall always obey you except where the question of my marrying is concerned. But if you ill-treat me I shall leave your house and not return. I am of age, and I have my aunt to go to. Now, unless *you* promise *me* that you will never raise your hand to me again, I will leave for Santa Barbara to-night."

Again Don Roberto stared at her. But his surprise passed quickly. He was too shrewd a judge of human nature to doubt her. If she had inherited the iron of her mother's ancestors, she had also inherited the pride of the Yorbas: she would not permit her womanhood to be outraged. But he could have his revenge in other ways; and he would take it. He gave the promise and ordered her sullenly to send the butler to help him up to bed.

XVI

During the following week Don Roberto was very ill. The doctor came three times a day. Mrs. Yorba and Magdaléna sat up on alternate nights. Mr. Polk was constantly at the bedside. When he retired to snatch an hour's sleep, Don Roberto's temperature became alarming; of the presence of his wife and daughter he took no notice whatever.

As the ego must enter into all things, Magdaléna, despite her alarm and pity, was grateful for the diversion. The interview with her father had roused her abruptly and finally; and during that night her misery had raged in every part of her. It is true that in the long watches thought fairly stamped in her brain, but it was rudely brushed aside every little while by the imperious wants of the sick man, or the whispered remarks of the professional nurse. At other times she slept heavily or received the numerous friends who came to inquire for the eminent citizen who had dined out too often during the gayest season in many years.

Don Roberto recovered, and his convalescence was as memorable as his previous social activity. No nurse would remain more than thirty-six hours at any price; and even his wife, whose ideas of marital duty were as rigid as her social code, lost her patience upon one occasion and rated him soundly. Mr. Polk was the only person he treated with common decency. As for Magdaléna, he might have been a sultan and she his meanest slave. But Magdaléna was rather pleased than otherwise. Her conscience had flagellated her as the immediate cause of his illness, and she strove by every act of devotion to make amends.

As soon as he was sufficiently recovered, he was taken, in a special car, to Fair Oaks, to absorb the sun on his spacious verandahs. Magdaléna had asked the doctor to order Southern California, but the order had been received with such a roar of fury that the subject was not resumed. Magdaléna was forced to return to Menlo Park.

She spent the night walking the floor of her room, struggling for endurance to face the places eloquent of Trennahan. There were so many of them! Helena simply would not have returned; no power short of physical force could have compelled her. More than once Magdaléna wished that she was cast in her friend's anarchic mould. She felt that did her grip upon herself relax she should scream aloud and grovel on the very boards that had had their share in her brief love-life. But she was Magdaléna Yorba, th proudest woman in California; in the very hour of her discovery, when sh had been possessed of a blind terror rather than grief, she had remembere to be thankful that the world could not pity her. Even the genuine sympath of Tiny would have been gall in a raw wound. She was looking thinner an plainer than ever, but her father's illness would account for that. She mus set her features in steel and lock them, keep her emotions for the night.

The next day she visited every spot associated with Trennahan,—no once, but many times. She had made up her mind with the right instinc that the thing to do was to blunt her sensibilities. By the third day she had ordered the earlier associations on duty, and managed to confuse then somewhat with those which had held possession for so brief a time. She was determined to succeed. She had no right to love the husband of anothe woman, and suffering was something so much more terrible than anything her imagination had ever hinted that she was frantic to get rid of the load as quickly as possible. By and by she would go back to her writing; and that and her duties, should be every bit of her life henceforth.

At the end of a week she discovered that she was still receptive to the æsthetic delights. It was early spring. The soft air caressed the senses perfumed with violet and lilac, Castilian roses, new clover, and the breath of mountain forests, brought on the long sighs of the wind. Never was there such a *bouquet* since Time began. Over a high bush on the lawn opposite her window the long "bridal wreaths" tumbled. The meadows were full of mustard, the bright green leaves hardly visible, so thick were the yellow blossoms.

Once she rode to the foot-hills, escorted by Dick. They were covered with yellow and purple lupins, miniature jungles which harboured nothing more sanguinary than the gopher and the cotton-tail. The tawny-poppies had hills all to themselves, a blaze of colour as fiery as the sun to which they lifted their curved drowsy lips. The Mariposa lilies grew by the creeks, in the dark shade of meeting willows. The gold-green moss was like plush on the trees. From the hills the great valley looked like a dense forest out of which lifted the tower of an enchanted castle. Not another signal of man was to be seen, nothing but the excrescence on the big wedding-cake house of a Bonanza king. Beyond the hills rose the slopes of the mountains, with their mighty redwoods, their dark untrodden aisles, their vast primeval silences. Magdaléna was thankful that Nature had not ceased to be beautiful, and pressed her hands against her heart to stifle its demand; Nature commands union, and has no sympathy for aching solitude.

Meanwhile Don Roberto was recovering rapidly. From the hour that he could walk briskly about the garden his voluble irascibility left him, and he reverted to something more than his old taciturnity; he rarely opened his mouth except to put the plainest of food into it, even to speak to Mr. Polk. His brows were lowered constantly over heavy brooding eyes; his lips seemed set with a spring. When he finally addressed his wife, it was to tell her that she must manage with one butler and one housemaid. Coincidently he dismissed two of the gardeners and commanded the one retained, and Dick, to plant in a part of the lawns that there might be less water used. Himself came from town every evening and worked in the garden for two hours, besides arising at five in the morning and working until breakfast. He sold his finest carriage horses to Mr. Geary; and when one of the two remaining was temporarily disabled, he rode to and from the station in the spring wagon. The monthly allowance of his wife and daughter was suspended for the summer.

Mrs. Yorba, tall, garbed in black, stalked about the house with the expression of an outraged empress; Magdaléna, being the cause of the outrage, was rarely addressed. She ostentatiously made over several of her old frocks and coldly requested her daughter to make her own bed. She kept all the windows in the house, with the exception of one in each room, closed and shuttered, as she was deprived of both service and water. The house seemed perpetually expectant of funeral guests, its silence only broken by Mrs. Yorba's heavy sighs.

Magdaléna had certainly succeeded in making three people miserable; she could only hope that she had been more fortunate with the other two. She spent most of her time out of doors, riding or walking until her strength was exhausted. She was profoundly grateful that she was to take little part in the socialities of the summer. To dance and picnic and tennis and ride to the hills, exactly as she had done when quite another person! She infinitely preferred the disapproval of her parents and the freedom they gave her.

XVII

Trennahan had written to Magdaléna from the Islands, acknowledging the letter she had written him after her interview with her father, and accepting his dismissal. He returned to San Francisco the last of May. Almost immediately she received a letter from Helena announcing her engagement to him.

Helena, while in Southern California, had written to Magdaléna with her accustomed regularity. The letters were bitter with self-reproach alternated with the very joy of being alive in that opulent southern land. When she wrote of the engagement she assured the dearest friend she had on earth that if things had turned out differently she should have gone away and got over it somehow, but as Magdaléna's decision was irrevocable she intended to be the happiest girl in the world; it wouldn't do anybody a bit of good if she wasn't. Magdaléna felt no bitterness toward her. She had lost Trennahan; the woman mattered nothing. She would rather it were Helena than another; for who else could make him so happy? But she knew that she should see less of Helena in the future, and she hardly knew whether she were glad or sorry. She wished that she had the courage to ask her to keep him away from Menlo Park this summer.

The other girls moved down, bringing many guests, and she saw them daily; habit is not broken in a moment. They passed through Fair Oaks as usual on their afternoon drives, stopping for a chat; in their char-à-bancs or on the verandah. It was some time before they discovered the changes in the Yorba household, and when they did they merely shrugged their shoulders at the old don's eccentricities. The big parlours were certainly to be regretted; but there were other parlours that were not half bad, and it was terribly up-hill work entertaining Don Roberto. They were profoundly sorry for Magdaléna, and were so insistent in their demands that she should spend much of her time with them that she found her solitude far less complete than she had hoped. But Helena and Trennahan were not to come down until the first of July; they had gone with Colonel Belmont to the Yosemite, Geysers and Big Trees.

XVIII

Trennahan in that first month thought little of Magdaléna. He hardly knew whether he were happy or not; he certainly was intoxicated. Helena was both impassioned and shy, a companion to whom words were hardly a necessary medium for thought, and magnificently uncertain of mood. Moreover, whether riding a donkey up the steep dusty grades of the Yosemite, or half veiled in a mist of steam, reeking of Hell, or standing with wondering eyes and parted lips among the colossal trees of Calaveras, she was always beautiful. And Trennahan worshipped her beauty with the strength of a passion which had sprung from a long and recuperative sleep. That he was twice her age mattered nothing to him now. Nothing mattered but that she was to be wholly his.

The morning after his return to Menlo he awoke with a confused sense that he should be late for his morning ride with Magdaléna. He laughed as his senses rattled into place, but he sighed just after; and both the laugh and the sigh were Magdaléna's, grim as the former may have been. That had been a time of peace and perfect content, and he could never forget it, not though he lived long years of unimaginable bliss with Helena—which he probably would not. A part of his life, limited and stunted a part as it was, belonged irrevocably to Magdaléna. He concluded, after some hard thinking, that it was his best part. He had given her something of his soul, and he had no wish to take it back. He had given her the reviving aspirations of an originally noble nature; the sun of her had shone upon the barren soil, and the harvest was hers. He was an unimaginative man, but he was inclined to believe that if there was a future existence, Magdaléna would belong to him then and for ever, that something even less definable than the soul of each belonged to the other. For there was nothing to be ashamed of in his love for Helena. She appealed as powerfully to his mind and heart as to his passion. But there was something beyond all, and he had no name for it,—unless it were that principle of absolute good as distinguished from its grades and variations; and it belonged to the girl whom he certainly no longer wanted in this life.

He wished that he had suggested to Helena to spend the summer in San Rafael or Monterey. Menlo Park belonged to Magdaléna; he found himself hating the thought of having a series of very perfect memories disturbed, even by the most passionately loved of women. And so Magdaléna had he first revenge.

He went reluctantly enough to Fair Oaks in the afternoon. The very leaves whispered as they drove through the woods. He had protested, bu Helena must see 'Léna at once; she could never be entirely happy until she had looked into 'Léna's eyes and convinced herself that they were quite unchanged. And Trennahan must go, too, and have it over. Trennahan who only crossed her whims for the pleasure of making up with her later admitted that she was right, and went.

Mrs. Yorba was on the verandah receiving Mrs. Geary and Mrs. Brannan Magdaléna was upstairs in her room. The monotony of those afternoor receptions had taken its place among the distasteful things of life, and she was determined not to go down until she was sent for. Each time she heard wheels she went to the window and looked out. The third time she saw Trennahan and Helena. The very bones of her skeleton seemed to fall upon each other; she sank to the ground with less vigour than a shattered soldier. But in a moment she gave a hard gasp and pressed her hands to her face. Then she heard Helena's voice,—that sweet husky voice which was not the least potent of her charms.

"'Léna! 'Léna! Well, I'll go look for her."

Magdaléna scrambled to her feet and fled down the hall to her mother's dressing-room. There, in a cupboard, was always a decanter of sherry; for Mrs. Yorba, after her neuralgic attacks, was often faint. Magdaléna filled a glass, drank it, and blessed the swift fire which shook her will free and made a disciplined regiment of her nerves. She was so delighted at her sudden mastery over herself that she ran out into the hall, caught Helena in her arms, and kissed her demonstratively. Helena burst into tears. "You are the best girl on earth," she sobbed. "And I feel so wicked,—but I am so happy."

Magdaléna dried her tears, a part she had filled many times. "You are the dearest and most honest girl in the world," she said.

"Oh, I try to be honest, but I get so mixed up. I wish I could have a new set of commandments handed down all for myself, and that I could have made the rough draft of them. Then I'd be quite happy. But come down and see Jack,—I couldn't stand John. He's awfully brown and looks splendid."

Trennahan gave Magdaléna's hand a friendly shake and asked her what the plans for the summer were.

"Papa has a frightfully economical fit and says we are not to entertain any more. He doesn't even allow us enough water to wash the windows;

and if this supply of gasoline gives out before the end of the summer, we've got to burn oil."

"Magdaléna!" gasped Mrs. Yorba. She wondered if her contribution to the Yorbas had suddenly gone mad. But the sherry was in Magdaléna's head. She was quite conscious of it, but recklessly decided to let it have its way so long as it helped her to convey to Trennahan the information that he was no more to her than the browning tuberoses on the lawn.

"It's only what everybody knows," she replied. "I am sure everybody in Menlo has discussed him threadbare. Mr. Trennahan, you happened upon him in the oasis of his life; you never could stand it to dine here now. We can scarcely see to eat, and he never opens his mouth except to swear at the servants."

Mrs. Yorba was speeding her guests. When she returned, she gave her daughter an annihilating glance and went into the house. Trennahan stared at Magdaléna. He saw her object, but could not guess the motive-power behind. A sudden, sickening fear assailed him: Was Magdaléna deteriorating? And he the cause? But Magdaléna was rattling on. The sherry seemed to have a marvellous power over one's wits and tongue. Why had she not known of it in the days when she had longed to shine? But her mother did not approve of girls drinking wine, and she had rarely tasted it, although until recently it had always been on the table.

"You both look so well," she said. "You don't look so tired as most engaged people do. I suppose you don't sit up every night until twelve talking about yourselves, as they generally do, I am told. That must be so fatiguing. Mr. Trennahan, you are actually stouter. You don't look as if you had been climbing perpendicular mountains. Is it true that a man stepped over the Bridal Veil backward? Do tell me all about it!"

Helena was staring at Magdaléna with her mouth half open. She was the least obtuse of mortals, but although she knew that pride was at the root of Magdaléna's extraordinary behaviour, she concluded that love had fled, and marvelled, for she had believed Magdaléna to be the deepest and most tenacious of women. But she was very glad.

"Well!" she exclaimed. "Something has improved you! You will be fairly brilliant by next winter. And do for goodness' sake, 'Léna, give Don Roberto to understand that he's not to have his own way. He's like all bullies: he'd soon give in if you bullied him. I adore papa, and would do anything on earth for him; but if he had been born a different sort, and gave me trouble, I'd find more than one way of bringing him to terms. Just flash your eyes at Don Roberto as you're flashing them at us, and you'll see the difference it will make."

Has she ceased to love me? thought Trennahan. Thank God!—at least I ought to.

When they had gone, the sherry had run its course, and Magdaléna felt very much ashamed of herself. I overdid it, she thought in terror, as she recalled her scintillating remarks and elaborate manner. He must have suspected! I'll drink no more, and next time I'll be just what I would have been if I had never laid eyes on him—if I die in the attempt. And how talked! What things I said! Great Heaven, I made a complete fool of myself!

And the knowledge that for once in her life she had thrown her dignity and pride to the winds put her other pain to flight, and she had at least one night unracked by the record within her.

XIX

Two days later she met Trennahan on the Montgomerys' verandah. She was her old sedate self, to his unspeakable relief. That Magdaléna should change, be less than the admirable creature he had loved when he was something more than himself, would have seemed no less a calamity than had the stars turned black. She sat up very straight in her prim little way and talked of Helena's new project; which was to build bath-houses down by the lagoon at Ravenswood and bathe when the tide was in. He told her that he too had a project: to persuade the men of Menlo to build a Club House, and thus have some sort of informal social centre. She told him that she thought that would be nice, and added that she wished she had a project too, but she was hopelessly unoriginal. Trennahan assured her that she did herself injustice; and in these admirable platitudes they pushed along a half-hour like a wheel-barrow, while both thought of the great oak staring at them from the foot of the garden.

It will come easier with time, she thought that night, as she pulled her clothes off with heavy fingers. I can almost look him in the eyes without wanting to fling myself at him. His voice does not matter so much, for I always hear it anyway. They say that when you no longer hear a person's voice in your memory the love has gone too. They will be away for a year after they marry. Perhaps I shall forget then. My memory is not very good.

She opened the upper drawer of her bureau and lifted out her large handkerchief box. In its lower part, carefully hidden away, were Trennahan's letters, several of his faded boutonnières, and one of his gloves. She had made up her mind the day she heard of his engagement to Helena that these things must be burnt, but had dreaded their sight and touch. Now, however, they must go. She was always conscious of their presence; something of her weakness might pass with their destruction. As she lifted out the handkerchiefs she came upon the dagger. It was a beautiful toy, but she pushed it aside resentfully. Its magic was not for her. She gathered up her tokens with trembling fingers, resisted the impulse to sit down and weep over them, laid them in the grate, and flung a bunch of lighted matches into the pyre.

Helena immediately gave a party. The Belmont house, like most of the others of Menlo, had been designed for comfort rather than for entertaining, but the dining-room was large, and when stripped of the many massive pieces of furniture which Colonel Belmont had brought from his Southern home, would have accommodated more dancing folk than the neighbours and their guests. The famous Four were not present; nor were they seen in Menlo that summer. Immediately after the announcement of Helena's engagement some cruel wag had sent each a miniature tub with "For Tears' inscribed with black paint upon the bottom. It was generally supposed that the afflicted quartette were spending their leisure over these tubs, for they had retired into as complete an obscurity as their various callings would permit. Helena told Magdaléna that she lived in terror of their poisoned or perforated bodies being found in the dark byways of Golden Gate Park; but the youth of the modern civilisation, while amenable to suffering, thinks highly of himself as a factor in current history.

Trennahan was not allowed to spend the evening in the smoking-room with the older men; he must keep himself in sight even while his Helena was dancing with another. He wandered about with a grim smile on his mouth, talking occasionally to the older ladies who sat in a corner; wall-flowers there were none. He wished that Magdaléna would take pity on him, for he was unmercifully bored; but she danced with exasperating regularity. Occasionally Helena slipped her hand through his arm and took him out in the garden, purring upon his shoulder and begging him not to be bored; but she must look at him! If he insisted upon it, she would not dance. He refused to countenance such a sacrifice, and protested that he was just beginning to understand the pleasure of evening parties. Once he did slip away, and was lying, with his coat off, a cigar between his lips, crosswise on a bed upstairs with Colonel Belmont and Mr. Washington, when he received a peremptory message to go downstairs at once. He threw his cigar away, jerked himself into his coat, and left the room with jeering condolences in his wake. He felt cross for the moment; but when he reached the hall below he smiled humorously as he met the protesting eyes of his lady.

"I can't bear to have you out of my sight!" she exclaimed. "It's horribly selfish, but I feel as if everything were a blank when you are out of the room."

What could a man do in the face of so much beauty and so much affection, but to vow to hold up the wall for the rest of the evening?

As he was taking Magdaléna to her carriage a little after midnight, she said to him shyly, —

"I hope you are quite happy."

And he answered with unmistakable fervour, "I am indeed."

Mrs. Yorba was detained by Mrs. Cartright, who was delivering herself of many words.

"Do you believe that love is everything in life?" Magdaléna asked him.

"By no means. Not even to woman, in spite of the poets. It induces intense concentration for the time, consequently looms larger in the affairs of life than the million other scraps that go to make up the vast patchwork. But it is as well to remember that it is but an occasional patch in the quilt, even if it be of the most vivid hue. And there is a lot to be got out of the other patches!"

"If you lost Helena, could you feel like that?"

"In time; beyond a doubt. Memory simply cannot hold water beyond a certain strain; there comes a rift at last, and the flood pours through."

"Then if you lost Helena, should you feel as—as—you did when you came here first? You were—tired of everything—you remember. You told me—you don't mind my speaking of it?" She was aghast at her inconsistency, but the magnet in the man was as irresistible as ever.

"Mind? From you? I have never talked to a human being about myself as I have talked to you. I don't know what would happen to me in such an event. I am neither a fool nor a drunkard, remember. I think I should seek entirely new, barely comprehended, lands,—the South Sea Islands, for instance. I have wasted my life. I have neither the energies nor the ambitions to pull up now. I should simply seek new oranges and squeeze them dry. There are always the intellectual pleasures, you know. I should not be proud of myself, but I should get through the remaining years somehow."

"There was something else—I should not speak of it—"

They were standing in the shadow of the char-à-banc. Trennahan raised her hand to his lips. "I was in a state of moral chaos when I met you,— that is what you mean. I do not think I ever shall be again. Even Helena could never do for me what you did. You and I made a great mistake, but we generated one of those singular friendships which no circumstances nor time can annihilate. Some day we shall take up the threads where they broke off. I always look forward to that. A man may be contented with one woman's love, but not with one woman's friendship. I am glad that you are as dear to Helena as you are to me. In time, perhaps we may all three live more or less together."

He was a man of humour, but he said that. She was a woman of little humour, but she laughed.

XX

The breathless state of Helena's affections did not interfere with her desire to lead in all things those favoured of her acquaintance. Although in deference to Trennahan's emphatic wish, she forswore eccentricities, she taxed her fertile brain to keep Menlo Park in a whirl of excitement.

"It can't be done," said Rose. "The climate has poppy dust in it instead of oxygen, but she may wake us up for a while."

She did. The bath-houses were built, and the big char-à-bancs rolled down the dusty road to Ravenswood every morning. The salt water and the sun brought out the red in the girls' hair, so the pastime promised to weather one season, at least. She gave dances and picnics on alternate weeks, and her hospitality in the matter of luncheons and dinners was unbounded. The Colonel built a bowling-alley and a proper tennis-court; in short, there was no doubt about "The Belmonts'" being the nucleus of Menlo Park. Several times Helena persuaded the owner of the stage line between Redwood City and La Honda to let her drive; and she took a select few of her friends on the top of the lumbering coach, relegating the uneasy passengers to the stuffy interior. The road is one of the most picturesque in California, but the grades are steep, the turnings abrupt, dangerous in many places. Nevertheless, Helena, balancing on her narrow perch high above the wheelers' heels, managed her rapid mustangs so admirably that Trennahan, balancing beside her, wondered if he should be able to manage her one half so well.

"What Helena Belmont needs," said Mrs. Montgomery, with some asperity, "is six babies; and I hope for Mr. Trennahan's sake she'll have them. Otherwise, I should like to know where the poor man is to get any rest; she's a human cyclone."

"I never thought she'd marry so soon," replied Mrs. Brannan. "It looked as if she were going to be a regular old-time belle; and it took them years to get through."

"She's not married yet," remarked Mrs. Montgomery.

But these enormous energies, as Rose had predicted, reached their meridian in something under two months, after which, much to Trennahan's relief, Helena succumbed to Menlo Park, and manifested an increasing desire for long hours alone with him under the trees on the lawn, although she by no means allowed her neighbours to rest for more than seventy-two hours at a time.

XXI

Don Roberto and Mr. Polk took no part in these festivities; Mrs. Yorba and Magdaléna took less and less; the picture made by Don Roberto in his shirt-sleeves, manipulating a hose as the char-à-banc drove off, finally forbade his wife to riot while her husband toiled. She was angry and resentful; but she was a woman of stern principles, and she had a certain measure of that sort of love for her husband which duty prompts in those who are without passion.

"I don't pretend to understand your father," she said to Magdaléna "The bees he gets in his bonnet are quite beyond me, but if he feels that way he does, and that's the end of it; and he makes me feel uncomfortable all the time I am anywhere. I sha'n't go out again until he gets over this. You can go with somebody else."

"I would a great deal rather stay home. I don't enjoy myself. People work so hard to be amused. I'd much rather just sit still and do nothing."

"You're lazy, like all the Spanish. Well, you'll have to do a good deal of sitting still, I expect; and in a sick room, I'm afraid. Poor Hiram looks thinner and greyer every day. Almost all our relations died of consumption."

"I wrote to aunt how badly he was looking, but she has not answered."

"She won't, the heartless thing. She never loved him. But if he takes to his bed with slow consumption, she'll have to come up and do her share of the nursing. She ought tō like it. Fat women always make good nurses."

Magdaléna was more than glad to fall out of the gaieties. She was beginning to feel that most demoralising of all sensations,—the disintegration of will. Pride, a certain excitement, and novelty had kept her armour locked for a time; but each time she met Trennahan, the ordeal of facing him with platitudes, or, what was worse still, in occasional friendly talks, and of witnessing Helena's little airs of possession, suggested a future and signal failure. She came to have a morbid terror that she should betray herself, and when in company with him kept out of the very reach of his voice. She never went to the woods, lest she meet him, with or without Helena. In those rustling arbours of many memories, she knew that she should let fly the passion within her. She was appalled that neither time nor will nor principle had authority over her love. She had made up her mind that she would, if not tear it up by the roots, at least level it to the soil from which it had sprung, and she was quite ready to believe that love was not all; that with her youth, intellect, and wealth there was much in life for her. But the plant flourished and was heavy with bloom. Even while she avoided him, she longed for the moment when he must of necessity speak to her. She welcomed the excuse to secede from the ranks of pleasurers, but even then she started up at every sound of wheels that might herald his approach. She longed for the wedding to be over; but Helena would not marry before December, that being her birth month and eminently suitable, in her logical fancy, for her second launching. Colonel Belmont, having satisfied himself that everyone in the little drama had acted with honour, was well pleased with his son-in-law; but he was much distressed at the attitude of the old friend who had hoped to fill a similar relation to Trennahan. Don Roberto, taciturn with everybody, refused to speak to Colonel Belmont, to return his courtly salutation.

"I suppose it is natural," said Colonel Belmont to Helena. "Don is not only eccentric, but he would almost rather lose a hundred thousand dollars than his own way. But I hope he'll come round in time, for it makes me feel right lonesome in my old age. He and Hi were the only real intimates I have had in California, and now Hi is going, poor old fellow! and of course I can do little to cheer him up until Don thaws out."

"Do you feel quite well yourself?" asked Helena, anxiously. "You often look so terribly pale."

"I never was better, honey, I assure you. But remember that you must expect to lose your old father some day. But I've been pretty good to you, haven't I? You'll have nothing but pleasant things to remember?"

"You're the very best angel on earth. I don't even love Jack so much. I thought I did, but I don't."

"Don't you love him?" asked her father, anxiously. He was eager for her to marry; he knew that his blood was white.

"Of course! What a question!"

XXII

It was an intensely hot September night. Magdaléna, knowing that sleep was impossible, had not gone to bed. She wandered restlessly about her large room, striving to force a current of air. Not a vibration came through the open windows, nor a sound. The very trees seemed to lean forward with limp hanging arms. Across the stars was a dark veil, riven at long intervals with the copper of sheet lightning. Her room, too, was dark. A light would bring a pest of mosquitoes. The high remote falsetto of several, as it was, proclaimed an impatient waiting for their ally, sleep.

Last night, Tiny had given a party, and wrung from Magdaléna a promise that she would go to it. Rose had called for her. At the last moment Magdaléna's courage had shrunk to a final shuddering heap, and as she heard the wheels of the Geary waggonette, she had run upstairs, and flung herself between the bedclothes, sending down word that she had a raging toothache. It was her first lie in many years, but it was better than to dance with despair and agony written on her relaxed face behind the windows of the garden in which Trennahan had asked her to marry him.

To-night she was seriously considering the proposition of going to her aunt in Santa Barbara, with or without her father's consent. Her sense of duty had not tumbled into the ruins of her will, but she argued that in this most crucial period of her life, her duty was to herself. Helena had not even asked her to be bridesmaid; she took her acquiescence for granted. Magdaléna laughed aloud at the thought; but she could not leave Helena in the lurch at the last moment. When she got to Santa Barbara, she could plead her aunt's ill health as excuse for not returning in time for the ceremony. She was in a mood to tell twenty lies if necessary, but she would not stand at the altar with Trennahan and Helena. Her passionate desire for change of associations was rising rapidly to the dignity of a fixed idea. To-morrow there must be a change of some sort, or her brain would be babbling its secrets. Already her memory would not connect at times. She felt sure that the prolonged strain had produced a certain congestion in her brain. And she was beginning to wonder if she hated Helena. The fires in Magdaléna burned slowly, but they burned exceeding hot.

She paused and thrust her head forward. For some seconds past her sub-consciousness had grasped the sound of galloping hoofs. They were on the estate, by the deer park; a horse was galloping furiously toward the house.

She ran to the window and looked out. She could see nothing. Could it be a runaway horse? Was somebody ill? The flying feet turned abruptly and made for the rear of the house, then paused suddenly. There was a furious knocking.

Magdaléna's knees shook with a swift presentiment. Something had happened—was going to happen—to her. She stood holding her breath. Someone ran softly but swiftly up the stair, and down the hall, to her room. She knew then who it was, and ran forward and opened the door.

"Helena!" she exclaimed. "What is the matter? Something has—Mr. Trennahan—"

Helena flung herself upon Magdaléna and burst into a passion of weeping. Magdaléna stood rigid, ice in her veins. "Is he dead?" she managed to ask.

"No! He isn't. I wish he were—No, I don't mean that—I'll tell you in a minute—Let me get through first!"

Magdaléna dragged her shaking limbs across the room and felt for a chair. Helena began pacing rapidly up and down, pushing the chairs out of her way.

"Would you like a light?" asked Magdalena.

"No, thanks; I don't want to be eaten alive with mosquitoes. Oh, how shall I begin? I suppose you think we've had a commonplace quarrel. I wish we had. I swear to you, 'Léna, that up to to-night I loved him—yes, I know that I did! I was rather sorry I'd promised to marry so soon, for I like being a girl, not really belonging to anyone but myself, and I love being a great belle, and I think that I should have begged for another year—but I loved him better than anyone, and I really intended to marry him—"

"Aren't you going to marry him?"

"Don't be so stern, 'Léna! You don't know all yet. Lately I've been alone with him a great deal, and you know how you talk about yourselves in those circumstances. I had told him everything I had ever done and thought—most; had turned myself inside out. Then I made him talk. Up to a certain point he was fluent enough; then he shut up like a clam. I never was very curious about men; but because he was all mine, or perhaps because I didn't have anything else to think about, I made up my mind he should come to confession. He fought me off, but you know I have a way of getting what I want—if I don't there's trouble; and to-night I pulled his past life out of him bit by bit. 'Léna! he's had *liaisons* with married women; he's kept house with women; he's seen the worst life of every city! For a few years—he confessed it in so many words—he was one of the maddest men in Europe. The actual things he told me only in part; but you know I have the instincts of the devil. 'Léna, *he's a human slum*, and I hate him! I hate him! I hate him!"

"But that all belongs to his past. He loves you, and you can make him better—make him forget—"

"I don't want to make any man better. I love everything to be clean and new and bright,—not mildewed with a thousand vices that I would never even discuss. Oh, he's a brute to ask me to marry him. I hate myself that I've been engaged to him! I feel as if I'd tumbled off a pedestal!"

"Are you so much better and purer than I? I knew much of this; but it did not horrify me. I knew too, what you may not know, that he came here in a critical time in his—his—inner life, and I was glad to think that— California had helped him to become quite another man." Her voice was hoarse, almost inarticulate.

Helena flung herself at Magdaléna's feet. She was trembling with excitement; but her feverish appeal for sympathy met with no response.

"That is another thing that nearly drove me wild,—that I had taken him away from you for nothing. I know you don't care now; but you did— perhaps you do now—sometimes I've suspected, only I wouldn't face it— and to think that in my wretched selfishness I've separated you for ever! For your pride wouldn't let you take him back now, and he's as wild about me as ever: I never thought he could lose control over himself as he did when I told him what I thought of him and beat him on the shoulders with both my fists. He turned as white as a corpse and shook like a leaf. Then he braced up and told me I was a little wild cat, and that he should leave me and come back when I had come to my senses, that he had no intention of giving me up. But he need not come back. I'll never lay eyes on him again. While he was letting me get at those things, I felt as if my love for him burst into a thousand pieces, and that when they flew together again they made hate. He told me he was used to girls of the world, who understood things; and that the girls of California were so crude they either knew all there was to know by experience, or else they were prudes—"

Helena paused abruptly and caught her breath. She had felt Magdaléna extend her arm and stealthily open a drawer in the bureau beside her chair. There was nothing remarkable in the fact, for in that drawer Magdaléna kept her handkerchiefs. Nevertheless, Helena shook with the palsy of terror; the cold sweat burst from her body. In the intense darkness she could see nothing, only a vague patch where the face of Magdaléna was. The silence was so strained that surely a shriek must come tearing across it. The shriek came from her own throat. She leaped to her feet like a panther, reached the door in a bound, fled down the hall and the stair, her eyes glancing wildly over her shoulder, and so out to her horse. It is many years since that night, but there are silent moments when that ride through the woods flashes down her memory and chills her skin,—that mad flight from an unimaginable horror, through the black woods on a terrified horse, the shadow of her fear racing just behind with outstretched arms and clutching fingers.

Helena's sudden flight left Magdaléna staring through the dark at the Spanish dagger in her hand. Her arm was raised, her wrist curved; the dagger pointed toward the space which Helena had filled a moment ago.

"I intended to kill her," she said aloud. "I intended to kill her."

The mental admission of the design and its frustration were almost simultaneous. Her brain was still in a hideous tumult. Weakened by suffering, the shock of Helena's fickleness and injustice, the sudden perception that her sacrifice had been useless, if not absurd, had disturbed her mental balance for a few seconds, and left her at the mercy of passions hitherto in-existent to her consciousness. Her love for her old friend, long trembling in the balance, had flashed into hate. Upon hate had followed the murderous impulse for vengeance; not for her own sake, but for that of the man whose weakness had ruined her life and his own. In the very height of her sudden madness she was still capable of a curious misdirected feminine unselfishness.

When she came to herself, chagrin that she had failed to accomplish her purpose possessed her mind for the moment, although she had made no attempt to follow Helena, beyond springing to her feet. Then her conscience asserted itself, and reminded her that she should be appalled, overcome with horror, at the awful possibilities of her nature. The picture of Helena in the death struggle, bleeding and gasping, rose before her. Her knees gave way with horror and fright, and she fell upon her chair, dropping the dagger from her wet fingers, staring at the grim spectre of her friend. Then once more the sound of galloping hoofs came to her ears. Both Helena and herself were safe.

In a few moments her thoughts grouped themselves into a regret deeper and bitterer still. She was capable of the highest passion, and Circumstance had diverted it from its natural climax and impelled it toward murder. She sat there and thought until morning on the part to which she had been born; the ego dully attempting to understand, to realise that its imperious demands receive little consideration from the great Law of Circumstance, and are usually ignored.

XXIII

The next morning Magdaléna did as wise a thing as if inspired by reason instead of blind instinct: she got on her horse and rode for six hours. When she returned home she was exhausted of body and inert of brain. She found a note from Helena awaiting her.

> Dearest 'Léna, — What a tornado and an idiot you must think me! I cannot explain my extraordinary departure. I suppose I was in such a nervous state that I was obsessed in some mysterious manner and went off like a rocket. I can assure you I feel like a stick this morning. You will forgive me, won't you? for you know that although my affections do fluctuate for some people, they never do for you.
>
> Well! this morning I had a scene with papa. He was very angry, talked about honour and all that sort of thing, said that I was an unprincipled flirt, and that I expected too much of a man. But when I said I could not understand how so perfect a man as himself could wish his daughter to marry a rake, he never said another word, but went off and wound up with Mr. Trennahan. I don't know what they said to each other; I don't care. It's all too dreadful to think about, and I never want to hear the subject mentioned again.
>
> We're going to Monterey this afternoon to remain till the end of the season, and then we'll go to the Blue Lakes for a little before settling down for the winter. I'm tired of Menlo. Can't you come to Monterey for a week or two? Do think about it. I haven't a minute to go over to Fair Oaks to say good-bye, but perhaps you'll come to the train. Helena.

Magdaléna got some luncheon from the pantry, then went to bed and slept until six o'clock. At dinner Mr. Polk said to her,—

"I saw Trennahan this afternoon in a hack with a lot of luggage on behind, and I stopped the driver and got in, and went to the ferry with him. His engagement with Helena Belmont is broken, it seems, and he is off for Samoa. Looked like the devil, but was as polite as ever, and asked me to say good-bye to all of you."

Don Roberto looked up. "When he coming back?" he asked.

"You know as much about that as I do; or as he does, I guess. He told me that he was going to explore the South Seas thoroughly, and that ought to take as many years as he's got left, and more too."

It was two or three days before Magdaléna realised what a relief it was to have Trennahan out of the country. It moved him back among the memories, and struck from her imagination agitating possibilities. And he belonged to no woman! He could never be hers, but at least she could love him. Already she had begun to do so with a measure of calm. She could hide him in her soul and count him wholly hers; and the prospect seemed far sweeter and more satisfactory than she should have imagined of such immaterial union. And some day, she believed, he would write to her. He had spoken authoritatively of the permanence of their friendship, and of its necessity to him. He had not loved her, as men count love, but for a little she had been to him something more than other women had been. The spiritual sympathy which had been rudely interrupted, but had surely existed, taught her this. In time he would become conscious again of the bond, and his letters alone would be something to live for.

And she had much else. In the evenings when her father was weeding on the lawn, she devoted herself to her uncle; and he seemed grateful for her attentions, slight as was his response. He was visibly shrinking to his skeleton, although he neither coughed nor complained, and went to town every morning with the regularity of his youth. But his gaunt face was less savagely determined, his eyes had lost the hard surface of metal; and one evening when Magdaléna slipped her hand into his, he clasped and held it until Don Roberto, gloomy and perspiring, came panting across the drive.

And almost immediately Magdaléna began to write. She did not go to her nook in the woods, but after her morning ride she wrote in her room until luncheon. She told her mother of her literary plans and asked her advice about making a similar announcement to her father. Between astonishment and consternation Mrs. Yorba gasped audibly, and her impassive countenance looked as if the hinges had fallen out of its muscles.

"For God's sake don't tell your father!" she exclaimed; and she was not given to strong language. "I don't believe you can write, anyhow, and we should only have a terrible scene for nothing."

Magdaléna accepted the advice. Her father showed so little sense of his duty as a parent that her own was growing adaptable to circumstances, although she was still determined not to publish without his knowledge. She had not returned to her English romance: that had been consigned to the flames, and was now meditating in that limbo which receives the wraiths of the lame, the halt, and the blind of abortive talent. She was at work upon the simplest of the Old-Californian tales.

On the Saturday afternoon after Helena's departure for Monterey Rose called and invited Magdaléna to drive with her to the train to meet Mr. Geary. Tiny and Ila, who were with her, added their insistence, and Magdaléna, having no reasonable excuse, joined them. As they drove through the woods Ila confided her engagement to young Washington, and was kissed and congratulated in due form.

"I'm going to live in Paris," she announced. "No more California for me. You might as well be on Mars, in the first place, and everybody cackles over your private affairs, in the second. For the matter of that, you haven't any."

"I think it's disloyal of you to desert California," said Tiny. "I have a feeling that we should all keep together, and to the country."

"That's a very fine sentiment, but though I love you none the less, I want to live. I intend to be the best-dressed American in Paris. That's a reputation worth having."

"I'm going East to find a husband," said Rose, shamelessly. "There's no one to marry here. Alan Rush would not have been half bad, but he might as well be in an urn on Helena's mantel-piece. I like Eastern men best, anyhow."

"Why not go to Southern California?" asked Tiny. "It's not so far as New York; and there are always plenty of them there."

"I should feel like a ghoul,—man-hunting in One-lungdom, as Mr. Bierce calls it. Besides, I'd rather die an old maid than have a sick man on my hands for five minutes. I'm not heartless, but—well, we've all had our experiences with fathers and brothers. A sick man's an anomaly, somehow: he doesn't fit into a woman's imagination."

"I'm not going to marry at all," said Tiny. "Fancy what a lot of bother. It's so comfortable just to drift along like this."

"Tiny," said Rose, "you're a Menlo Park poppy."

They had arrived at the station, the pretty station under its great oak, and flanked by its beds of bloom. Eight or ten other equipages were there, waiting for the "Daisy train,"—the fast train from town which on Saturday afternoons carried many San Franciscans to Monterey.

The women were in their bright summer attire and full of chatter; as the train was not due for some moments, several got out of their carriages and went to other carriages to gossip. It was a very lively and agreeable scene:

there being no outsiders, they were like one large family. In the middle of the large open space beside the platform stood several of the phaetons and waggonettes, whose horses stepped high at sight of the engine. On the far side was a row of Chinese wash-houses, in whose doors stood the Mongolians, no less picturesque than the civilisation across the way. Behind them was the tiny village of Menlo Park. On the opposite side of the track was a row of high closely knit trees which shut the Folsom place from the passing eye. Caro, under a big pink sunshade, had walked over to chat with her friends and escort her visitors home.

The train rolled in and discharged its favoured few. The wait was short, and Mr. Geary was still mounting the steps of his char-à-banc when Magdaléna sat forward with a faint exclamation. The smoking-car was slowly passing. Four hats at four consecutive windows were raised as they drifted past. They were the hats of Alan Rush, Eugene Fort, Carter Howard, and "Dolly" Webster.

XXIV

The Yorba house on Nob Hill was the gloomiest house in San Francisco in any circumstances; upon the return of the family to town this year it suggested a convent of perpetual silence. Mrs. Yorba, bereft of her full corps of servants, herself shook the curtains free of their loops and pinned them together. "Ah Kee can play the hose on the windows from the outside once a month," she remarked to her daughter; "but Heaven only knows when they will be washed inside again, or how often poor Ah Kee will have time to sweep the rooms. I shall make an attempt to keep the reception-room in some sort of order; and as it is comparatively small and I can dust it myself, I may succeed, but I don't suppose anyone will ever enter the parlours again. There seems no hope of your father coming to his senses."

Magdaléna flung her own curtains wide, determined to have light if she had to wash the windows herself. But the rest of the house chilled and oppressed her. Even her mother's bedroom was half-lighted, and the halls and rooms downstairs were echoing vaults. One was almost afraid to break the silence; even the soft-footed Chinaman walked on his toes. Magdaléna conceived the whimsical idea that her father's house had been closed to receive all the family skeletons of San Francisco, of which many whispers had come to her. Sometimes she fancied that she heard their bones rattling at night, as they crowded together, muttering their terrible secrets. But the idea only amused her; it did not make her morbid, although there was little but her own will to keep her spirits on a plane where there was more light than bog. It was a very grey and rainy winter. She was forced to spend the afternoons after four o'clock in idleness: Don Roberto himself turned off the gas every morning before he went down town, and on again at seven in the evening. The meals in the dining-room, naturally the darkest room in the house, were eaten in absolute silence. In fact, it was seldom that anyone spoke except on Mrs. Yorba's reception day. Herself wore the air of a stoic. Don Roberto's keen eyes searched his wife and daughter now and again for any sign of extravagance in attire, but he rarely addressed them except on the first of the month, when he demanded their accounts. He peremptorily forbade them to go out after dusk, as the night air was bad for the horses. The evenings he spent in his study with his brother-in-law. Mrs. Yorba and Magdaléna sat in their respective rooms until nearly half-past ten; when Don Roberto went the rounds to see that the lights were out. Were it not for his fear of earthquakes, he would have turned off the gas at that hour, but he permitted a tiny spark to burn in the halls all night. Occasionally Mr. Polk came home early and went to Magdaléna's little sitting-room, the old schoolroom, and sat with her for an hour or two. He said little and never talked of himself. She longed to bring her aunt back to this lonely old man, but did not know in the least how to go about it, and the subject never was mentioned between them; he might have been a bachelor or a widower. But as he sat staring into the fire, Magdaléna was convinced that he was thinking of his wife. She had never entered his house since the day of her strange discovery; delicacy kept her away, but her feminine curiosity often tempted her to go in and see if the fires were burning, the flowers and magazines on the table. Sometimes at night she heard footsteps in the connecting gardens behind the houses, and fancied they were those of her uncle, gone on what pilgrimage she dared not imagine.

She and Helena met again early in November. They greeted each other with all their old cordiality, but there was a barrier, and both felt it. Still, they exchanged frequent visits, and Magdaléna was always interested in Helena's new conquests and dazzling regalities. Helena was enjoying herself mightily. She had all her old admirers exhausting and coining adjectives at her feet, and a number of distinguished foreigners, who were spending the winter in San Francisco. She could not drive, nor yacht, nor run to fires on account of the weather, but she unloosed her energies upon indoor society, and started a cotillion club, and an amateur opera company. She gave a fancy dress ball, to which all her guests were obliged to come in the costumes of Old California, and laughed for a week at the ridiculous figure which most of them cut. She also gave many dinners and breakfasts, kettle-drums and theatre parties, and, altogether, managed to amuse herself and others. She never mentioned Trennahan to Magdaléna. Nor did he write. The Pacific might have been climbing over him, for any sign he gave.

XXV

It was midnight, and Magdaléna was still awake; a storm raged prohibitive of sleep. The wind screamed over the hills, tearing the long ribbons of rain to bits and flinging them in great handfuls against the windows; from which they rebounded to the porch to skurry down the pipes and gurgle into the pools of the soaked ground below. The roar o the ocean bore aloft another sound, a long heavy groan,—the fog-horn o the Farallones. Magdaléna imagined the wild scene beyond the Golder Gate: the ships driven out of their course, bewildered by the fog, the loud unceasing rattle of the rigging, the hungry boom of the breakers, the mountains and caverns of the raging Pacific. Her mind, open to impressions once more, stirred as it had not during its period of subservence to the heart, and toward expression. Suffering had not worked those wonders with her literary faculty of which she had read; but she certainly wrote with something more of fluency, something less of attenuated commonplace She had finished her first story; and although it by no means satisfied her, she had passed on to the next, determined to write them all; then, with the education accruing from long practice, to go back to the beginnings and make them literature. To-night she forgot her stories and lay wondering at the ghostly images rolling through her brain, breaking upon the wall which stood between themselves and speech,—hurled back to rise and form again What did it mean? Was some dumb dead poet trying to speak through her brain, inextricably caught in the folds of her ravening intelligence before recognising its fatal limitations? Or was that intelligence but the half of another, divided out there in eternity before being sucked earthwards? It was seldom that such fancies came to her nowadays, but to-night the storm shrieked with a thousand voices, no one of which was unfamiliar to these ghosts in her mind. She had heard the expression "hell let loose" variously applied. Were those the souls of old and wicked mates tossed into the wild playground of the storm, helpless and furious shuttle-cocks, yelling their protests with furious energy? The idea that she too might have been wicked once thrilled Magdaléna unexpectedly: she had had a few sudden brief lapses into primal impulse, accompanied by a certain exaltation of mind. As she recalled them the rest of her life seemed flat by comparison, and unburdened with meaning; something buried, unsuspected, left over from another existence, shook itself and made as if to leap to those doomed wretches, heavy with memories, buffeting each other on the tides of the storm.

A crash brought her upright. It had been preceded by a curious bumping along the front of the house. She realised in a moment what it meant: the flag-pole had snapped and been hurled to the ground. She thought of her father's dismay, and shuddered slightly; she was in a mood to greet omens hospitably.

Suddenly her eyes fixed themselves expandingly upon the door. She was cast in a heroic mould; but the storm and the vagaries of her imagination had unnerved her, and she shook violently as the knob was softly turned and the door moved forward with significant care. Had her father gone suddenly mad? The possibility had crossed her mind more than once. She would lock her door hereafter.

"What is it?" she faltered.

The door was pushed open abruptly. Her uncle stood there. For a moment she thought it was his ghost. The dim light of the hall shone on a ghastly face, and he wore a long gown of grey flannel. He held one hand pressed against his chest. In another second she heard the rattling of his breath. She sprang out of bed and ran to him.

"I am going to die," Mr. Polk said. "Telegraph and ask her to come."

She led him to his room, roused her father and mother, telephoned for the doctor and a messenger boy, then went to her room, dressed, and wrote the telegram. She had little time to think, but the approach of death made her hands shake a little, and lent an added significance to the horrid sounds without. Death had been a mere name before these last few moments; he suddenly became an actual presence stalking the storm.

The bell rang. She went down to the door herself. It was the messenger boy. She gave him the telegram to despatch, and told him to return and to remain on duty all night. Then she went to her uncle's room. Her mother and a dishevelled maid were compounding mustard plasters and heating water. Her father was huddled in an armchair, staring at the gasping form on the bed. Magdaléna shuddered. His face was more terrible to look on than the sick man's.

"It's pneumonia, of course," said Mrs. Yorba, in the hushed whisper of the sick room, although her hard voice was little more sympathetic in its lower register. "He was wet through when he came home this afternoon. I should think it had rained enough for one year."

The doctor came and eased the sufferer with morphine; but he gave the watchers no hope.

"He has no lungs, anyhow," he said. "This abrupt climax is rather a mercy than otherwise."

Magdaléna remained by the bedside during all of the next day. Early in the morning a telegram came from Mrs. Polk, saying that she was about to start on a special train. The message was read to her husband, and he whispered to Magdaléna, "I should live until she came,—if she took a week." That was the only remark he made until late in the day, when he motioned to Magdaléna to bend her ear to his lips. "Don't waste your youth," he whispered; and then he coloured slightly, as if ashamed of having broken the reticence of a lifetime.

Don Roberto barely moved from the chair which commanded a view of the dying man's face. His own shrank visibly. He neither ate nor drank. His sunken terror-struck eyes seemed staring through the passing face on the high pillows into an inferno beyond.

"I declare, he gives me the horrors, and I'm not a nervous woman," said Mrs. Yorba to her daughter. "I never could understand your father's queer ways. Who would ever have thought that he could care for anyone like that? Poor Hiram! No one can feel worse than I do; but he has to go, and as the doctor says, this is a mercy; there's no use acting as if you had lost your last friend on earth."

"Perhaps that's the way papa feels; and as you say, he's not like other people."

The only other person in the sick-room was Colonel Belmont. He came over as soon as he heard of the attack, and sat on the other side of the bed all day, when he was not attempting to make himself useful. His old comrade smiled when he entered; but Mr. Polk took little notice of anyone. Occasionally his eyes rested with an expression of profound pity on the face of his brother-in-law: once or twice he pressed Magdaléna's hand; but his attention chiefly centred on the door, although he knew that his wife could not arrive until after midnight.

Magdaléna went to the train to meet her aunt. It was still raining, but calmly. There was no gay and chattering crowd in Market Street, not even the light of a cable car flashing through the grey drizzle. Magdaléna recalled the night of the fire. Her inner life had undergone many upheavals since that night; even her feeling for Helena was changed. And her aunt was a mere memory.

At the station she left the carriage and walked along the platform as the train drew in. Mrs. Polk, assisted by a Mexican maid, descended from the car. She was very stout, but as she approached Magdaléna, it was evident that her carriage had lost nothing of majesty or grace. She kissed her niece warmly.

"So good you are to come for me, *mijita*. And when rain, too—so horriblee San Francisco. Never I want to see again. And the uncle? how he is?"

"He says he will live until you come; but he won't live long after."

"Poor man! I am sorry he go so soon. But all the mens die early in California now: work so hard. Live very old before the Americanos coming."

They could talk without restraint in the carriage, for the maid did not speak English; but Mrs. Polk merely asked how her husband had caught cold. Her fair placid face and sleepy eyes showed no print of the years. She seemed glad to see Magdaléna again.

"Often I wish have you with me in Santa Barbara," she said. "But Roberto is what the Americanos call 'crank.' No is use asking him. Santa Barbara no is like in the old time, but is nice sleep place, where no have the neuralgia, and nothing to bother. Then always I have the few old families that are left, and we are so friends,—see each other every day, and eat the Spanish dishes. I no know any Americanos; always I hating them. So thin you are, *mijita*; I wish I can take you back."

But Magdaléna felt no desire to go with her; her aunt seemed to belong to another life.

When they reached home, Mrs. Polk went to Mrs. Yorba's room to remove her wraps and drink a cup of chocolate. She smoothed her beautiful dusky hair and arranged the old-fashioned lace about her throat, then sailed in all her languid majesty across the hall.

"Aunt," said Magdaléna, with her hand on the door of the sick room, "will—will—you kiss uncle?"

Mrs. Polk raised her eyebrows. "Why, yes, is he wanting; but I never kiss him in my life. Why now?"

"He is dying, and he has wanted you more than anything."

"So queer fancies the seeck people have. But I kiss him, of course."

As she entered the room, Mr. Polk raised himself slightly and stared at her with an expression she had never seen in his young eyes. It thrilled her nerves within their mausoleum of flesh. She bent over and kissed him. "Poor Eeram!" she said. "So sorry I am. But you no suffer, no?"

He made no reply. He sank back to his pillows; and after greeting her brother, she took a chair beside the bed and sat there until her husband died, in the ebb of the night. He held her hand, his eyes never leaving her beautiful face, never losing their hunger until the film covered them. What thoughts, what bitter regrets, what futile desires for another beginning may have moved sluggishly in that disintegrating brain, he carried with him into the magnificent vault which his widow erected on Lone Mountain.

His will was read on the day following the funeral, in the parlour where his coffin had rested, and by the light of a solitary gas-jet. Magdaléna had never heard a will read before: she hoped she might never hear another. The three women in their black gowns, the four executors and trustees in their crow-black funeral clothes, — her father, Colonel Belmont, Mr. Washington, and Mr. Geary, — the big rustling document with its wearisome formalities, — made a more lugubrious picture than the lonely coffin of the day before. The terms of the will were simple enough: the interest of the vast fortune was left to Mrs. Polk; upon her death it was to be divided between his sister and niece, the principal to go to Magdaléna upon Mrs. Yorba's death. When Mr. Washington finished reading the document, Don Roberto spoke for the first time in four days.

"I go to resign. I no will be executor or trustee. No need me, anyhow." And he would listen to no argument.

The next day he called a meeting of the bank's board of directors and resigned the presidency, requesting that Mr. Geary, a cautious and solid man, should succeed him. His wish was gratified, and he walked out of the bank, never to enter it again. His many other interests were in the hands of trustworthy agents: neither he nor his brother-in-law had ever made a mistake in their choice of servants. When he reached home, he wrote to each of these agents demanding monthly instead of quarterly accounts. He had a bed brought down to a small room adjoining the "office," and in these two rooms he announced his intention to live henceforth. At the same time he informed his wife and daughter that their allowance hereafter would be one hundred dollars a year each, and that he would pay no bills. Ah Kee, who had lived with him for twenty years, would attend to the domestic supplies. Then he ordered his meals brought to the office, and shut himself up.

On the third day Mrs. Polk said to Magdaléna, —

"Si I stay in this house one day more, I go mad, no less. Is like the dungeons in the Mission. *Madre de Dios!* and you living like this for years, perhaps; for Roberto grow more crank all the time. Come with me. I no think he know."

"You may be sure that he knows everything. And I cannot leave them. Shall you go back to Santa Barbara? Don't you want to travel?"

"*Dios de mi alma;* no! I think I go to die on that treep from Santa Barbara — so jolt. I am too old to travel. Once I think I like see Spain; but now I only want be comfortable. Well, si you change the mind and come sometime, I am delight. But I go now: feel like I am old flower wither up, without the sun."

XXVI

Mrs. Polk's large white face and throat had seemed to shed a measure of light in the dark house; when she left, the gloom seemed to get down and sit on one. Helena refused to enter by the front door, and lamenting that she was too big to climb the pillar, paid her visits by way of the kitchen and back stairs.

After the calls of condolence visitors came more and more rarely to the Yorba house. They said it depressed them for days after, and that while there they sat in mortal terror of hearing Don Roberto burst out of his den with the yell of a maniac. And as for dear Mrs. Yorba and Magdaléna, they never had had much to say, but now they had nothing. They would not drop off altogether, for the old don was bound to follow his brother-in-law in course of time, and then his widow would once more be a useful member of society. Mrs. Montgomery, Mrs. Geary, and Mrs. Cartright were more faithful than the others, but the affections Mrs. Yorba had inspired during her long and distinguished sojourn in San Francisco were not very deep and warm.

The girls were sorry for Magdaléna, and called frequently, conquering their horror of the gloomy echoing house; but they had less to endure than their elders, for they were received in Magdaléna's own sitting-room, which, although sparsely and tastelessly furnished, was always as cheerful as the weather would permit. They brought her all the gossip of the outside world, discussed the new novels with her, and occasionally induced her to spend a day with them.

At the end of the winter Ila was married; very grandly, in Grace Church. All her friends but Magdaléna were bridesmaids. The omission was a serious one, and all felt that it robbed the function of a last fine finish: each of the girls had counted upon having the last of the Yorbas for chief bridesmaid. Magdaléna went and sat in a corner of the church and saw the first of her friends break the circle of their girlhood. Her present had been very meagre: it had come out of her monthly allowance. Mrs. Polk was much too indolent to consider whether her niece was allowed an income suitable for her position or not, and Magdaléna was much too proud to ask favours. She slipped out of the church just before the end of the ceremony, feeling like a poor relation.

She rarely saw her father. Occasionally she met him in the hall; he drifted past her like a ghost. Mr. Polk died in February. On the first of June Don Roberto had not been out of the house for three months, nor had he exchanged a word with his wife or daughter.

"He'll blink like an owl when he does go out," said Mrs. Yorba. "I wonder if he remembers that it is time to go to the country?"

"He never forgets anything. I'll pack his things if you like."

But the day passed and the next, and Don Roberto gave no sign of remembering that it was time to move. Then Mrs. Yorba drew several long breaths, went downstairs, and knocked at his door. There was no response, but she turned the knob and went in. Don Roberto's face was between the large pages of a ledger. He looked round with a scowl.

"Everything is ready to move down. Are you not coming?"

"No; and you no going either. Letting the place."

If the President of the United States had let the White House, Mrs. Yorba could not have been more astounded.

"Let Fair Oaks! Fair Oaks?"

"Yes."

"And where are we to go this summer?"

"We stay here."

"Robert! You cannot mean that. No one stays here in summer. The city is impossible—those trade-winds—those fogs—"

"Need not go out. Can stay in the house." And Don Roberto returned to his ledger.

Mrs. Yorba went straight to Magdaléna's room, and for the first time in her daughter's experience of her, wept.

"To think of spending a summer in San Francisco! How I have looked forward to the summer! Things are always bright and cheerful in Menlo even with the house shut up, for one can sit on the verandah. But here! And not a soul in town! And the house like a prison! What in Heaven's name ails your father? He's not crazy. He's reading his ledgers, and what he says is to the point, goodness knows! But I shall follow Hiram if this keeps up. You're a real comfort to me, 'Léna. I don't know what I should do without you."

Magdaléna said what she could to console her mother. The two had drawn together during these trying months. She was bitterly disappointed that she could not go to Menlo Park. She was tired of its efforts to amuse itself but she could live in its woods, its soft gracious air, find companionship in the distant redwoods swimming in their dark-blue mists.

The girls all invited her to visit them, but she would not leave her mother, even could her father's consent be obtained. Mrs. Yorba was genuinely unhappy. Without mental resources, and deprived of even an occasional hour with her friends, she was further harassed by the fear that her husband would die and leave her with a pittance: he certainly appeared to hate the sight of his family. It consoled her somewhat to reflect that wills were easily broken in California. Why had her brother left her nothing? With a full purse she could at least have the distractions of philanthropy. She took to novel-reading with a voracious appetite, and her taste grew so exacting that she would have nothing that was not magnificently sensational. She thought on Boston with a shudder, but concluded that it was enough to have been intellectual when young.

Magdaléna plodded on with her work. She described the customs and manners of the old times with much accuracy, and felt that her beloved creations were rather more than puppets; and it was as much for their sake as for her own that she wanted these little histories to be triumphs of art, that they might arrest the attention of the world. Alvarado and Castro were great heroes to her: it was unjust and cruel that the big world outside of California should know nothing of them; to the present Californian, for that matter, they were not even names. And forty years before the Californias had bent to their nod! They had lived with the state of princes, and the wisdom with which the one had ruled and the other had managed his armies would have given them lasting fame had not their country then been as remote from Earth's greater civilisations as had it been on Jupiter. If she could only immortalise them! That would be a sufficient reason for living, compensate her for the wreck of her personal life. It might take a lifetime, but what of that if she succeeded in the end?

She took long walks daily; alone, for the French maid had been dismissed long since. The walks were not pleasant, for when the sand from the outlying dunes was not swept through the city by the bitter trades, the fog was crawling into one's very marrow. And the hills were steep. Sometimes she took the cable car to the end of the line, then walked to the Presidio; but that brought the sand-hills nearer, and she went home with smarting eyes. Protected by her window, she found beauty even in the summer mood of San Francisco; and sometimes she went up into the tower of the Belmont house and watched the long clouds of dust roll symmetrically down the streets of the city's valleys; or the delicate white mist ride through the Golden Gate to wreathe itself about the cross on Calvary, then creep down the bare brown cone to press close about the tombs on Lone Mountain; then onward until all the city was gone under a white swinging ocean; except the points of the hills disfigured with the excrescences of the rich. Into the cañons and rifts of the hills beyond the blue bay the fog crept daintily at first, hanging in festoons so light that the very trades held aloof, then advancing with a rush,—a phantom of the booming ocean whence it came.

And Trennahan? He made no sign. Whether he were dead or alive, the victim or the captor of his old familiars, careless, or nursing an open wound, Magdaléna was miserably ignorant. The time had come when she waited tensely as mails were due, feeling that an empty envelope covered with his handwriting would give her solace. She cherished no hope that he would ever return to her, but he had promised her his lasting friendship. Sometimes she wondered at the cruelty of men. Why should he not help her? Even if he really believed in the extinction of her love, he might guess that she needed his friendship. She had yet to learn that the one thing that man never gives to woman is spiritual help.

Helena wrote that her father was so anxious for her to marry Alan Rush that she was officially engaged to that much-enduring youth and really liked him. Menlo Park was the same as ever; not so gay as last year, but the same in quality. No one had called on the lessees of Fair Oaks. They were new people whom nobody knew, and it would be horrid to go there, anyhow. Caro was engaged to marry an Englishman who had bought a grape-ranch some twenty miles from Menlo. Tiny was prettier and more bored than usual. Rose wrote that she certainly could not stand another summer of Menlo and should go East in the autumn. Ila wrote from Paris, London, and Homburg that life was quite perfect. It was so interesting to be named Washington,—everybody stared so; as the English had never read a line of United States history, they thought her George was a lineal descendant of the immortal head of his house; and she had thirty-two trunks of Paris clothes and ever so many men in love with her.

And Magdaléna lived this life for three years. Its monotony was broken by one event only.

XXVII

During the winter following Mr. Polk's death, Colonel Belmont was driving his coach along the beach beyond the Park one afternoon when Helena, who sat beside him, saw him give a long shudder, then huddle. She grasped the reins of the four swiftly trotting horses and spoke over her shoulder to Alan Rush.

"Pull my father up to the top," she said.

Rush did as he was bid, and the body of Colonel Belmont was laid out between the two rows of young people, whose gaiety had frozen to horror.

"Now take the reins," said Helena.

Rush took the reins. Helena followed her father swiftly and stooped to take his head in her arms. But she dropped her ear to his lips instead, then to his heart. For a moment longer she stared at him, while the others waited for the outburst. But she returned to the front seat, and caught the reins from Rush's hands.

"I must do something," she said; and he knew better than to answer her, or even to look at her.

It was some time before she could turn the horses, and then she was several miles from home. She drove with steady hands; but when they had reached the house and Rush lifted her down, she was trembling violently. She pushed him aside.

"Go and get Magdaléna," she said.

Magdaléna remained with her a week. This was Helena's first real grief, and there was nothing cyclonic about it. "I'll never get over it," she said. "Never! And I'll never be quite the same again. Of course I don't mean that I'll have this awful sense of bereavement and keep on crying all my life: I know better than that; but I could never forget him, nor forget to wish I still had him, if I lived to be a hundred. If I had anything to reproach myself for—anything serious—I believe I'd go off my head; but I *was* good to him; and I am sure mamma never could have taken better care of him than I did. When he was under doctor's orders I gave him every drop of the medicine myself, and I never would let him eat a thing I thought wouldn't agree with him. He used to say his life was a burden, poor darling, but I know he liked it. And who knows?—if I hadn't watched him so, he might not have lived as long as he did. That is my one consolation.... This terrible grief makes everything else seem so paltry; I could not even think of being engaged to Alan Rush any longer. Poor fellow! I feel sorry for him, but I can't play for a long time to come. As for papa's wishes in the matter, Mr. Geary and Mr. Washington will take care of my money, and I am quite able to take care of myself. If papa is near me now, he will understand how I feel, and agree with me. I wish I had some heroic destiny. Why has the United States ceased to make history? I'd like to play some great part. Papa used to say there was bound to be another upheaval some day, but I'm afraid it won't be in my time."

"It may," replied Magdaléna. "There's a good deal of history-making, quiet and noisy, going on all the time. I've been reading the newspapers this last year. They're horrid sensational things, but I manage to get a few ideas from them. No one can tell what may happen ten years hence. You may have a chance to be the heroine of a revolution yet."

"I'm afraid I'll never be anything but a belle, and I'm tired of that already, although I never could stand being shelved. But if there is a revolution during my life I'll be a factor in it. Just you remember that."

"I really do believe that you were intended for something extraordinary."

"I believe I was. That's the reason I'm so restless and dramatic. I don't feel as if I ever could be so again, though,—not for ages, anyhow."

The old close and affectionate intimacy between the two girls was restored during that week. At its end Helena went East to visit her aunt, Mrs. Forbes. She was the untrammelled mistress of something under a million dollars; and as her private car, filled with flowers, bonbons, and books, pulled away from a sorrowing crowd of friends on the Oakland side of the ferry, it must be confessed she reflected that the future would appear several shades darker if she were arranging her belongings in a half-section, a small quarterly allowance in her pocket. Nevertheless Colonel Belmont had his reward. His daughter's grief was deep and lasting; and perhaps he knew.

XXVIII

Caro married her Englishman, and on a thriving grape-farm entertained other Englishmen. Rose went East and triumphantly captured a Baltimorean of distinguished lineage and depleted exchequer. Tiny went to Europe again Magdaléna was practically alone. Her father still lived in his two rooms downstairs and never spoke to anyone but Ah Kee. Once he forgot to close his study door, and Magdaléna, who happened to be passing, paused and looked at him. His face had shrunken and was crossed with a thousand fine and eccentric lines; like the palm of a man singled out for a career of trouble He had let his hair and beard grow, and he looked uncouth and dirty.

Mrs. Yorba still read novels. She no longer paid calls, for her allowance, now reduced to fifty dollars a year, was quite inadequate to meet the requirements of a dignified member of society. She received her few intimate and faithful friends in her bedroom; the first floor was never dusted nor aired. The house smelt musty and deserted; the lower rooms were as cold and damp as underground caverns; the spiders spun unheeded; when the front door was opened, the festoons in the hall swung like hammocks. Even the gloom of the house seemed to accentuate with the years. Magdaléna wondered if the inside of the old Polk house looked any more haunted than this; and even the Belmont house was acquiring an expression of pathos, peculiar to desertion in old age. Magdaléna fancied that the three houses must be pointed out to visitors as the sarcophagi of the futile ambitions of three Californian millionaires.

In her own rooms she toiled on, absorbed in her work, loving it with the beggared passion of her nature, experiencing two or three moments of creative ecstasy and many hours of dull discouragement. She wrote her stories and rewrote them; then again, and again. Her critical faculty took long strides ahead of her creative power, and she rarely ceased to be uneasy at the disparity between her work and her ideals. But Trennahan had said that it would be ten years before she could attain excellence, and she was willing to serve a harder apprenticeship than this. Had it not been for her work and the books of those who had climbed the heights and slept beneath the stars, she might have become morbid and melancholy in her unnatural surroundings. But although the monotony of her life was never broken by a day in the country, she had always the beauty of bay and hill and sky beyond her window; and there are certain months in the spring and autumn when San Francisco is as lovely and brilliant as the southern shores of California. The trades are hibernating in the caves of the Pacific, and the fogs exist only in the spray of the ponderous waves. On such days and evenings Magdaléna sat for hours on her little balcony, forgetting her work, dreaming idly. It was inevitable, in her purely mental and imaginative life, that she should apprehend in Trennahan the lover again. She wove her own romance as ardently and consecutively as that of any of her heroines. In time he would forget Helena; his love for her had been one of those sudden insane passions of which she had read,—which she tried to depict in her Southland tales,—and in time it would fall from him, and he would hear the tinkle of the chain forged in long hours of perfect sympathy. They would both be older and wiser and more sad: the better, perhaps. Loneliness and the peculiar circumstances of her life inclined her to borderland sympathies; she believed that if he died suddenly she should become immediately aware of the fact.

Her love for Trennahan by no means interfered with her literary ambitions. All others had failed her; she knew now that with the best of opportunities she should never have cut a brilliant figure in society. But she did not care; letters were a far more glorious goal. Helena adored great military heroes, great imperialists like Clive and Hastings, even great tyrants like Napoleon. Herself reverenced the great names in literature, and could think of no destiny so exalted as to be enrolled among them. And if she succeeded, what would have mattered these long years of dull loneliness, of denial of all that is dear to the heart of a girl? Sometimes she even thought the tarrying of Trennahan mattered little; for there is no tyrant so jealous as Art.

Once she read her stories aloud to her mother; and Mrs. Yorba was pleased to observe that they were much better than she could have expected, but that on the whole she preferred "The Duchess." She had grown quite fond of her daughter, and often sat in her room while she wrote. The intimacy and isolation of the two women had made it easy and natural for Magdaléna to confide in her mother, but she was forced to confess that she had not inherited her critical faculty from her maternal parent. Nevertheless, she was glad of the meagre encouragement and plodded on.

XXIX

It was early in the fourth year that Henry James swooped down upon San Francisco. He arrived in the train of Helena's triumphant return, under her especial patronage. Not that a few choice spirits in California had no discovered James for themselves long since; but James as a definite entity known and approved by Society, awaited the second advent of Helena. He immediately became the fad; rather, Society split into two factions and was threatened with disruption. One young woman of the disapproving camp even went so far as to call an ardent advocate a "Henry James fool." All o which was doubtless due to the fact that the traditions of action still lingered in California. Strangely enough, Tiny, who returned almost immediately after Helena, was one of the first to take Mr. James under her small but determined wing. She regarded well-read people as an unnecessary bore, and ambition of any sort as unsuited to the Land of the Poppy, but she had a feminine faith in exceptions, and joined the cult with something like enthusiasm. It was she who introduced him to Magdaléna.

Magdaléna cared nothing for American latter-day authors, and gave no heed to Helena's emphatic approval of Mr. James. In fact, she and Helena had so much else to talk about that they found little leisure for books. Helena had been abroad again, and the belle of a winter in Washington. She was more beautiful than ever, and, although somewhat subdued, was full of plans for the future. Her first ball—she arrived at the end of the winter season—determined that her supremacy, socially and sentimentally, was unshaken. Immediately after, she bought an old Spanish house in the northern redwoods and provided new surprises for her little world. But there is no more room for Helena in this chronicle. Perhaps, if history shapes itself around her, she may one day have a chronicle to herself.

Tiny called on Magdaléna one afternoon with two volumes of Henry James under her arm. She took to her toes as the front door closed, and ran down the long hall and up the stair to Magdaléna's room.

"I feel like a book agent," she said, trying not to pant, and hoping Magdaléna would go down to the door with her when she left. "But you really must read him, 'Léna. He's so fascinating: I think it's because nothing ever happens, and that's so like life. I think I must always have felt Henry Jamesish, and it seems to me that he is singularly like Menlo,—when Helena is not there,—just jogging along in aristocratic seclusion punctuated by the epigrams of Rose and Eugene Fort. I'm sure Mr. James could, write a novel of Menlo Park; he just revels in irradiating nothing with genius. There! I feel so guilty, for I really do love Menlo,—with intervals of Europe,—but I've been visiting Rose, and I'm afraid I'm plagiarising a little; you know I'm not one bit clever. Only I really feel so when I read Mr. James. And he'll be such company in Menlo this summer. Just think, I shall be all alone there, when I'm not visiting Helena or Caro. Is—is—" she glanced about fearfully—"is there no hope of dear Don Roberto relenting?"

"I am afraid not. But it is such a comfort to have you back. I heard you were engaged—to an Englishman, or something?"

Tiny blushed. She was on her way to a tea, and looked exquisitely pretty in a fawn-coloured *crêpe de chine* embroidered with wild roses, and a bonnet of pink tulle crushed about her face. Magdaléna wondered why some man had not married her out of hand, then reflected that Tiny was likely to dispose of her own future.

"I'm not quite sure," said Miss Montgomery, looking innocently at a lithograph of the Virgin which still decorated the wall. "You see, he has a title, and it's so commonplace to marry a title. But if I decide to, I'll let you know the very first."

Shortly after she went away—and left Magdaléna alone with Henry James.

She took up one of the volumes. As she did so, something stirred in the cellars of her mind—beat its stiff wings against the narrow walls—struggled forward and upward.

She stood on the porch in the late evening: alone in a fog. Her young mind opened to literary desire—preceding it was a swift disturbing presentiment; it had recurred once, and again—but not for several years. What did it mean, here again? And what had Henry James to do with it? She dropped into a chair. Her hands trembled as they opened the book.

XXX

It was a week before she squarely faced the relation of Henry James to her own ambitions. Then she admitted it in so many words: she could not write, she never could write. The writers who were dust had inspired her to emulation; it took a great contemporary to bring her despair. It is only the living enemies we fear; the dead and their past are beautiful unrealities to the smarting ego.

Magdaléna realised for the first time the exact value she had placed upon the art of expression,—a value that was in inverse ratio to her limitations. Literature to her was, above all else, the art of words. Stories were to be picked up anywhere: had she not found a number ready to her hand? The creative faculty might, in its unique development, be something supremer still, although crippled without the perfected medium of this writer, who seemed above all writers to be the master and not the servant of words. She re-read her own efforts. They represented the hard thought and work of six years; not a great span, perhaps, but long enough to determine the promise of a faculty. The stories were wooden. Her work would always be wooden. There was not a phrase to delight the cultivated reader, not a line that any moderately clever person, given the same material, might not have written. After as many more years of labour she might become a praiseworthy writer of the third rank. She put her manuscripts in the fire.

After that, life turned grey indeed. Her imagination might have gone into the flames with the stories, for her illusions about Trennahan fell to ashes coincidently. She no longer believed that he would return, that he would even write demanding her friendship. She could hardly recall his face; the sound of his voice was gone from her. Indubitably he had forgotten her long since. Why not? She had ascended above the rosy stratum of youth, where delusions were possible.

Then began a long struggle against despair and its terrible consequences. It was a summer of raging trades which seemed to lift the sand dunes from their foundations and hurl them through the choking city. She could take little exercise. The Library was her only resource, but one can read only so many hours a day. If she could but travel, as Helena did, when anything went wrong! Or if her uncle had only left her an income that she could expend in charity! Her sympathy for the poor had never ebbed, and she would have gladly spent her life in their service, although she doubted if they were more miserable than herself. It was true that she had enough to eat, a roof to her head, and clothes to wear,—extremely plain clothes; but that was all. A nun or a prisoner had as much.

There were times when she was threatened with a consuming hatred of life, and then she fled out into the dust and battled with the storms within and without; for her ideals were all that were left her. She knew the ugly potentialities in the depths of her ill-compounded nature: the day she ceased to be true to herself there would be a tragedy in that dark house on the hill. Sometimes she wondered toward what end she was persevering, striving to perfect the better part of her. A quarter of a century or more of meaningless earthly existence? A controvertible hereafter? But she ceased to analyse, knowing that it could lead nowhere until the human mind ceased to be human.

And one day, in the end of the summer, she lost her grip on herself.

For three days the trade-winds had raged; she had not been able to leave the house. Twice she had set forth, desperate with the nervous monotony of her hours, and been driven back by the blinding dust. It was on the third day that she happened to catch sight of herself in the glass. She saw her face plainer than ever, but her attention passed suddenly to her shoulders and rested there. They were bent. Her carriage was dejected, apathetic. The sluggish tide mounted slowly to her face as she realised that this physical manner must have fallen upon her gradually, and been worn for some time; and its significance. She made an effort to reassume her old erect haughty poise, which had been partly the manifest of inherent pride, partly of half-acknowledged defiance of the beauty-worship of the world. Her shoulders sank before the spine had risen to its perpendicular. What did it matter? Again she experienced that disintegration of will which once had left her at the mercy of that instinct for destruction which is one of the essential particles of the ego.

Her brain was almost torpid. The want of exhilarating exercise, the long dearth of companionship, the terrible monotony of her life, the restless nights, the dank gloomy atmosphere in which she had her perpetual being, were, she told herself dully, doing their work. And she did not care. But if her brain was sodden, her nerves felt as if on the verge of explosion. She noticed that her hands were not steady, and sat for hours, wondering what was coming upon her. She cared less and less.

Ah Kee tapped at her door. She replied that she did not want any dinner, loathing the unvarying bill-of-fare.

The hours dragged on, and darkness came; but she did not light the gas, whose jet was but a feeble point in these times, hardly worth the waste of a match. She strained her ears, fancied she heard whisperings in the hall below. If San Francisco's skeletons really were down there, she wished they would go in and throttle her father. He was the author of all her misery, and was any woman on earth so miserable as she? Why should he live, exist down there like a beast in his cave, when his death would give her liberty?—a poignant happiness in itself. She wondered did she kill him should she be hanged? They rarely hanged anybody in California, never when there was gold to rattle contemptuously in the face of the law; why should she not deliver her mother and herself? They would both be in an asylum for the mad, or dead before their time, unless he went soon; and their lives were of several times more value than his. They, at least, had ruined the lives of no one, and with his hoarded unsavoury millions they would gladly do good to hundreds.

She tiptoed out into the hall, and leaned over the circular railing, and peered down into the space below. Only an old-fashioned waxen taper burned in a cup of oil; it emitted a feeble and ghostly light. The large webs of the spiders quivered in a draught. They assumed strange distorted shapes and seemed to point long fingers at her father's door.

They are the ghosts that once animated the skeletons, she thought; and they think it time he joined them.

She stood there for a long while, her eyes narrowed in a hard searching regard; the trembling gloom with the tiny sallow flame in its middle suggested the purgatory of imaginative artists. Should she go down and thrust the dagger into his neck?

Her thoughts were torn apart by the abrupt loud shouts of the wind. She wondered if there were such winds anywhere else on earth, or if this were the voice of some fiend prisoned in the Pacific,—the spouse whom California had taken to her arms when the fires in her body were hewing, and shattering and rehewing her, and divorced in an after-desire for beauty and peace.

Magdaléna went back to her room and turned the key in the drawer which contained the dagger.

"I must get out of this house," she said aloud, with the sensation of dragging her will from the depths of her brain and shaking it back to life. "If I don't, I'll be in an asylum to-morrow. Something is certainly wrong in my head."

She put on her jacket and hat with trembling fingers. Her nerves seemed fighting their way through her skin. Her ears were humming. Something had begun to pound in her brain.

She ran downstairs and let herself out, averting her eyes from her father's door. Her fingers were rigid, and curved.

As she reached the sidewalk, a squall caught and nearly carried her off her feet. It bellied her skirts and loosened her hair. She lost her breath and regained it with difficulty; she could hardly steer herself. But the wind filled her with a sudden wild exaltation, not of the soul, but of the worst of her passions,—those tangled, fighting, sternly governed passions of the cross-breed.

She cursed aloud. She let fly all the maledictions, English and Spanish, of which she had knowledge. The street was deserted. She raised her voice and pierced the gale, the furious energy of her words hissing like escaping steam. She raised her voice still higher and shrieked her profane arraignment of all things mundane in a final ecstasy of nervous abandonment.

When the passion and its voice were exhausted, her obsession had passed. Her head felt lighter, the danger of congestion was over; but her protest was the keener and bitterer. Her father's life was safe in her hands, but she had no desire to return to his house. She determined to walk until morning, and to drift, rudderless, in the great sea of the night.

She caught her skirts close to her body and walked rapidly to the brow of the hill. The twinkling lights were all below. The wrack of cloud torn by the wind into a thousand flapping sails skurried across a sky which the hidden moon patched with a hard angry silver. Far away and high in the storm the great cross on Calvary seemed dancing an inebriated jig above the ghostly tombs of Lone Mountain.

Magdaléna walked rapidly down the hill. Once or twice she paused before a house and stared at it. What secrets did it hold? What skeletons? Were any within so desperate as she? Why did they not come out and shriek with the storm? She pictured a sudden obsession of San Francisco: every door simultaneously flung open, every wretched inmate rushing forth to scream his protest against the injustice of life into the ecstatic fury of the elements.

High on a terrace, or rather an unlevelled angle of the hill, and reached by a long rickety flight of steps, was an old ugly wooden house. It was unpainted; the shutters were shaking on their rusty hinges; the chimneys had been blown off long since; but it had cost much gold in its time. It had been the home of a "Forty-niner," and he was dead and forgotten, his dust as easily accounted for as his winged gold. Doubtless every room had its patient skeleton, grinning eternally at the yellow lust of man.

As she passed Dupont Street, she paused again and regarded it steadily. Sheltered in the steep hillside, it took no note of the storm; its sidewalks were not empty, and its windows were broken bars of light. Magdaléna wondered if the painted creatures talking volubly behind the shutters were not happier and more normal than she. They were the rejected of their native boulevards, beyond a doubt, but they were free in their way, and they certainly were alive.

I am nothing, she thought; neither to myself, nor to any one else. I wonder will the wind blow me in there some night? What if it does?

But when a man started toward her with manifest intent to speak, she fled down the hill.

When she reached Kearney Street she turned without hesitation to the left, and walked toward those regions which are associated in the minds of every San Franciscan with lawlessness and crime. She had given a swift glance to the right before turning; the region of respectable shops and fashionable promenade was as black as a tunnel; the eccentric economy of the city forbade the light of street lamps when the moon was out, whether clouds accompanied her or not.

Ahead was a line of lights twisting and leaping in the wind,—the vagrant gas-jets before the row of cheap shops on the east side of the Plaza. Magdaléna hardly glanced at the medley of curious wares and faces as she hurried past; the wind was roaring about the open square, interfering with sight and hearing and headway. And beyond—her blood leaped to that mysterious disreputable region.

She left the Plaza and passing under the shelter of the heights upon which stood her home slackened her steps. There was a discordant crash of music in the crowded streets. Light was streaming from music-halls, above and below stairs, and from restaurants and saloons. But everybody seemed to be on the sidewalks. It was a strange crowd, and Magdaléna forgot herself for the moment: she had entered a new world, and her tortured soul lagged behind.

The riff-raff of the world was moving there, and when not apathetic they took their pleasures with drawn brows and eyes alert for a fight; but the only types Magdaléna recognised were the drunken sailors and the occasional blank-faced Chinaman who had strayed down from his quarter on the hill. There were dark-faced men who were doubtless French and Italian; what their calling was, no outsider could guess, but that it was evil no man could doubt; and there were many whose nationality had long since become as inarticulate as such soul they may have been born with. Many looked anæmic and consumptive, but the majority were highly coloured and frankly drunk. And if the men were forbidding, the women were appalling. There was no attempt at smartness in their attire; they were dowdy and frowsy, and even the young faces were old.

The din of voices, the medley of tongues and faces, the crash of music, the poisoned atmosphere, confused Magdaléna, and she turned precipitately into a restaurant. It was almost empty; she sat down before a dirty table and ordered a cup of coffee. The only waiter in attendance—the rest were probably in the street—was old and bleared of eye, but he stared hard at the new customer.

"You'd better git out of this," he said, as Magdaléna finished her unpleasant draught. "You ain't pretty, but you're a lady, and they don't understand that sort here. Have you got much money with you?"

"About a dollar, and I certainly do not give the impression of wealth. Most nursery maids are better dressed."

"You'd better git out, all the same."

But the strong coffee had gone to Magdaléna's head, and she cared little what became of her. Nevertheless, a moment later she was shrieking and struggling in the arms of a big golden-bearded Russian. She barely grasped the sense of what followed. There was a volley of screams and laughter; the man was cursing and gripping her with the arms of a grizzly. Then there was a flash of knives, and she was stumbling headlong through the crowd, hooted at and buffeted. But no one attempted to stop her, for a fight with bowie-knives was more interesting than a sallow-faced girl who had happened upon foreign territory. She ran up a dark side-street, and then, as her breath gave out and forced her to moderate her pace, she glanced repeatedly over her shoulder. No one was in pursuit, but it was some moments before she realised that it was not relief she experienced, but something akin to disappointment. She was in the ugliest mood of which her nature was capable, and that was saying much. With one exception, better forgotten, this blond ruffian who had insulted her was the only man who had ever desired her; doubtless, she reflected bitterly, even Trennahan might be excepted. And when an unprepossessing woman of starved affections and implacably controlled passions sees desire in the eyes of a man for the first time, her vanity of sex responds, if her passions do not.

She half turned back and stood looking down the hill to the brilliant noisy street.

Why should I not go back and live with him, and disappear from a world which takes no interest in me, and in which I am no earthly use she thought. And no life could be worse than mine, nor more immoral, for that matter. I have never fulfilled a single one of the conditions for which woman was born, and I'd be more normal as that man's mistress, and less unhappy even if he beat me, which he probably would, than living the life of a blind mole underground.

Then she wondered who her deliverer was, and wondered if he too had wanted her. Some portion of the blackness in her soul receded suddenly, and she smiled and trembled slightly. Involuntarily her back straightened, and she lifted her head. But with the sudden rush of sexual pride the magnetism of its creators receded, and she turned her back on the flare below and continued to mount the hill. In a moment she turned into a badly lighted alley thinly peopled. Here there was but a tinkle of music, and it came from the guitar. Fat old women with black shawls pinned about their heads sat on the doorsteps of ramshackle houses talking to men whose flannel shirts revealed hairy chests. The women looked stupid, the men weather-beaten but the prevailing expression was good-natured. In the middle of the street was a tamale stand surrounded by patrons. The aroma of highly seasoned cooking came from a restaurant at the foot of a rickety flight of steps. Every dilapidated window had its flower-box.

This, then, was Spanish town. Magdaléna had dreamed of it often, picturing it a blaze of colour, a moving picture-book, crowded with beautiful girls and handsome gaily attired men. There was not a young person to be seen. Nothing could be less picturesque, more sordid.

An old crone with a face like a withered apple followed her, whining for a nickel. The others stared at her with the stolid dignity of their race. She gave the woman the nickel and interrupted the invocation.

"Are there no girls here?"

"Girl come from other place sometimes, then have the baby and is old queeck. Si the señorita stay here, she have the baby and grow old too."

Magdaléna hastened on. She neither knew nor cared where she went, but after a time struck down the slope again, judging that she was beyond the centre of social activity. Once, at the corner of two sharply converging streets, she passed a house whose lighted windows were open, for the wind had gone and the night was hot. But she only stood for a moment. Fat Mexican women half dressed were lolling about, and the front door was open to many men. The women were not as evil appearing as the French dregs of Dupont Street, possibly because they wore flowers in their hair and looked more frankly sensual and less commercial. Again Magdaléna felt an almost irresistible attraction, but hastened on. Once, in a dark street, she was flung against a wall and her pockets turned inside out, but she made no protest and was allowed to go without further indignity. It was a woman who had robbed her, and Magdaléna, having come off with the mere loss of seventy cents, indulged in a pleasurable thrill of adventure.

After a time she found herself climbing a steep hill and felt a sudden desire to reach the top, and that the climb should be a long one. Here and there she passed a tumble-down house, but the rest of the hill under the brilliant moon showed bare and brown. From the other side came the sound of lapping waves, and she knew herself to be on Telegraph Hill.

She reached the top and sat down on the ground. The clouds had flown with the wind, and the moon revealed the quiet bay and the black masses of cliff and hill and mountain beyond. An occasional gust made a loud clatter in the rigging of the many crafts below, or an angry shout arose from the water-front; but otherwise the night from the summit of Telegraph Hill was peaceful and most beautiful.

Magdaléna, who loved Nature and had yielded to its influence many times in her life, made a deliberate attempt to absorb the peace and beauty of the night into her own scarred and troubled soul. But she gave up the attempt in a few moments. The fierceness of her mood had passed, and some of its blackness, but she was still bitter and hopeless. There was nothing to do but to face the problem of her life, and thinking was easier on these altitudes, where the air was fresh and salt, and the stars seemed close, than in the ill-ventilated prison which she called her home. She determined to remain until morning and to restore her brain to its normal condition, if possible.

She looked back upon the mental and moral inertia into which she had sunken during the past month, and its sequence of morbid and criminal instinct, with terror and horror. Before an hour had passed, she had herself in hand once more, for she had deliberately forced herself to face her own soul, and she believed that she could put her character together again and accept the future without further luxation or debility of will. But she made no attempt to close her eyes to the ugly fact that in that future of interminable years there were only two small stars of hope; and it required an effort of imagination to drag them above the horizon,—her father's death and the return of Trennahan. Her father belonged to a long-lived race, and Trennahan during an absence of three years and some months had given no indication that he remembered her existence; moreover, he had gone into exile for love of another woman. But without the faint white twinkle of those stars the future would be not a blank, but an infernal abyss, which Magdaléna, without the society of her kind, without talent without occupation, without religion, refused to contemplate. And she had all a woman's capacity for fooling herself with the will-o'-the-wisps of the imagination.

Her eyes had been clear and her logic relentless so long as the man ha been within sight and touch, but his absence, combined with his abrupt and final eviction from the toils of the other woman, had lifted him from practica life into the realms of the imagination; in other words, he was no longer so much a man as an ideal,—a soul whom her own soul was free to await or pursue in that inner world where realities are bodiless and forgotten.

She longed for the old comfortable irresponsible sensuous embrace of the Church of Rome. Its lightest touch was hypnotic, its very breath a balm Why, she wondered bitterly, could she not have been given less brains, or more? If her talents had been genuine, she would have had that magnificent independence of religion and worldly conditions which only art—and love—can create in the human mind. And if her logic had been a trifle less relentless, she would have had hours of ecstatic forgetfulness these last long years. Of course there was always the Almighty Power to whom one could pray, and who certainly could grant prayer if He chose. But it seemed to her an impertinence for ordinary insignificant beings to importune this remote and absolute God, so forbidding in His monotonous mystery. She had all the arrogance of intellect despite her remorseless limitations. Had she been granted the gift of creation,—in other words, a spark from the great creative force commanding the Universe,—she felt that she should have no hesitation in begging for further favours; a certain sense of kinship, of being in higher favour than the great congested mass, would have given her assurance and faith. She sighed for a new religion, for that prophet who must one day arise and rid the world of the abomination of dogma and sect, giving to the groping millions a simple belief, in which the fussiness, sentimentality, and cruelty of present religions would have no place.

She sat there until the dawn came, grey and appalling at first, then touching the bay and the dark heights with delicate colour, as the sun struggled out of the embrace of the ocean. She was obliged to walk home, as she had no money, and the long toilsome tramp in the wake of the eventful night gave her appetite and many hours of rest. When she awoke she felt that, whatever came, the most formidable crisis of her life had been safely passed.

XXXI

In the autumn she found an occupation which gave her a temporary place in the scheme of things. Mrs. Yorba fell ill. The sudden and complete change from a personage to a nobody, the long confinement,—she rarely put her foot outside the house lest her shabby clothes be remarked upon,—and a four years' course of sensational novels induced a nervous distemper. Magdaléna, hearing the sound of pacing footsteps in the hall one night, arose and opened her door. Mrs. Yorba, arrayed in a red flannel nightgown and a frilled nightcap, was walking rapidly up and down, talking to herself. Magdaléna persuaded her to go to bed, and the next morning sent for the doctor. He prescribed an immediate change of scene,—travel, if possible; if not, the country. Magdaléna undertook to carry the message to her father.

Knowing that a knock would evoke no response, she opened the door of the study and went in. Don Roberto, dirty, unshaven, looked like a wild man in a mountain cave; but his eyes were steady enough. His table and the floor about his chair were piled high with ledgers. On everything else the dust was inches thick, and the spiders had spun a shimmering web across one side of the room. It hung from the gas-rod like a piece of fairy tapestry, woven with red and gold here and there, where the sun's rays, scattering through the slats of the inside blinds, caressed it. On the mantel-piece, supported on its broken staff, was the big American flag which had floated above the house of Don Roberto Yorba for thirty years. It had been carefully washed, and although broken bits of spiders' weavings hung to its edges, there were none on its surface.

Magdaléna felt no desire to kiss her parent, although it was the first time for several years that she had stood in his presence. She disliked and despised him, and thought no less of herself for her repudiation. If she, a young, inexperienced, and lonely woman, could fight and conquer morbid fancies, why not he, who had been counted one of the keenest financial brains of the country? She felt thoroughly ashamed of her progenitor as she stood looking down upon the little dirty shrunken shambling figure.

"Well?" growled Don Roberto, "what you want?"

"My mother is very ill. This life is killing her. The doctor says she must have a change."

"All go to die sometime. What difference now or bimeby?"

"Will you let us go to Santa Barbara to visit aunt?"

"Si she send you the moneys, I no care what you do with it. I no give you one cents."

"Very well; I shall ask my aunt."

But Mrs. Yorba declared that she would not go to Santa Barbara: she detested her sister-in-law, and would accept no favours from her, nor be forced into her society. There was nothing for Magdaléna to do but to nurse her, and a most exasperating invalid she proved. Nevertheless, Magdaléna, although a part of her duties was to read her mother's favourite literature aloud by the hour, was almost grateful for the change. She seldom found time for her daily walk, but at least she had little time to think.

When Mrs. Montgomery, Mrs. Geary, and Mrs. Brannan returned to town, they came frequently to sit with the invalid, and cheered her somewhat with talk of the coming summer, when they should take her down to their own houses in Menlo.

"And I shall go," said Mrs. Yorba to her daughter, "if I *haven't* a decent rag to my back. They think nothing of that; I was a fool not to go before. And I'm going to get well—against the time when that old fiend dies. There I never thought I'd say that, for I was brought up in the fear of the Lord, but saying it is little different from thinking it, after all. I've been thinking it for two solid years. California's not New England, anyhow. When I do get the money, won't I scatter it! I've been economical all my life, for I had it in my blood, and it was my duty, as your father wished it; as long as he did his duty by me, I was more than willing to do mine by him: he can't deny it. But we all know what reaction means, and it has set in in me. When I am my own mistress, I'll give three balls and two dinners a week. I'll have the finest carriages and horses ever seen in California. I'll have four trousseaux a year from Paris, and I'll go to New York myself and buy the most magnificent diamonds Tiffany's got. I'll refurnish this house and Fair Oaks. The walls shall be frescoed, and every stick in them will come from New York—"

She paused abruptly, springing to her elbow. The door was ajar. Through the aperture came a long low chuckle. Magdaléna jumped to her feet, flung the door to, and locked it.

"Do you think he's gone mad at last?" gasped Mrs. Yorba.

"It sounded like it."

"For Heaven's sake, don't leave me for a minute. You must sleep here at night. There's a cot somewhere,—in the attic, I think, if the rats haven't eaten it. What a life to live!" She fell to weeping, as she frequently did in these days. Suddenly her face brightened. "If he should make a will disinheriting us, we could easily enough prove him insane after the way he's been acting these four years. Thank Heaven, this is California! General William could break any will that ever was made."

Mrs. Yorba took an opiate and fell asleep. Magdaléna went out, locking the door behind her. She determined to ascertain at once if her father was insane. If he was, he should be confined in two of the upper rooms with a keeper. The world should know nothing of his misfortune; but it would be absurd for herself and her mother to live in a constant state of physical terror.

As she descended the stair, the door of her father's study opened abruptly and a man shot out as if violently propelled from behind. The door was slammed to immediately.

Magdaléna ran downstairs and toward the stranger. He was a tall man greatly bowed, and as she approached him she saw that he was old and wore a long white beard. His head was large and suggested nobility and intellect; but the eyes were bleared, the flesh of the face loose and discoloured, and he was shabby and dirty. He looked like a fallen king.

"Was—was—my father rude?" asked Magdaléna. "He is not very well. Perhaps I can do something." The man appealed to her strangely, and she had a dollar in her purse.

"We were great friends in our boyhood and youth," replied the stranger. He spoke with an accent, but his English was unbroken. "And he has been my guest many times. There was a time when he thought it an honour to know me. When the Americans came, everything changed. My career closed, for I would have nothing to do with them. I had held the highest offices under the Mexican government. I could not stoop to hold office under the usurpers—many of whom I would not have employed as servants. Then they took my lands,—everything. But I am detaining you, señorita."

"Oh, no, no, indeed! How could they take your lands? Who are you? Tell me everything."

"They 'squatted,' many of them, almost up to my door. The only law we could appeal to was American law, and California was a hell of sharpers at that time. It is bad enough now, but it was worse then. And then came the great drought of '64, in which we lost all our cattle. We never recovered from that, for we mortgaged our lands to the Americans to get money to live on with,—everything was three prices then; and when the time came they foreclosed, for we never had the money to pay. And we were great gamblers, señorita, and so were the Americans—and far better ones than we were. We were only made for pleasure and plenty, to live the life of grandees who had little use for money, and scorned it. When the time came for us to pit ourselves against sordid people, we crumbled like old bones. Your father has been very fortunate: he had a clever man to teach him to circumvent other clever men. Years ago, when I was prouder than I am now, I put my pride in my pocket and wrote, asking him for help. I wanted a small sum to pay off the mortgage on a ranchita, upon which I might have ended my days in peace, for it was very productive. He never answered. To-day I came to ask him for money to buy bread. He roared at me like a bull, and vowed he'd blow my brains out if I ever entered his house again. He looks like—" He paused abruptly. There was much of the old-time courtliness in his manner.

"I—I—am so sorry. And I have little money to spend. If you will leave me your name and address, I will send you something on the first of each month; and if—if ever I have more I will take care of you—of all of you. I suppose there are many others."

"There are indeed, señorita."

"Some day I will ask you for all of their names. And yours?"

He gave it. It was a name famous in the brief history of old California,—a name which had stood for splendid hospitality, for state and magnificence, for power and glory. It was the name of one of her beloved heroes. She had written his youthful romance; she had described the picturesque fervour of his wooing, the pomp of his wedding; of all those heroes he had been the best beloved, the most splendid. And she met him,—a broken-down old drunkard, in the dusty gloom of an old maniac's wooden "palace," in the fashionable quarter of a city which had never heard his name.

"O God!" she said. "O God!" and she was glad that she had burned her manuscripts. She took the dollar from her pocket and gave it to him.

He accepted it eagerly. "God bless you, señorita!" he said. "And you can always hear of me at the Yosemite Saloon, Castroville."

He passed out, neglecting to shut the door behind him, but Magdaléna did not notice the unaccustomed rift of light. She sank into a chair against the wall and wept heavily. They were the last tears she shed over her fallen idols. When the wave had broken, she reflected that she was glad to know of the distress of her people; it should be her lifework to help them. When she came to her own she would buy them each a little ranch and see that they passed the rest of their lives in comfort.

She leaned forward and listened intently. Loud mutterings proceeded from her father's room. She wondered if there was a policeman in the street. She and her mother were very unprotected. The only man in the house besides her father was the Chinaman, and Chinamen are as indifferent to the lives of others as to their own. Don Roberto had ordered the telephone and messenger call removed years ago. The sounds rose to a higher register. Magdaléna, straining her ears, heard, delivered in rapid defiant tones, the familiar national cry, "Hip-hip-hooray!"

She went over softly, and put her ear to the thick door. The tones of the old man's voice were broken, as if by muscular exertion, and accompanied by a curious bumping. Magdaléna understood in a moment. He was striding up and down the room, waving the American flag, and shouting, "Hip-hip-*hooray*! Hip-hip-*hooray*! *hooray*! *hooray*! *hooray*!"

She ran down the hall to summon Ah Kee and send him for a doctor, but before she reached the bell she heard the front door close, and turned swiftly. A man had entered.

She went forward in some indignation. So deep was the gloom of the hall that she could distinguish nothing beyond the facts that the intruder was tall and slight, and that he wore a light suit of clothes. When she had approached within a few feet of him, she saw that he was Trennahan.

For the moment she thought it was the soul of the man, so ghostly he looked in that dim light, in that large silence.

His first remark was reassuring: "I rang twice; but as no one came, and the door was open, I walked in,—as you see."

"We have so few servants now. Won't you come and sit down?"

He followed her down to the reception-room. She jerked aside the curtains, careless of the bad house-keeping the light would reveal. It streamed in upon him. He was deeply tanned and indescribably improved.

They sat down opposite each other. Magdaléna, recalling her tears, placed her chair against the light. "When did you get back?" she asked.

"The ship docked an hour ago."

"You look very well. Have you been enjoying yourself?"

"I have been occupied, and useful—I hope. At least, I have collected some data and made some observations which may be new to the world of Science. I found the old love very absorbing. And, you will hardly credit it, I have lived quite an impersonal life."

"Have you come back to California again because you think it a good place to die in?"

"I came back to California, because it is a good place to write my book in, and because you are here."

"Ah!"

"Don't misunderstand me. I am not so conceited as to imagine that I can have you for the asking. But—listen to me: I had a brief but very genuine madness. When I recovered I knew what I had th—lost. I argued—even during my convalescence—that I had been wholly right in believing that you were the one woman for me to marry, and, that fact established, you must believe it no less than I. But for a long time I was ashamed to come back, or to write. Later, I went where it was impossible. Moreover, in solitude a man comes into very close knowledge of himself. After a few months of it I knew that I should never be contented with mere existence again. I determined to take advantage of what might be the last chance granted me to make anything of my life; I had thrown away a good many chances. I also argued that if you loved me, you would wait for me; that you were not the sort to marry for any reason but one. At least, perhaps you will give me another trial."

"I shall marry you, I suppose; I have wanted to so long, and I never had any pride where you were concerned. A few months ago I should have flown into your arms; and I had felt sure that you would return. But lately I have not been able to care about anything. I am not the least bit excited that you are here. It merely seems quite natural and rather pleasant."

"Is anything the matter?" he asked anxiously. "You look very thin and worn, and the house—it was like entering the receiving vault on Lone Mountain. I thought when I came in that you were having a funeral, at least."

"It has been like that for four years. Uncle died, and papa was afraid to trust himself in the world for fear he would relapse into his natural instincts. So he shut himself up, makes us live on next to nothing, and of course we go nowhere, for we have no clothes. Mamma has been ill with nervous prostration for months, and now I feel sure that papa has gone insane. I have only spoken to him once in four years; but I have been certain that he would lose his mind finally, and I have just discovered that he is quite mad."

"Good God! We'll be married to-morrow. I never imagined your father would hit upon any new eccentricities. You poor little hermit! I fancied you going to parties and plodding at your stories. I never dreamed that you were shut up in a dungeon. I shall see that you are happy hereafter."

"I feel sad and worn out. I don't think I can ever feel much of anything again."

"Oh, you'll get over that," he replied cheerfully; he was as practical as ever. "What you want is plenty of sun and fresh air and a rest from your family. If your father is insane, he'll go into an asylum; and a rest cure is the place for your mother. That will dispose of her while we are taking our honeymoon in the redwoods. Do you think you could stand camping out?"

"I could stand anything so long as it was the country once more," she said, with her first flash of enthusiasm. "But there is something I should tell you. Perhaps after you hear it you won't want to marry me. I tried to kill Helena once."

"You did what?" he said, staring at her.

"She came to me just after leaving you, on the night of your last interview. I was very much worked up before she came, had been for a long while; and when she told me that she had treated you badly and had thrown you over, after taking you away from me, I suddenly wanted to kill her, and I took my dagger out of the drawer beside me. It was very dark, but she had an instinct, and she jumped up and ran away. I never knew I could feel so; but every bit of blood in my body seemed shrieking in my head, and if she had not gone I should have jumped on her and hacked her to bits. I must go up to my mother now. You can think it over and come back again."

"I don't need to think it over," he said, smiling. "That was all you needed to make you quite perfect. You are a wonderful example of misdirected energies. Where is your father? I will go and look after him at once."

He took her suddenly in his arms and compelled her to kiss him; and then Magdaléna knew how glad she was that he had come.

She went with him to the door of the study.

"He is quiet," she whispered. "Perhaps he is asleep."

She left him and went down the hall, turning to wave her hand to him. Trennahan knocked. There was no answer. He opened the door softly, then gave a swift glance over his shoulder, entered hurriedly, and closed the door behind him.

Suspended from the gas pipe, which was bent and leaking, was Don Roberto. The light was dim. The purple face on the languidly revolving body was barely visible; but as it turned slowly to the door, it occupied a definite place among the shadows. Trennahan flung back the curtains and opened the window, closing the lower inside blinds. A cloud hurried across the face of the sun, as if light had no place in that ghastly room. About the limp body and sprawling hands clung the delicate prismatic tapestry of the spiders. It was rent in twain, and it quivered, and threatened to drop and trail upon the floor. The little weavers were racing about, full of anger and consternation, bent on repair. A number had already gathered up the broken strands and were fastening them across the body. Had Don Roberto remained undiscovered for twenty-four hours, he might have been wrought into the tissue of that beautiful delicate web, a grotesque intruder over whom the spiders would doubtless have held long and puzzled counsel.

The cloud passed. The sun caught a brilliant line of colour. Trennahan went forward hastily, and examined the long knotted strip between the body and the ceiling.

Don Roberto had hanged himself with the American flag.